THE TRUTH ABOUT ANTON VAN ZYL

ALSO BY THE AUTHOR

The Chanteuse from Cape Town

THE TRUTH ABOUT ANTON VAN ZYL

John Constable

Copyright © 2025 John Constable

The moral right of the author has been asserted.

Apart from any fair dealing for the purposes of research or private study, or criticism or review, as permitted under the Copyright, Designs and Patents Act 1988, this publication may only be reproduced, stored or transmitted, in any form or by any means, with the prior permission in writing of the publishers, or in the case of reprographic reproduction in accordance with the terms of licences issued by the Copyright Licensing Agency. Enquiries concerning reproduction outside those terms should be sent to the publishers.

The manufacturer's authorised representative in the EU for product safety is Authorised Rep Compliance Ltd, 71 Lower Baggot Street, Dublin D02 P593 Ireland (www.arccompliance.com)

This is a work of fiction. Names, characters, businesses, places, events and incidents are either the products of the author's imagination or used in a fictitious manner. Any resemblance to actual persons, living or dead, or actual events is purely coincidental.

Troubador Publishing Ltd
Unit E2 Airfield Business Park,
Harrison Road, Market Harborough,
Leicestershire. LE16 7UL
Tel: 0116 2792299
Email: books@troubador.co.uk
Web: www.troubador.co.uk

ISBN 978 1836281 948

British Library Cataloguing in Publication Data.
A catalogue record for this book is available from the British Library.

Printed and bound by CPI Group (UK) Ltd, Croydon, CR0 4YY
Typeset in 11.25pt Garamond by Troubador Publishing Ltd, Leicester, UK

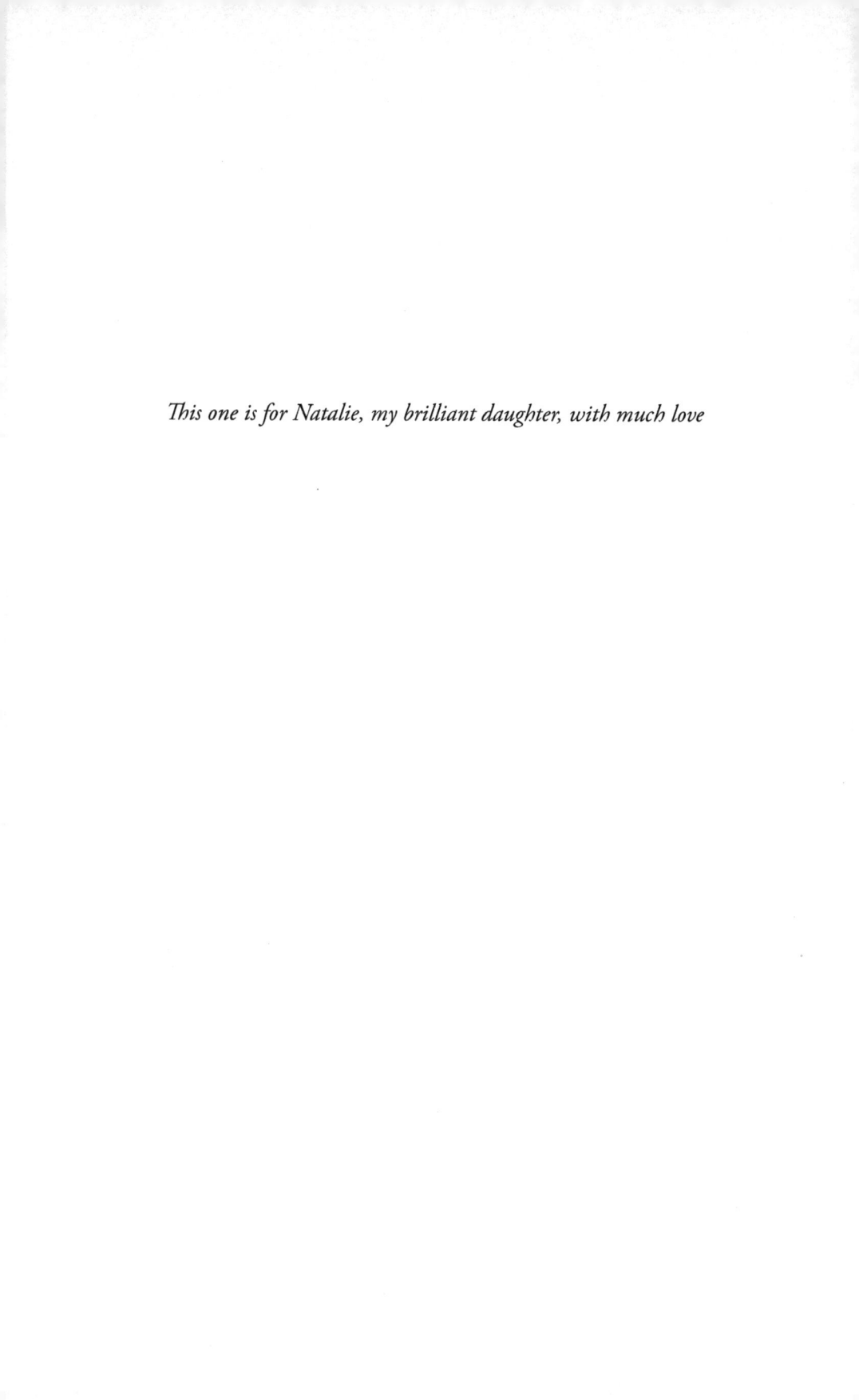

This one is for Natalie, my brilliant daughter, with much love

CHAPTER ONE

As soon as I realised where Moti lived, I should have turned the car round and headed home. Only hubris, influence and money, a lot of money, could have authorised a development on land designated a nature reserve by the regional government in Cape Town. And the fact this compliant administration was headquartered in the capital of the Western Cape should have set additional alarm bells ringing. The truth was Moti's real power base rested hundreds of kms away in PE, where he was on prattling terms with the suits who ran City Hall.

But, on that fine February morning, I wasn't ahead of the game. In fact, I wasn't in the game and to be honest I wasn't even in the ballpark. And that was all down to my low mood and a tension headache.

At the end of my journey, close to Plettenberg Bay, I pulled the Mustang off the highway and halted in front of a pair of wrought-iron gates. They were anchored to pillars set within an impenetrable screen of thorn and wild fig that ran as far as the eye could see on either side. Beyond the gates lay a track of beaten earth which led downhill between walls of scrub until it was lost to sight. In the distance, I discerned a crane mast with a long jib which, framed against the wide blue yonder, was lifting a steel girder.

Given the cloudless sky, I shouldn't have been surprised by the heat when I opened the car window. But I'd been sitting in the car's air-conditioned cabin for over three hours so the hot air that hit my face was a shock. Stretching my arm across to a white box mounted on a post in front of the gates, I opened it and lifted the receiver inside.

The phone rang a long time before I heard the one word, '*Ja?*'

'I've an appointment at ten,' I said. 'My name's Nemo.'

'Come again.'

'My name's Nemo. Sol Nemo.'

'Wait.'

With the eight pots of the Mustang's five litre engine burbling merrily beneath my right foot, I waited. Idly, I watched as a vervet monkey ran from the branch of a wild fig and perched itself on one of the pillars. When he yawned, I found myself reciprocating and when I scratched my nose he followed suit. I knew then the mystics were right when they say we are all One.

'No Nemo,' said a tinny voice at last from the other end of the line.

I focused with an effort, my headache worse. 'The meeting was fixed two days ago,' I said. 'I'm here to see Mo...' I quickly corrected myself. '...Mr. Matsunyane.'

'Not site services then?'

'Site services?-No, I'm a private investigator.'

'Wait.'

'Again?'

'I guess.'

Eventually the gates opened, and I began the long descent down the hillside. The track ran more or less straight for half a kilometre with a few passing places along the way. At the bottom there was a wide plateau cleared of vegetation above the sea. It was dominated by the high mast of the crane and parked near it was a long five-axle artic carrying girders. As I watched, a couple of black guys standing on the back of the lorry pulled in hawsers from the crane's jib and attached them to one of the steel joists. The men were dressed in shorts and T-shirts but wore hard hats and heavy-duty gloves. On the far side of them, I noticed Kwikspace cabins, several vehicles and an array of building materials including timber frames and fancy aquamarine tiles. Standing around a trestle table, three men were poring over what I assumed were blueprints or plans.

As nobody paid me any mind, I left the car in front of a single storey building of tired appearance and walked through a small *loggia* and open double doors. These were matched by others on the far side and, unchallenged, I strode across a carpeted lounge and out onto an expanse of tiered decking bordered by low bushes. The distant sea lay below me with a view all the way down to the Southern Ocean and Antarctica. Despite this, the breeze that ruffled the long hair at the nape of my neck was warm and an antidote to the intensity of the sun.

I turned my face away from the brightness and found my eyes drawn to the scene farther along the cliff face, or rather to the area below it. On the rocks, about ten metres above the sea, a vast concrete plinth had been laid and steel uprights sunk into the rock beneath. The girders I'd seen on the artic were being transferred by the crane to a holding area at the side of what was becoming a large construction site.

My musing as to what the building might in future look like was interrupted by a figure I saw out of the corner of my eye. He was built like a sumo wrestler but dressed like a waiter in a white shirt, open at the collar, and a pair of black pants. The pants and the 44 Mag Ruger he carried in a shoulder holster matched the colour of his skin. To match mine they'd have been tobacco brown.

'We got a doorbell,' he said shortly as he moved in, before planting himself in front of me. I recognised the voice I heard on the phone.

'Door was open,' I said.

'You Nemo?'

'I guess.'

I think for not much more than the price of a match, he'd have slugged me into the middle of next week. But he decided against and instead gave me a look that would have vaporised granite.

Looks are like words though: they don't break bones. Hell, he had the appearance of a waiter, and I needed a service. 'Could I trouble you for a glass of water?' I asked sweetly.

Large podgy hands became fists and a vein in the man's neck throbbed like a puff adder with St.Vitus's dance. 'You trying to be funny?'

I ignored him. 'Yeah, and some aspirin wouldn't go amiss,' I added, flashing a smile that usually melts hearts. 'I *am* sorry, but I've got the bitch of a headache.'

He pondered that one for long seconds. 'You better hope, Nemo, I forget your name real quick,' he said at last. With that he turned on his heel and, at a speed surprising for a man of his size, I watched as he propelled heavy buttocks towards a low table and half a dozen cane chairs. On the far side was a glass door which he flung open before disappearing inside.

He was gone a while. A while during which the pain in my head started to pulse with the regularity of a metronome. Concluding I was dried out wasn't difficult, but I was also as tired as a marathon runner grinding out those last hundred metres. The cause was my recurring problems with sleep. Shrinks variously ascribed it to any one of several disorders but the root cause was anxiety. It left me swallowing pills, and sometimes taking sedatives; anything to kill the churning in my stomach and feelings of suffocation.

My new-found friend returned eventually at the same speed at which he'd left. I took the aspirin with the water he thrust in my face and then let him direct me to a gap in the bushes. 'Take the path to the steps,' he ordered. 'Walk down to the beach. Moti will meet you there.' He squared up in front of me. 'But, before you go,' he said aggressively, 'I'm gonna take your piece.'

The piece was a Beretta Tomcat in a soft pouch pushed into the waistband at the back of my shorts. It was concealed by my T-shirt and because the weapon's small and light you needed sharp eyes to spot it. Very sharp eyes.

I retrieved the gun and passed it over. The contempt in his eyes plain, the man laid it on the palm of his hand where its insignificance was exaggerated. 'What's this for?-Icing crickets?'

I ignored him and then, under his lowering eyes, found the path that descended steeply before leading onto cement stairs. I paused at the top to view a rocky foreshore and an area behind where it looked as though somebody had imported truckloads of sand to make a beach. Discreetly posted on an outcrop of rock was an armed guard cradling a rifle like it was his first born. I took no notice of him because beyond chairs, tables and a damask red umbrella was a tidal pool where I noticed someone bathing.

Descending the steps, I strolled towards the water. Closer to, I discerned the bald head of a man, but his face was turned away, so he didn't see me. As I watched, he launched himself across the water, his arms turning over and over in a lazy crawl. At the far end of the pool and beneath a buttress of red sandstone, he lifted himself out and retrieved a white towel. In a leisurely fashion, he dried himself off and not until I raised an arm in a silent greeting did he acknowledge me by waving. With a further gesture of his hand, he indicated I should join him by the chairs and beach umbrella.

We converged over the sand from our separate directions at the same time. By then he'd draped the towel round his neck and composed his features into an expression of overblown friendliness. Such displays instil in me suspicion, but I went along with him as he pumped my hand and declared with a broad smile, 'Thanks for rocking up. It's a pleasure to meet you, man. Mind if I call you Sol?'

I shook my head and pushed my shades up onto the top of my head. At his invitation, I sat down opposite him under the umbrella and accepted an iced tea from a portable fridge. As he passed it over, I noticed the large ruby in a silver mount on his little finger.

'Really bin looking forward to this, Sol' he went on. 'My people say you've got the juice.' Then, like a cloud suddenly obscuring the sun, I saw his face fall and his smile evaporate. This denied me further contemplation of implants that showcased our Rainbow Nation's dentistry at its extortionate best. 'Pity we have to hook up this way,' he added.

'I was told this is about your son-in-law,' I prompted, sipping my drink. Sitting in the shade and with the aspirin beginning to work its magic, I was already feeling better.

Moti would have answered but his cell sang out. In that instant, I ceased to exist because without excuse or apology he glanced at the screen and took the call. I gleaned nothing from the exchange in Zulu, except an appreciation of his quick temper.

The interlude though gave me an opportunity to look him over. No doubt, there were many that would have envied me my opportunity. Celebrity these days has its legions of fans and getting up close and personal is the dream of every camp-follower who believes physical proximity somehow sprinkles a little stardust. Like the poor, the deluded are ever with us.

Moti was shorter than me but must have been at least 20 kgs heavier. Dressed in Bermuda shorts with a contrasting blue and yellow diamond pattern, his sleek and muscular torso reminded me of a well-nourished porpoise. On the other hand, his wrinkled and pockmarked skull which sat on a neck of loose skin invited other comparisons; the one that stood out was a Galapagos tortoise.

But, if there was doubt about whether Moti might ever shed weight, in the matter of his name, shedding those excess syllables had been ruthlessly addressed. The catalyst had been the press who'd quickly determined that even if they could spell Mahumapelo Matsunyane it kinda stymied snappy headlines. Who exactly had come up with the handle Moti was lost in the mists but there was no understating its grab factor. Headlines like *Moti donates a million; Moti wins mega Metro contract; Moti brokers a settlement* all made for saleable copy.

My host ended the call at last and threw the phone down onto the table. He was angry about something, so angry he'd forgotten about me.

'Problems?' I asked with my usual rapier-like insight.

My voice brought him back from the place his mind had sent him. 'Nothing I can't pack away,' he said dismissively. 'But your being here now's real timely.'

'How so?'

'Call was from my head honcho. He's been sniffing around some cash issues in one of my companies. Seems the smell's all bad.'

'How does this concern your son-in-law?'

'He's been siphoning off the dough.'

'You sure?'

'Sure!-What you mean am I sure?'

I ignored him. 'What are we talking about?'

'North of five million bucks. But it's not that.' Moti's expression became mournful. 'No, it's the abuse of trust.'

'And there've been other incidents?'

Moti looked puzzled. 'You got an angle on this I don't know about.'

It was my turn to be confused. 'If this is the first one, how come you asked me here?'

'I thought the meet was explained.'

I shook my head.' I was told it was highly confidential. Me, I was travelling to Plett anyway. I'm taking time out.'

Moti levelled his gaze, his eyes the colour of obsidian and the whites streaked with yellow. 'My son-in-law's missing, Sol,' he said flatly. 'Has been for over a month. That's why I need help. It's uber urgent.'

'OK,' I said, 'now I understand. What are the police doing?'

'SAPS don't stress in these cases. Not unless a party's at risk.'

He was right. I knew that from having worked for Detective Services for years. Resources had always been stretched and that meant choosing priorities. I guessed someone like Moti might be able to pull strings for a while but the relentless pressure from the daily toll of murders, rapes, armed robberies, abductions and so forth would soon have pushed any plea of his out of mind.

I drained the tea and levered myself upright in the chair. There was a large envelope sitting on the table. It had been there throughout our discussion and yet again my eyes alighted on it. 'That's the low-down,' said Moti, following my gaze.

I lifted the envelope and opened it. 'What's your son-in-law's name?' I asked.

'Anton van Zyl.'

In the act of retrieving the envelope's contents, my hand stopped. Van Zyl is a Dutch name while Matsunyane is Zulu. In the bad old apartheid days, marriage between members of different racial groups was illegal. It was the sort of proclamation that had echoes of those chilling enactments the Nazis signed off in Nuremberg between world wars. Decades on in SA and the law has long since changed, but behaviour by and large hasn't. Marriage across the racial chasms remains remarkable because of its infrequency.

The envelope contained a photograph and a sheet of paper. 'When was the picture taken?' I asked.

Moti shrugged. 'I don't recall, but he's not changed much.'

Van Zyl was handsome and stared boldly into the lens of the camera. He was tall and slim with fair hair parted at one side and was dressed in a blue sports jacket and beige chinos. Open-faced with a high forehead and strong jaw, he wore heavy glasses with black frames. He looked like a school teacher or college lecturer.

'What were the circumstances of his disappearance?'

'After a while he got missed.'

'You were that close?'

Moti grimaced. 'Our paths used to cross but it wasn't planned.'

I looked down at the sheet of paper in my lap. 'OK, I'll start with your daughter,' I said. 'Is the PE address the marital home?'

Distracted by trying to work out where exactly Anton's home was, it took me a few seconds to realise Moti hadn't responded.

When I did lift my eyes, I found his countenance cemented into a mask, his dark eyes bulging and dangerous. 'No way you shoot the breeze with my daughter,' he hissed. 'Namzano's bin real choked up by what's happened and…'

I put up a restraining hand, but it only halted the tirade momentarily before he was off again.

I let it all wash over me and waited for him to regain his composure. When he had, I said quietly, 'Namzano may hold the key to this. And even if she doesn't, I'm sure she'll know something. It's essential I talk with her.'

Moti breathed hard before I witnessed a transformation. The congestion in his face vanished as quickly as it had appeared. Soon, I was treated to a renewed display of his pearly whites as he expanded his lips in a wide smile. 'I'm real sorry, Sol,' he said ingratiatingly. 'Really, I am. Namzano's my only child so I find this whole thing uber painful. My baby's health's so fragile. Bin that way a while. As of now, I gotta say she's not around. She's been in Europe a time now. Anyways Anton's walkout isn't connected to Namzano.'

Later, I came to understand the significance of what he said but, at that moment, I attached no importance to it. 'What's Anton's line of work?' I asked.

'Project management.'

'In one of your companies?'

Moti nodded.

'What would have motivated his stealing?'

'Why would I know?'

I smiled into his vexed face. 'What I meant was did he need to steal?'

'What's your point, Sol?'

'I'm just working up a background, that's all.'

'He's dough of his own, but who's to say? Some guys just can't help themselves, can they?'

'Is the timing significant?'

Moti shrugged and sculpted his face into an expression of paternal concern. 'This is about my daughter, Sol. It's about Namzano and her happiness. I only mentioned his ripping me off as you were here.' He paused and scratched his sleek stomach with a manicured fingernail. 'It pains me, but it's not the whole reason Anton's no bro.'

'How's that?'

'He puts it around. You know what I mean. He's been at it for years.'

'Maybe he's run off with someone,' I ventured.

Moti spread questioning hands and the ruby on his finger sparkled for an instant as it caught the sun. 'Beats me, but it's a line. You might get bites from fishing the places he hangs out.'

I looked down at the sheet of paper and saw the names of two golf clubs, a gym, a glider school, and a racquets club. All the locations were in the Eastern Cape. 'Where did you get this?'

'Picked it up from the house. I had it searched.'

'There's no financial stuff.'

'Could be he lifted it when he took off.'

'Yeah,' I said, but I was distracted. The thing was I'd now heard enough to decide whether the job was for me. I came to a decision. 'I've gotta tell you this isn't for me. I reckon it's going to take time to find your son-in-law. Maybe a lot of time. And time's not something I've a lot of right now. Not for this sort of case.'

Once more, I got the eye-bulging routine as Moti's peepers registering something I call hatred. 'So why the fuck are you here?'

This sort of *kak* doesn't faze me. What messed with my head was being sleepless at three in the morning. 'I'd no idea what this was about,' I said.

Moti wasn't mollified. 'You think I've got time to socialise! Time's money, man.'

'I heard that someplace before,' I said coolly, making to get up. Making to get up that was until his voice interrupted and I sat down again.

'I can really make it worth your while,' Moti said, his face once more cast into an expression of empathy, indeed bordering on supplication.

'Making it worth my while doesn't really come into it,' I said. Fact was I'd inherited a fortune from a father who wanted nothing to do with me. Even after giving up most of it, I was still left, as they say in the circles I don't move in, very well-heeled.

'You telling me my bucks ain't gonna swing this?'

'That's right. Thing is I work *pro bono*.'

'That's no problem,' said Moti chuckling. 'You can work for me for nothing.'

I smiled thinly. 'The people I work for have nothing, so I charge nothing.'

From his expression, it seemed Moti thought this a novel idea. But he hadn't got where he was by being a dunce in the art of negotiation or by being slow on the uptake. 'Suppose we work this out different,' he suggested.

I shrugged. 'Before we get to that: why me?' I asked.

'Like I said, you got the juice and besides you know PE.'

'There's other guys.'

'I want somebody trained like you but who goes his own way. Other guys are up to no more than snapping back door men and sleepwalking checks on new hires. I need a pro and your record's ace.'

It wasn't flattery made me take the job: it was the size of the charitable donation I extracted. I did that with no compunction after Moti boasted about what he was worth.

Before we parted, he gave me the keys to the house and the codes for the security system. It also prompted him to direct my attention to the construction site below the cliffs. 'What do you think of my little project?' he asked proudly, a sheen of sweat glistening on his bald pate.

'I'd say you're building too close to the water.'

'Only if you've no faith in modern building techniques.'

'Faith's not something I place a whole lot of trust in.'

He shot me a hard look and clapped me patronisingly on the arm. 'You mind your back,' he said, before his hand gripped my elbow, 'and be sure you keep me in the loop.' With that, his features dissolved into a smile. 'You and me, Sol, are gonna become real close.'

Somehow, the prospect left me distinctly underwhelmed.

CHAPTER TWO

It took me half an hour to drive from Moti's to the Beacon Island Hotel. To get there, I had to negotiate Main Street in Plettenberg Bay, the traffic reduced to a crawl by angle-parked vehicles pulling out into the stream from both sides. It was always like that during the summer season when visitors from all over crammed the place tighter than sticks of gum in a pack. But bring it on I say: our Rainbow Nation needs all the dollars, Euros, sterling and whatever else it can get its mitts on to keep the wheels of our impoverished democracy turning.

On the far side of town, I took the steep downhill right-hander that gave me first sight of the hotel, its lofty elevations painted a brilliant white, its bulk immovable against the endless azures of sea and sky. Standing proud on a peninsula, the place always put me in mind of an ocean liner breasting the waves. It had been doing that for decades ever since the new building went up 50 years ago.

Moments later, I crossed the bridge over the Piesang River and parked behind Robberg Beach grabbing the space vacated by a white *bakkie* displaying Guateng plates.

As I approached a barrier leading up to the reception area, a security guard levered himself off the adjacent wall. 'I'm expected,' I said. The guy gave me a gap-toothed smile and wiped a hand across his beaded brow in the 35-degree heat.

Beyond the lobby and forgoing the sun, I made for the dining room. It overlooked the grass, and the palms, and the massed loungers, and the umbrellas, and all the people. Fold-away doors to the space where I sat down stood open and I heard the shrieks of children from the pool near the rocks mingle with raucous cries from gulls overhead in the palms.

I got as far as the third forkful of a chicken salad before I was interrupted by Effie. She's my girl Friday back in PE, though the term didn't adequately describe the range of her accomplishments. 'Hi Sol,' she said. 'Is this a good time?'

'It's fine.' I put a finger into the ear that wasn't covered by my cell as a small boy at an adjacent table screamed. 'The meeting's finished. This about Xavier?'

'I'm sorry but it is. You OK with me going to SAPS with the original birth certificate? They won't accept the faxed copy.'

I breathed hard. Xavier had been arrested for burglary and remanded to St. Albans. But the prison was for adults and Xavier was no more than sixteen years of age. Getting him released though was taking a long time, far too long, particularly as the only evidence against him for burglary was his palm print on the next house to the one robbed. 'There was no need to ask,' I said. 'Take the original to them. But before you do, please talk to Grunewald. Ask about making a court application today.'

'Under the Bill of Rights?'

'Search me. You're the one studying law.'

'Maritime law's unlikely to help much in this case.'

'Yeah, I know,' I said with a laugh. 'Just see what Grunewald can give you so you can beat SAPS' brains out with it. That's if you need to. I'm tired of this screwing around.'

'OK, I'll do that. What did you make of Moti?'

'In a word volatile. Says his son-in-law's missing. He wants me to find him.'

'When you return next week?'

'No, I'm travelling back later.'

'I thought you said you needed a break.'

'I guess, but this is urgent.'

And that was the way I left Effie believing my return was only because of the new case. But, even had there been no urgency, the looming prospect of spending time idle and disengaged had already lost its allure. It's said it's better to travel than to arrive and, as I looked around me, I could see the truth of that. Don't get me wrong, it wasn't about the place, it was about me. Time off provided the opportunity to fret and with that came a downward spiral. I'd been endlessly counselled to keep busy, to keep moving, and so dispel the demons.

I finished my meal and slowly drank a double espresso. I washed it down with mineral water before turning my back on the holiday throng and walking out.

CHAPTER THREE

'I can pick Xavier up at St. Albans this morning,' said Effie.

'Are you sure?' I asked, taking another sip of *rooibos* tea.

'I was told it's been cleared with the prison. I had a call from SAPS last thing yesterday afternoon.'

Effie and I were standing together in the workspace allocated to Nemo Investigations. It comprised two rooms within the double storey penthouse I own in Summerstrand. From the roof garden, complete with *faux* grass, there are views over Algoa Bay and the centre of PE. It was bought after I disposed of property in Lovemore Heights. That place had been full of memories, and I needed to move on.

'You'll have to be straight with them,' I said. 'Otherwise, they may give you a lot of bullshit about getting clearance. That means a referral to the DCS in Pretoria.'

'Trust me, Sol. I can handle it.'

I smiled at her determined expression and was happy to believe her. Effie hadn't been with me long, but she had a forthright approach and the sort of physical presence, despite using a walking stick, which gave that impression credence. She was a mature student at the Nelson Mandela Metropolitan University along the road pursuing studies for a doctorate in law. With nowhere to live, I gave her the lower floor of the penthouse and paid her something to look after the phone part-time; provide a reception service on the occasions it was required; run errands; and help out. My largesse wasn't particularly altruistic as having her around had a beneficial effect on my monophobia.

'OK, I'll leave it to you,' I said. 'I'm going to look over the van Zyl place. Ring me when you know how you made out.'

I took the elevator down to the basement garage and fired up the Mustang. With the snarl of the engine bouncing off the walls and low ceiling, I took the ramp and used the remote to raise the grille at the top. I'd been uncompromising about buying a place with secure parking having had a bomb detonate in my car a couple of years before.

The van Zyl residence in Sunridge Park was at the end of a street where wayward blades of grass along the verges were decapitated, probably daily. The houses standing behind consisted of detached villas with high walls, tall iron gates and usually either razor wire or electric fences. It was an area where if you had the misfortune to pass by on foot, barking dogs menaced your every step until you were out of sight and sound.

Number Twenty-Three seemed no different from its neighbours but, once I entered the grounds, the house struck me as desolate as a mausoleum in an abandoned churchyard. The windows were dusty and shut tight, the water in the swimming pool was covered in dry leaves and the shrubs planted out in large pots on the L-shaped terrace had all withered and died.

Entry to the house proved easy as the silence that greeted my opening the front door told me the alarm was unset. The air though was hot and oppressive as I stood in the hall and saw my face in a bevelled mirror. It wasn't a sight for which I much cared. There were black smudges beneath my eyes, and I looked kinda tired of life. Maybe it was a mistake not to have taken time out.

A slow drip from somewhere at the back of the place shook me out of my reverie. I went as far as the kitchen and traced the source of the leak to a tap above a butler sink. I turned it off, but not before pouring myself a glass of water. I drained it in one long gulp and took my time over a second while idly counting the number of dead bugs on the tiled window sill.

As I neither knew what I was looking for nor what there might be to find, I went through the house with the attention of a miser tallying his assets. An early win was the discovery of a laptop in a case that I found on top of a wardrobe at the rear of the house. Covered in dust, it looked as though it hadn't been handled in years. I set it up but found it was password-protected; it would need an IT geek to unlock.

Paperwork in the house was scattered in various places. There was stuff in the main bedroom, in the kitchen, in a drawer in the dining room and even in a box in the double garage. This last was stored on a shelf hard by a new *bakkie* and an old Mazda hatchback whose paintwork, once red, was now salmon pink. Unless there were other vehicles, and I found no evidence of any, it seemed Anton had left without wheels.

Nor did he seem to have departed with any personal effects. I discovered various items all of which spoke of his having cleared out in a great hurry. What added further credence to this was the discovery of a golf bag. A man who belonged to two golf clubs would surely not be parted from his driver and irons unless he'd had no choice.

What also became clear as I worked my way through the various rooms was that the house had already been searched, but not just for documents and paperwork. My conclusion was that something bulkier had been sought, like a package or a container or a box of some description and that it was the quest for this which could have been the main thrust of the effort expended.

I first noticed it in the dining room where there was a view of the terrace with those dead shrubs. Matching chairs set around a walnut dining table had been moved but not put back in the depressions their weight had originally made in the pile carpet. It was as if someone had lifted each of them and presumably turned them upside down to see if anything was hidden beneath; the same disturbance was apparent as regards other furniture. What I did wonder was whether it had been done by Moti's people at the same time as the search for clues to his son-in-law's whereabouts. It was something to be raised with him later.

In the meantime, I cast an eye over every piece of paper I could lay my hands on. It's sometimes through attention to the smallest details that the biggest breakthroughs are achieved. I'd been taught that truth early on by a SAPS Warrant Officer when I'd first joined Detective Services.

But, despite my diligence, the pickings were as disappointing as finding intact pansy shells after a storm. Nevertheless, when I did discover something, I made an entry in a small notebook. Yet what I gleaned were no more than a few names, addresses and telephone numbers and in one instance a place name noted twice that meant nothing to me. Of course, I'd check everything out later, but nothing leapt off the page.

It was mid-afternoon when I finally made the breakthrough. Concealed amongst five years' worth of bank statements was a document just two pages in length. Briefly drawn without the endless recital of covenants respectively applying to lessor and lessee, it was a rental agreement.

Specifically, it granted a tenancy in respect of identified residential property to one Anton van Zyl and had been dated three and a half years earlier. It seemed my quarry had an alternative address in another part of the city.

CHAPTER FOUR

Unlike, for instance, the summer sweat box of Durban, PE offers an equable climate. Generally, it's neither too hot nor too cold and so has none of the visibly well-defined seasons encountered in central Europe. For that reason, many people regard it as one of the best places in the country.

But exceptions always prove rules, and it was so when I parked in the Central district and searched out Anton's other address. I was only a half kilometre from the ocean and its cooling breezes, but as I stepped from the car the heat bounced off the pavement and tried to suffocate me. Not even the few dry leaves underfoot as much as trembled as I walked along the length of a dusty street bathed in a harsh yellow light.

Chandler Court was a six-storey block built in the *art deco* style. Its faded exterior gave some hint of how its fortunes had declined down the years, as did the satellite dishes secured to its sun-blasted walls. These deficiencies though weren't uppermost in my mind when I discovered the lift was out of order and that I needed to access the fifth floor.

I took my time over the ascent up long flights of stairs. I took about as much time as an octogenarian with double vision, impaired lungs and arthritic knees; it was that hot and airless.

I fetched up at last outside a stained door at the end of a gloomy corridor. As I pressed the bell, I wiped my forehead with an arm slick with perspiration. Then, while I waited, I saw wet patches appear on the front of my T shirt and felt trickles of sweat run down my back in the stifling atmosphere.

I rang several times. Thinking the bell wasn't working, I tried rapping but that got me nowhere. At that point, I had a choice as to whether to stay or go.

There were several apartments on the fifth floor. I tried announcing my presence at each in turn but either nobody was at home or, more likely, they weren't in the habit of opening up to uninvited callers.

I returned to van Zyl's. The door was a stout affair though ill-fitting, and I noticed a chink of light between it and the jamb. It also let me see that the mortise and tenon lock wasn't engaged, leaving the place secured by no more than the latch.

This sort of breaking and entering isn't my forte but a five-year-old could have used a credit card to push the latch away. Admittedly, the card ended up bent but by then I was on the inside.

In front of me, a corridor ran into a living-cum-dining room and beyond I spotted a recessed balcony drowned in sunlight. The door to it stood open and mercifully I detected a gentle breeze.

Moving closer, I let puffs of air fan my wet face and torso. While I cooled off momentarily, my gaze lifted above a rack full of damp clothes and took in the coastal highway below, the rail tracks, and in the distance the expanse of the Charl Malan Quay with its opposing breakwater.

In the next instant, the scream from a motorcycle racing through a close ratio box obliterated all other sounds.

That was why I didn't hear her approach. It was why I didn't hear her call out. And it was why she got the drop and left me feeling like a rookie. The first rule in my line of work is to keep your wits about you. I think mine had melted in the heat. That door left on the latch should have told me someone had slipped out for no more than a short while.

'Put your hands on your head,' said a soft voice that tore a hole in my composure like a torpedo striking a ship.

Startled, I put my hands on my head and began to turn.

'Don't move! Did I say you could move!'

She hadn't, so I didn't. I waited. Somehow the breeze and the view across Algoa Bay had ceased to matter very much. I waited some more. It seemed like a very long time.

'Now you can turn,' she said at last, 'but you make it slow. Very slow.'

I did as she ordered and confronted a diminutive figure pointing an equally diminutive gun. But small or not, such weapons kill as surely as ones that are bigger, heavier and possessed of greater muzzle velocity. It made me compliant, particularly as the distance between us was no more than three or four metres and her dark eyes were hard and angry.

'I can explain,' I said.

'You can do that to the police.'

This wasn't what was wanted. I needed to grab the initiative and quickly. What gave me immediate hope was that I couldn't see a phone. She was wearing a plain cerise singlet, which complemented her white skin, and a pair of boxer shorts. Both garments bulged over her pregnant stomach.

'Yes, I certainly can,' I said in as casual a voice as I could summon. 'But how long do you think it'll be before SAPS put in an appearance?'

'Put in an appearance?-What the hell do you mean?'

'Think about it,' I said. 'It's early evening on one of the hottest days of the year. You phone and maybe someone will happen by in the next hour or two. Maybe not. I mean you can't exactly tell them you're in imminent danger, can you?'

'You broke into this apartment!' she shouted.

'I'm sorry, but I must correct you there,' I countered. 'If you wish, I can give you an argument about what constitutes breaking in. That would of course be from the standpoint of law enforcement, about which I happen to know something. In this case…'

'You sound like police,' she interrupted.

I smiled. 'I was with the Detective Service for a while.'

'But not now?'

I shook my head and would have thought I was making some progress but for the gun that remained pointed at my chest.

'So, who are you?' she asked.

'My name's Nemo. I'm a PI.'

She looked surprised and her small firm mouth registered the fact by making an O shape. 'Prove it.'

'If I can get to my wallet?'

'Which is where?'

'Front pocket. Left hand side.'

'OK, Nemo. Lower your right hand and very slowly take it out.'

I retrieved my Burberry bifold with difficulty as the pocket was deep and the wallet wedged. At her instigation, I tossed it onto the floor at her feet before being ordered to replace my right hand on top of my head.

She bent her knees and, without taking her eyes off me, felt around for the wallet before lifting it. 'What am I looking for?' she asked.

'Silver ID card issued by PSiRA.' She looked puzzled. 'PSiRA are the regulators. It's illegal to work as a PI without accreditation.'

'But not illegal to force your way into other people's homes,' she snapped.

'I told you I could explain.'

'Go ahead. Explain away.'

'I'm looking for a party by the name of van Zyl. Anton van Zyl.'

In the act of appraising the detail on my plastic, she stiffened. 'That makes two of us,' she said with a catch in her voice. 'What's *your* interest exactly?'

'I was hired to find him.'

'Who by?'

'Mahumapelo Matsunyane.' Her expression told me this meant nothing. 'You might know him as Moti,' I added.

'Moti!-Isn't that the guy whose face pops up here, there and everywhere?'

'The same.'

'I think I've seen him on TikTok. What's the connection to Anton?'

'He's his father-in-law.'

She gasped and a look of bewilderment appeared on her pretty face. Distracted, and as though gun and wallet were too heavy for her to hold any longer, her arms dropped to her side. 'I don't understand,' was all she said in a tiny voice.

'You didn't know he was married?' I asked, taking the opportunity to lower my arms.

'Yes, but it ended. His wife had health problems. He told me she was in and out of a mental health facility. It was somewhere in the Northern Cape.'

This wasn't what Moti had told me, but I parked the information. The revelation that van Zyl's father-in-law had retained me to find him had deflated her spirit as fast as air escaping a popped balloon.

I tried to make her feel better. 'I got this address from a house in Sunridge Park,' I said. 'I don't think the place has been occupied for a long time. Can I ask how long you've known van Zyl?'

It was at that moment her face, framed by long straight hair, crumpled and she began to cry. 'For about eight months,' she sobbed. 'I-I've waited and waited to hear from him but there's been nothing. The t-time passes, and I don't know what to do anymore.'

'How long's he been gone?'

'Thirty-three days.'

There were other questions I needed to ask her, but first something more practical was needed. 'Why don't you sit down?' I suggested. An ivory leather sofa stood by a pinewood cabinet at the end of the room and, after gently retrieving the gun and my wallet from her hands, I steered her towards it. In return, I found a tissue in my pocket and passed it to her. She took it wordlessly and dabbed her eyes. 'I'll get you a drink. Maybe then we can talk.'

The kitchen lay across a stained wood floor. It was cramped and narrow with a single window looking out over the sun-drenched street. I placed the gun, which proved to be unloaded, in a drawer. After that, a hunt through several woodchip cupboards unearthed a bottle of Klipdrift. I poured a finger into a glass and added water from a tap that was tight and protested at being turned.

When I returned to the living room, she was sitting hunched in one corner of the sofa and hugging a large cushion to her chest; it depicted an orange cat with green eyes.

'Here,' I said. 'Drink this.'

She raised a tear-stained face. 'What is it?'

'Brandy and water.'

'But my baby...'

'...will be fine,' I interrupted her. 'I drowned the brandy.'

I got sort of a wan smile for that and a glimpse of white but irregular teeth. She accepted the glass and after that I sat down. Cautiously, she sipped the spirit, but it still made her cough, so she brought a tiny hand up to her mouth.

I smiled. 'What should I call you?'

'I'm Amy. Amy Smit.'

'OK Amy. You mind if I ask some questions?'

What she told me was that she had been living in the apartment with van Zyl for several months. Originally, she was his tenant because he told her, untruthfully it seemed, that he owned the place. Despite the age difference, I reckoned it must have been 15 or 20 years, they grew together, forged a bond, and became lovers. Amy said she worked in administration for a large distribution company off Govan Mbeki Avenue. She was home that afternoon because she fainted at work. She confirmed van Zyl was employed with a firm of consulting engineers but that he also did part-time charity work.

'What happened on the day he left?' I asked.

'What do you mean *happened*?'

I came straight to the point. 'Why did he go?' Her face told me she didn't know, but I had to prod her to at least think about it. 'For instance, how did he feel about the baby?'

It was a valid question but one perhaps better left unasked as it resulted in more tears. 'A-Anton was happy, really happy, when I told him I was p-pregnant,' Amy blubbed. 'H-he had no children from his marriage.'

'I'm sorry. I didn't mean to upset you.' I paused, before adding softly, 'Can you tell me how he was. I mean just before he left?'

Amy took another sip of brandy. 'That was just it,' she said in a firmer voice. 'Nothing about him changed. That's what makes this so difficult. He was as he always was.'

I'd switched on the ceiling fan when I crossed into the kitchen. It didn't seem to be doing much good because the air was as sticky as treacle. That was down to the changing weather because I noticed large black clouds moving in; clouds as heavy as the child Amy was carrying.

'Tell me what sort of a guy Anton was.'

Amy focused. 'He was really nice to be around and always made me feel special,' she began. 'He didn't have any issues or hang-ups. H-he was good fun and made me laugh. He just took life as it came along.'

'And you didn't notice any change?-I mean before he took off?' Amy shook her head sadly. 'What happened on the day he disappeared?' I persisted.

Recollection made Amy hug the cushion tighter and I found those cat's eyes boring into me. 'A-Anton took me to work same as always. I start half an hour before he does. I remember we agreed to go to Angelo's for dinner. I was really looking forward to it.'

'He took you to work by car?'

She nodded.

'What sort of car?'

Amy was embarrassed. 'I can't tell you,' she said lamely.

I smiled and hid my frustration. 'Was it perhaps white or a sun-faded red?' I was thinking of the garaged vehicles at Sunridge Park.

'No, it was blue. It had two doors. It wasn't anything special. Even I could see that. Anton always described it as a runabout.'

I had another idea. 'Is there any of his paperwork here?'

'No, he kept all his bits and pieces in the car.' I must have looked surprised because she added quickly, 'He said it was safer. Nobody would dream of breaking into the car because it was so old. They might think differently about the apartment.'

'And the car disappeared the same time he did?' I made it sound like a question, but I knew the answer she'd give me, so I didn't dwell on my disappointment. 'What did the police say?'

'What do you think?'

'I'm guessing they were none too helpful.'

She nodded her head, and her eyes flashed angrily. 'They went through the motions, that's all,' she said hotly. 'I could see from their expressions what they thought. Poor cow's got herself knocked up by a white guy old enough to be her father. He's had his fun and now…n-now…' At that juncture, Amy broke down again and tears coursed down her face uncontrollably.

I looked on helplessly. I knew enough to realise there was no point saying anything until the flood was over; she wouldn't be able to hear me. Wordlessly, I retrieved another tissue and passed it over to her.

She reached to take it and, with a strength I wouldn't have credited, grabbed my hand tightly. Lifting her tear-stained face, she asked vehemently, 'You will find him, won't you?'

'That's what I'm being paid to do.'

'And you get results, right?'

'I get results,' I agreed.

It seemed the easiest thing to say, given her fragility. But the truth wasn't as straightforward. People go AWOL in such large numbers that, when I first looked at the stats, I was shocked. Yet most of those who do go missing turn up within no more than a few days. And then offer varied explanations to account for their behaviour.

Van Zyl though had been gone almost five weeks with no word and the person seemingly closest to him had no idea as to his whereabouts. Also, the facts confirmed he'd gone in one hell of a hurry because, and Amy confirmed, he'd taken nothing with him. On the other hand, that theft from his employers implied his departure was premeditated, that he'd needed cash to facilitate whatever he planned to do next. But, there again, was his disappearance voluntary or had he perhaps been kidnapped? Hell, was he even still alive? At the moment, there was no evidence one way or the other.

I spent another half hour with Amy until she was calmer. I was happy to oblige but the additional time didn't do much to add to my knowledge. The sum of my additional insight was that van Zyl was a keen golfer, and his social life turned around his club activities, that and the time he spent doing work for the church. These pursuits had taken him away from Amy most Saturdays.

I left the apartment after dark, my mood matching the changed weather. By the time I descended to street level the rain, lit up by a street lamp across the road, had become a deluge. Standing irresolute for a few moments, I hoped it would pass but, as the minutes ticked by, the storm intensified with the onset of thunder and lightning.

Man's needs don't prioritise those falling within the category of physiological wants. That left me in a quandary as my twin needs were mutually exclusive. They comprised insistent pangs of hunger on the one hand and the loss of shelter if I attempted to fulfil them on the other.

Food won out so I stepped out into the night but found my recollection of the distance to the Mustang imperfect. Not that it would have made any difference. Within ten metres I was soaked to the skin and ten metres after that I was treading water.

I reached the car at last, climbed into the cabin, and pressed Start. As the engine fired up, I lifted my head and looked through the screen. I was in time to observe a dancing light show out at sea where tendrils of lightning were snaking across the sky and dropping fire to earth. Seconds later, I was terrorised by a violent crash of thunder that drowned out the engine and reverberated all around me.

Anxious to be gone, I threw the gear lever into Drive and put my foot to the accelerator. What happened next was unexpected. The car slithered, its forward momentum blunted as it slipped sideways. I tried again with the same result.

The reason wasn't difficult to spot once I walked with growing fury around the car. All four tyres had been slashed. Something like a large kitchen knife had been used judging by the cuts to the side walls.

As I stood there helplessly in the teeming rain, it might have occurred to me that this violent meeting of storm and sabotage was sounding a warning, a warning of which I was then wholly oblivious.

CHAPTER FIVE

'It's what I do,' I said for the third time. 'It's appreciated but it's really not necessary for you to thank me.'

Xavier's mother had rung early because she was a vegetable seller in Uitenhage and her days started before the rest of the world had opened its eyes. By doing so, she'd caught me on the hop as I was not long out of bed.

The previous day, Effie had gone to St. Albans prison and door-stepped Administration until they pulled their fingers out of wherever they'd stuck them and did the right thing. It had taken three hours but after that she drove away with a traumatised Xavier in the passenger seat. She was then the recipient of tearful thanks at the reunion between mother and son. What I was now getting was the backwash of all this gratitude.

'I'm really sorry,' I interjected quickly a couple of moments later when she paused for breath, 'but I must go. I've another call and it's urgent.'

Fortunately, she was satisfied with that and rang off but not before piling God's mighty blessings on my head. I've no strong opinion one way or the other about the efficacy of these though I reckon I could be worried if what were being piled were the devil's mighty curses.

I'd not called my breakdown service the previous night and instead got a taxi to bring me home. That left me with the task of retrieving the Mustang but only until I delegated the task to the Ford dealers off William Moffett. They said they'd send out a low-loader with a hoist and in the meantime source four replacement tyres. I toyed with the idea of calling my insurers to report the damage but saw little point in giving them a further excuse to jack up my already sky-high premium. For different reasons, there was equally little point in reporting the incident to SAPS.

I made French toast and coffee before moving out onto the roof garden. The storm had passed but ten floors up the wind was howling like a wild beast tangled in a net. Despite the sun on my face, the racket soon drove me back indoors.

Anton's laptop occupied me for longer than it should have done. As I've never had an aptitude for or interest in matters of IT, my efforts to gain access were doomed from the outset. I tried the password resetting routine three times, but it didn't work at which point I gave up. I left Effie a note asking her to see what she could do.

I headed out in the afternoon.

The offices of Newton Building Engineers & Quantity Surveyors were off the Grahamstown Road in an area known as the Deal Party Estate. Most of the companies based there were middlemen and factors of one sort or another. This made Newton, which made its money by charging consulting fees, look as though it was in the wrong part of town.

I arrived in the Fiesta at a tired, two-storey office block and parked out front adjacent to a vacant lot. On the far side were railway sidings, the N2 and the Bay. As I stepped out, the wind brought me the smell of the ocean and my eyes took in separated sheets of newspaper blowing around like dust devils beyond a rusted chain-link fence.

Brian Galway, one of Newton's partners, was tall and thin and exuded as much charm as a retarded mannequin. I wasn't surprised as his manner on the phone had been one beat short of hostile. But I think Moti had had a few words with somebody and told the company I might come knocking.

Secure in the superiority afforded him by his white shirt, plaid tie and long pants with razor-sharp creases, Galway viewed my T shirt and shorts with ill-concealed contempt. His gaze did linger though on my Omega Seamaster with its blue dial and matching strap.

After a perfunctory introduction and handshake, Galway turned on his heel and walked away. 'Follow me,' he said, spitting the words back over his shoulder.

I trailed after him, along a corridor, up a flight of carpeted stairs and across a secondary reception area to a glass-panelled door. Galway threw it open, flattened himself against the glass and invited me to pass by. As I did so, a whiff of something sweet and cloying assaulted my nostrils. It left me nauseous.

'There,' he snapped and pointed to a plain wooden seat with no arms set in front of an ancient desk. He settled himself on the other side in a *faux* leather executive chair. Devoid of decoration, the room seemed without purpose other than perhaps to remind the auditors, when they blew in once a year, that their work didn't need to take that long.

'I'll come straight to the point,' said Galway nastily. 'I regard your visit here as a complete waste of time. I've already spoken at length with SAPS.'

'I'm not the police.'

'Yet you're duplicating their function.'

'Not really,' I countered. 'Moti hired me because he was concerned about how Anton's disappearance would affect his daughter. Ergo he wants him found. The business about the theft is a side issue though it may prove relevant. Time will tell.'

'That justifies even less your reasons for being here!'

I shrugged. 'I'm sorry if there's been some misunderstanding. Now, would you mind if I ask a few questions?'

Galway consoled himself with an expression that would have killed the eternal flame. With that, he conceded defeat. 'All right,' he growled. 'You'd better get on with it.'

'OK,' I said with a smile. 'Tell me, were you surprised when van Zyl went missing?'

'Surprised?-Why should I be surprised?'

'So, he'd done it before?'

'Yes, he had but not in the same way. His absences were never this long. He'd usually disappear for two or three days at a time.'

'For what purpose?'

Galway gave me a crooked smile. 'I didn't manage him day to day, but I think it was because he had some woman in tow. That or it was golf related.'

'When was the last time he went absent?'

'It was a while back.' I looked askance, so Galway made an effort. 'Nothing that recent as I recall. The last time would have been during the winter.'

'What did the company do about it?'

'Other people covered for him.'

'And that was it? Nobody asked any questions?'

For that I got a look of condescension. 'Van Zyl's family connections gave him some latitude which he ruthlessly exploited,' said Galway. 'Also, you clearly don't have the first idea about business. This is a small professional services firm. Do you know how difficult it is to recruit appropriately experienced and/or qualified staff? -We operate here, not in Jo'burg or Cape Town. We must tread carefully and being heavy-handed isn't productive.'

'And I guess having your base here doesn't help recruitment.' I commented.

'That would be something for Dubazana, the Managing Partner. Or come to think of it you could talk to your client,' added Galway sarcastically. 'After all, he's the majority shareholder.'

I let that go. 'Was van Zyl on good terms with anyone here?'

Galway shook his head. 'He was tolerated by his professional colleagues, but hardly liked. He's never really pulled his weight. He was someone trying to get by through doing the bare minimum.'

'How long had he worked for you?'

'I've been here six years, and he was around then.'

'Did the fraud involve other people?'

I got a shake of the head. 'We think not.'

'How did it work?'

Galway had been sitting upright, no doubt so he could look superior across the width of the desk. Now he slumped back in the chair and began talking to his navel. 'We've been working with the Metro on several projects,' he began. 'Roads, health facilities, fire services etc. The work's billed quarterly in arrears but it's then payable within seven days. Van Zyl doctored a few high-value invoices, and the Metro paid into an account which wasn't ours.'

'Aren't there procedures to counter that sort of thing?'

'Of course there are,' snapped Galway. 'The problem is that our CFO has had several spells of sickness. By the nature of his work Anton worked closely with Finance. He only needed to choose his time.'

'How much have you lost?'

'It's already five million, but we're still checking.'

'Did he go missing because you found out?' I asked.

'No.'

'So, the fraud could have continued, perhaps indefinitely?'

Galway bridled and then became defensive. 'We do quarterly financial accounts,' he said. 'The embezzlement might have come to light then.'

That was as much as I was likely to get from him but as I turned to go a further thought struck me. 'Do you know anything about van Zyl's charity work?'

I'd expected Galway to say something but all he did was to choke on my words, the colour rising in his face. Perhaps, given our discussion about fraud, my question wasn't well-timed.

I descended the stairs thoughtfully. Two million bucks buys you a nice house in our Rainbow Nation. Double or treble that and for a time at least you've got a nice lifestyle to go with all those nice creature comforts. Everything considered, it seemed to me that van Zyl may well have lit out for good with the sort of money that would ensure he'd never be found.

At the bottom of the staircase, I caught the receptionist looking at me. It doesn't happen often with white women, but this one had an expectant expression on her face. 'Give you a hard time, did he?' she asked conversationally.

'Nothing I couldn't handle,' I said smiling at her.

She smiled back. 'I shouldn't worry. Brian's like that with everybody.'

'I came to talk to him about Anton van Zyl.'

'Ach, our very own charmer with the wandering hands.'

'If you say so.'

'And light fingers attached to them.'

'You heard about that then?'

'I should say. It was all over the company within a couple of hours. There's only about 30 of us so news travels fast. Are you with SAPS?'

I shook my head. 'Private investigator.'

'Do you think you'll find him?'

'It's early days,' I said without much conviction. 'Maybe you know something that might help?'

She shook her head, and I smiled to say it wasn't important. I started towards the door when her voice drew me back. 'T-There was one thing,' she said uncertainly.

'I'm listening.'

'There was a car,' she said. 'It was parked outside over a couple of days just before he vanished.'

'What of it?'

'People drive up and down the road, but they don't park on it. There's no need because if you're visiting there's generally off-street parking.'

I humoured her. 'Whereabouts exactly?' I asked, turning to face the road beyond the plate glass window.

'On the far side where you see the verge.'

'I don't suppose you could describe the car.'

'Mercedes with polished alloy wheels.'

'And the driver?'

'Heavy-set black guy. Chain-smoker.'

'Wow!-You saw all that from here?'

'My eyesight's pretty good and there was no wind. I saw cigarette smoke rising into the air. He was careful to blow it out of the window. Like maybe it wasn't his car.'

'Maybe you're in the wrong job,' I said impressed. 'How long was he parked?'

'Upwards of an hour, both mornings and afternoons.' She gazed at me quizzically. 'What do you think?'

I made a face. 'It could be something, it could be nothing. Who can say? Thanks for the heads-up though. It's much appreciated.'

I mulled over what she had to say for only as long as it took me to retrieve my phone from the Fiesta's cubby-hole. There were three missed calls from Amy followed by a text message which had arrived nine minutes earlier: *Please, please come!!! I'm very frightened.*

CHAPTER SIX

I tried Amy's cell several times, but it went to voicemail.

The distance from Deal Party Estate to Central is no more than a few kms. Do the journey at night and it takes ten minutes tops. That's unless the lights are against you. There are seven sets in Govan Mbeki Avenue. I got stopped at five. My impatient response was to blip the throttle. Impotently, I watched the minutes tick by.

The right I wanted to make off Baakens Street was closed. Instead, I drove up the hill by the Library where Queen Victoria stands stony-faced. At the top of the rise, I gunned the Fiesta past the SARS building. After that, I raced through the side streets behind the Donkin Reserve. In all it took almost 40 minutes to reach Chandler Court.

Frustrated and anxious, I braked hard and pulled up. The Glock in my hand, I retrieved a windbreaker from the boot. I put the jacket over the gun so as not to scare the locals. Then it was time to cross the street. A stiff breeze blew into my face.

Nothing had changed in the entrance hall. The lift remained out of order, my goal still up too many stairs. This time though I took them two at a time.

My chest heaving, I fetched up on the fifth. Straining my ears, I heard nothing so pushed the door open and slipped through unobtrusive as a ghost.

I stood once again in that gloomy corridor. There was a whistling from somewhere. I put that down to the wind. There were voices too, but they were faint. I soon realised they had American accents. Somebody in the apartments was watching TV.

I crept along the corridor towards van Zyl's place. The jacket still hid the Glock, but I now held the gun horizontally. My finger was inside the trigger guard. I felt sweat prickle on my brow and in my armpits. My body was so tense my neck began to ache.

The door to the apartment stood ajar. It was enough for light to leak from the far side. I noticed a jemmied lock. I stood clear at one side. Gun arm extended, I pushed the door open and watched it silently swing wide. Stock still, I listened for a time. It's fools that rush in.

When I was sure the apartment was empty, I moved into the doorway and then explored the interior room by room.

The place had been exhaustively searched. There'd been no attempt at subtlety, unlike van Zyl's marital home in Sunridge Park. Everything had been disturbed and displaced but not in a way which would have generated noise; noise that might have alerted neighbours bringing unwanted attention.

In the kitchen, each cupboard had been carefully turned out and the contents left on the worktops or on the floor. Jars and bottles had been unscrewed and the contents examined. Packets had been opened and their contents tipped indiscriminately into a large mixing bowl. Pots and pans had been hauled out of storage and the spaces they left searched. Likewise, the fridge had been emptied and the freezer cabinet unpacked.

Because of its quiet efficiency, the knife was the means of search everywhere. Mattresses and pillows had been hacked, soft furnishings ripped apart, the back of the sofa sliced open, and books slit at the spines before being discarded. Even the cushion depicting the orange cat with green eyes had been torn apart and its stuffing disinterred.

Deep in thought, I laid the gun and jacket down and perched on the edge of an upright chair, its cushion slashed. A sense of foreboding filled me as I gazed at the surrounding chaos. Given the amount of damage, I had serious concerns regarding Amy's safety. She'd left me a message saying she was frightened. Where had she sent it from? And more to the point where the hell was she now?

No answers presented themselves but there were consolations. At least there was no evidence of spilled blood and no evidence of a struggle either. But who was I kidding?-Amy was about 40 kilos and around 1.6m tall. It wouldn't have taken very much to subdue her and that was without factoring in her pregnancy which would have made her submissive.

I couldn't leave it there. Somebody must have heard something, so I went looking for answers along the length of the corridor.

Eventually, I eyeballed one resident who peered out at me from the narrow aperture created by a chained door. He was an old man dressed in a grimy string vest whose shaver hadn't been near his face in three or four days. A smell permeated from the interior, and it was one that spoke of neglect and abandonment.

'Police,' I shouted trying to compete with the sound of American voices spilling from his TV.

'Whatcha say?'

'Police. There was a break-in across the hall.'

'Break-in?-Where?'

'Across the hall.'

'You'll have to speak up. I'm deaf.'

It was a dispiriting conversation that yielded little other than the fact that his immediate neighbour was on holiday, one apartment was untenanted, and two others were occupied by people who he thought did shift work. Yes, he'd seen van Zyl and Amy Smit together once or twice but not to speak to. No, he'd not heard anything earlier that might be of help to me.

Certainly, he was disappointed he hadn't been able to help. I wondered idly how many people came to his door for any reason in the average week.

I left Central dejected and headed for home.

Only I didn't make it. A thought struck me passing the Piet Retief Monument in Marine Drive, so I stopped. Executing a clumsy U turn to the accompaniment of an irate horn, I drove once more to Sunridge Park.

Van Zyl's house looked as forlorn as before. The torrential rain of the previous night had done nothing to refresh its appearance. On the contrary, the clearer air made more palpable its lack of love and attention.

Inside though, everything had changed, and it wasn't for the better.

The interior had been subjected to similar treatment as the apartment in Central. In every room, I witnessed the same destruction which had as its key feature the slashing action of a sharp blade.

I didn't mark time as there was no point. What I did mark was that something had radically altered since my initial visit. No longer was the search seemingly for an item of size or bulk but rather for one that was small, yet of pre-eminent value to its seekers. Something perhaps like a key, or a cipher, or a computer stick, or a high value artefact such as a diamond or stamp.

Across the road from the house, a lady of indeterminate years but determined expression lifted her eyes from deadheading pink icebergs and called, 'Yours is the second car to stop by today. What's going on?'

I reciprocated her smile and strolled over. 'I've been hired to find your neighbour. He disappeared some weeks ago. You mind telling me when you last saw him?'

She pondered a moment while looking me up and down.' It was several months back,' she said at last. 'But he could have been here at other times. It's not like we're close. What's happened?'

I shrugged and spread my hands to signal defeat. 'I don't know. It seems he's vanished. His work's not seen him for over a month and neither has anybody I've spoken to. You mentioned there'd been a car earlier?'

'I did, didn't I? – There were two men in a large Mercedes.' She laughed self-consciously. 'I had to wonder if the car was stolen.'

This told me the men were probably black. 'Did you speak to them?'

'We passed the time of day when they first arrived. Like you, they wanted to know if I'd seen Anton. I asked why they were here, and they said it was to do with building works. But I think something inside the house upset them. When they came out, they ignored me completely and raced off.'

'Can you describe them?'

She gazed at me as though I'd asked for an explanation of moon tides. 'They were youngish,' she said uncertainly. 'And both of them were very well-dressed.' She paused a moment, before adding brightly, 'One of them was a smoker. He was standing where you are now, and I could smell stale tobacco. I've a very sensitive nose, you know.'

This and the make of car gave sudden significance to what the receptionist at Newton had told me. I changed the subject. 'Have you seen van Zyl's wife recently?'

She was surprised at that. 'Gosh,' she said. 'I don't think she's been here in two years or more. Of course, you'll already know about her health problems.'

'Something certainly,' I agreed. 'But it's a sensitive subject for any family.'

'It always is when it's mental health,' she replied quickly. 'We've been here 14 years and there've always been problems. She's been in and out of a facility up in the Northern Cape I don't know how many times.'

'It's very sad,' I said mechanically, my mind now somewhere else. Moti had told me nothing about a mental health issue as regards his daughter. Nor, come to think of it, had he told me other people were looking for Anton or for something he had in his possession. Pointedly, I looked at my watch. 'I'm afraid I have to go but thank you very much for your help.'

'You're welcome. Deadheading roses is very boring.' Then she looked me straight in the eye. 'Anton's a nice man,' she said. 'A charming man and there aren't enough of those in this world of ours. I hope you find him soon.'

For Amy's sake, and for mine, I could only agree.

CHAPTER SEVEN

For a reason unknown to me, but I suspect it was cost, the lift in my place only goes to the ninth floor. Access then to the upper floor of the penthouse is by a wrought-iron, spiral staircase. Because of her leg, it's not something Effie can negotiate except with great difficulty. This creates a physical barrier between us that guarantees my privacy but doesn't leave me feeling as though I am on my own.

I returned from Sunridge Park in a low mood. Apart from my concern about Amy's welfare, the trigger was the old man I'd exchanged a few words with at Chandler Court. Of course, I'd imbued his circumstances with assumptions that might have been false but there was no denying how he looked and no escaping the stench that drifted out of his apartment. It spoke to me of a sense of hopelessness and of the death of the spirit. His seemed an existence reduced to the blaring of a TV in a wasteland.

I guess all of us ask ourselves now and again what time has in store for us. I do and I know that as the years pass the burden this question exerts becomes heavier. Naturally, there are options. There always are. But the predicate for acting is a flexible mindset, an ability to see the positives any situation presents. And there, for me, is the rub. Too often, I'm fettered by an outlook that discounts the possibility of change and which leaves me boxed in. The shrinks and the mental health professionals call it depression. I call it what it can become: a life sentence without parole.

Wearily, I climbed the spiral staircase and crossed over to the cherry wood bar I'd inherited from the penthouse's previous owner. I tipped a generous measure of Richelieu into a crystal tumbler and dumped a less than generous measure of Coke on top of the brandy. I gulped a third of it down and felt the warm glow of the spirit take the edge off the rawness of my emotions.

I went back downstairs and trailed across to my work desk next to the room set aside for clients.

There was a single message from Effie. She said she'd given the laptop her best shot but hadn't made any progress. It was her view there was an additional layer of security that would need to be overcome. Specialist assistance was required so she'd made enquiries. One guy's name had come up and she'd got him on call back. In the meantime, and on her own initiative, she'd put the laptop into the floor safe. Evidently, her unspoken opinion was that the computer had some significance. I wasn't so sure.

Moti had given me a contact number where I could reach him, but I hadn't used it. Actually, I was surprised he hadn't called me. After punching digits into my phone, I got his messaging service. I came straight to the point: *This is Nemo. We need to talk. Call when you get this.*

Later, having tried Amy once more without success, I moved into the roof garden and grilled *sosaties*. These are lamb kebabs of Malayan origin, and the secret is in the marinade. Mine are usually pretty good but somehow that evening I lacked an appetite. It wasn't long before I pushed away uneaten the plate of skewers, sweet potato and salad.

It wasn't the same with the Richelieu where the level in the bottle went down with the sun which sank and finally disappeared behind the hills. Through glass panelling beneath chrome balustrades at the edge of the garden, I had a view 15 kms along the curve of the Bay. It stretched as far as Bluewater in the north and, as the light vanished, the sea darkened and became as mysterious as death. With my vision starting to swim, I gazed into this blackness and fell headlong into nothingness.

Because I was asleep, the sound of the ringtone didn't at first register. When it did, I wondered what it was and what it was to do with me. Only slowly did I make the connection and then identify where the sound was coming from.

At last, I lifted my cell from an adjacent chair. 'H-hey-hup,' I managed to say.

'Sol?'

'Y-Yeah?'

'Sol?-Is that you?'

I knew I was half out of it. 'Y-Yeah, it's me.' I was still trying to surface like a diver seeing the light above getting stronger. I made an effort. 'Amy?'

'It's Amy. What's the matter with you?'

'I was asleep. How are you? I was really worried.'

'You got my text?'

'I did but I was in the north of the city. It took me a long time to get to Central.'

'Thank you for making the effort.'

'But you weren't there, Amy. What the hell happened?'

'Two guys crashed into the place. When I went to the front door they grabbed me. They put a cloth over my nose and mouth. I don't know what it was, but it smelled sweet.'

'Maybe chloroform,' I volunteered, suddenly becoming conscious my mouth had dried out. I tried to get up but was unsteady on my feet. I fell back and listened as she started talking again.

'Whatever it was,' Amy went on, 'it knocked me out but not for long. I woke up after a few minutes. I was on the floor by the door and could hear them in the kitchen. They were searching for something. I felt sick, but I managed to slip out.'

'Slip out where?'

'I could hardly walk. I needed somewhere safe. There's a cleaning cupboard along the corridor. The door to it looks like another apartment. I crawled along to it and got inside. I closed it behind me and must have passed out. When I woke up, I heard them moving up and down outside. I was terrified. Then everything went quiet.'

I made a determined effort to get up from the chair. 'How long did you stay there?' I asked. Staggering, I crossed to the balustrade and leant against it. A gentle breeze bathed my face.

'It was over two hours,' said Amy. 'I had to be absolutely sure they'd gone.'

'Did you go back into the apartment?'

'The door was open, so I reckoned it was safe. I went back in and… and…' Amy's voice abruptly gave out. '…the place was a real mess, Sol. They'd r-ripped it all up and…'

'I know,' I said. 'I saw it. Amy, where are you now?'

'I collected a few things and took off. Anton told me if somebody wanted to hurt you, find a place where there are lots of people. I went to the Boardwalk.'

Groggy though I was, a sense of relief flooded over me. 'And you're there now?'

'No, not now. I got a taxi and came here to my sister's. I can't stay long as we don't get on. She lives in Despatch.'

For the first time, because the town of Despatch is an hour away, I looked at my watch. It was almost 11p.m. I must have slept for a couple of hours or more. 'Is it safe there, Amy?'

'It's fine but I'd like to catch up with you soon. Do you think you could come to me? Maybe tomorrow?-And as early as you like. I've been thinking a lot since we talked and there's more to say about Anton. I'll text you the address.'

To my shame, I let it go at that. I was befuddled, my thought processes slow and my perception of danger to Amy blunted by alcohol. Consequently, I failed to ask the obvious questions. Any of them. All I remember when I look back is my sense of relief that there was nothing more required of me that night, particularly as I knew I wasn't in a fit state to drive. I ended the conversation by wishing her well and saying I would see her tomorrow. I did it quickly, acutely aware I needed a pee.

CHAPTER EIGHT

Someone once said that sleep doesn't help if it's your soul that's tired. All I knew was that I'd suffered years of poor sleep, so it was likely by now my body was tired as well. As to the state of my soul, I make no comment.

Having slept earlier, I struggled to repeat the trick and so tossed and turned fitfully until around four in the morning. As I sobered up, half-formed questions started to nag at my brain, and these finally drove me out of bed in the pre-dawn.

I took a cold shower, drank a mug of strong coffee and left the apartment cradling a large bottle of water plus a couple of bananas.

I drove north-west along the coast road where the morning mist gave everything a hazy air. But that didn't last because the sun soon rose, its arrival heralded by a reddening sky slashed by brushstrokes of molten gold.

The town of Despatch got its name because it was from there that bricks manufactured locally were despatched by rail to PE. As an example of Afrikaner innovation, it touched a creative low rarely equalled since.

I skirted the south side of town via the R75 and pulled up a few minutes later on waste ground. I was within a couple of kms of my destination and it still wasn't seven o'clock.

I sent Amy a text saying I was on my way and asking her to get back to me. In the meantime, I drank some water and slowly ate one of the bananas. Despite this, lethargy overtook me, and my eyes closed.

I awoke some time later with a start. The strengthening sun had made the Fiesta's cabin uncomfortably warm, and I'd started to sweat. I checked, but there was nothing from Amy.

My destination lay on one edge of the Manor Heights estate facing distant, low-lying hills. I turned off an access road where piles of rubble and a yellow digger were parked. They were outside a vacant property with a half-finished extension.

Beyond was a track. At its end, stood a bungalow of modest proportions with hard standing for a couple of vehicles. Next to it was a grassed area where somebody had planted shrubs, each in a shallow hole to make watering easy. Closed-up windows stared me out as did the front door, its metal grille locked tight. If anybody was at home, they weren't doing a whole lot to advertise the fact.

As I stepped from the car, the raucous cry of a hadeda startled me. It was strutting about and pecking the ground in front of a wrought-iron gate that stood ajar. But it wasn't this which drew my attention so much as the glint of something lying in the grass. In a few quick steps, as the bird wheeled into the air, I crossed over and bent down.

What I found was a smart phone with a silver surround. I gawped at it for a few long seconds before switching it on and seeing a screensaver. It depicted a large ginger cat and, if I wasn't mistaken, the cat had green eyes.

With that revelation, I felt a tightness constrict my chest. It seemed I had Amy's cell but where was she?

The gate that stood ajar drew me to it. On the other side was a gravel path at the side of the bungalow. I passed scented thorn and young cabbage trees with their corky bark. Their foliage created an area deep in shadow.

At the back of the house, I found a crazy-paved patio. The length of the garden lay before me and was enclosed by a concrete slab fence. A high-voltage electricity pylon stood on the far side.

The garden's key feature was a swimming pool with a low diving board. I strode towards it past a couple of dwarf palms with brown fronds.

The pool was up a short rise. The grass in front of it was worn and marked. Closer to, I saw the rim on the far side of the pool. It was decorated with a mosaic of tiny blue tiles. Idly, I remember wondering how long it would have taken to lay them. I saw more and more the closer I got because the water level was so low.

How low became clear when I looked in. It seemed a long way down to the cement bottom. There was only a few cms of water around and under the diving board. Elsewhere the pool was dry.

But something else drew my gaze, a gaze that suddenly became horrified. Involuntarily, my hand flew to my mouth. All at once, the air seemed to be sucked out of my lungs. Then my brain started to scream. I realised it was screaming at me.

A figure lay prone at the bottom of the pool. It rested half in and half out of the water. Bare legs and the trainers attached to them were wet. Black shorts and a powder-blue singlet were dry. The head was twisted, and the eyes were staring into infinity. There was a mess of congealing blood around it, blood which had poured from the smashed head.

I'd found Amy.

CHAPTER NINE

I rushed to her. I don't know why. It was pointless. There was nothing to be done. There was nothing anybody could do. And if my instinct related to saving her unborn child, that too was a waste of time. Amy had been dead for hours. I found that out once I scrambled down into the pool and went to her. Kneeling by her side, I saw rigor mortis had set in. The speed of onset would be increased by the body's location. Already, I could feel the heat of the sun in that enclosed space.

I wondered what had happened. The distance to the rim of the pool above my head was perhaps five metres. It looked a long way up. Whether she'd been pushed or had fallen might would not have affected the outcome much. In either eventuality, the damage couldn't fail to be severe.

I marked one thing particularly. The pool was a wide one but her body relative to that width was closer to the far side. Did that mean she had been thrown in or had she, coming from the back of the house, been running? Running until she found that, terrifyingly, there was no longer any ground beneath her feet? It was a valid assumption as it would have been dark when she died. And, in this place, the night would have been inky black.

Numbly, I rose to my feet. I should have been hardened to all this by now. Fact was I'd seen enough not to be daunted by violent death.

The difference here was that Amy and I had been acquainted. However slight that association had been, I knew something of her history, and of her motivations, and of her dreams.

That made it hard: doubly hard because there were two deaths not one. But hard principally because of the responsibility I now had to accept. Had I not been drunk, I'd have turned out for her, made sure she was safe and secure. I'd seen what had been done to the apartment in Central and to the house in Sunridge Park. The savagery displayed didn't leave much doubt as to what the people involved were capable of.

I called it in like a good citizen. They asked two questions: was I sure the party found was dead and was there any sign of the perpetrators. Once I said no to both questions, I knew it could be a while before anyone showed up. But that suited me fine because it gave me time to look round.

First, I went back to the Fiesta and rummaged inside until I found a plastic evidence bag. I used that to secure Amy's cell before leaving it on the front passenger seat.

After that, I walked the perimeter of the bungalow.

The break-in was on the far side where a small pane of window glass had been removed using a cutting tool. It was as neat as anything I'd seen and would have made no noise. With the pane gone, access to the window catch would have been easy. There was a smudged footprint on the sill, but it was too indistinct to be of any value.

I went to the rear of the bungalow where aluminium sliding doors gave on to the patio and garden. There was a gap between them of about ten cms. Curtains drawn across made it impossible to see anything in the room.

I was tempted to go inside but held back. I figured there was an amount of explaining which would be required of me anyway and complicating matters by encroaching on a crime scene wasn't likely to serve my best interests.

SAPS uniforms arrived ten minutes later. Two of them climbed out of a *bakkie* whose side panels looked as though they'd been charged by a rhino. They were dressed in regulation blue shirts and trousers, and both wore peaked caps.

'Hi,' I said as they sauntered towards me.

'You the guy who called?' asked the female cop.

I nodded. 'I'm Nemo.'

'You touch anything?'

'Nope.'

'You sure?'

'I'm a PI. Before that I worked for SAPS.'

'Be helpful if you'd just answer the question.' It was the female cop again, now standing with her hands on her hips. Her male companion had half turned away, whether out of irritation or embarrassment was difficult to say.

I becamse short tempered. 'Sorry, what was it you asked?'

'I wanted to know if you'd touched anything.'

'Ach, that again. I thought I'd answered you already.' A flaring of the cop's flat nostrils warned me I might be on dangerous ground. 'For the record,' I went on, 'Nothing has been done to compromise your investigation. Now, maybe you'd like to see the body.'

Neither of the cops said anything, so I took the initiative and led the way avoiding the area between the house and pool. Wordlessly, we all stared into the abyss from a point adjacent to the diving board. I speculated on how hot it must have become down there. At least where we stood, there was a cooling breeze mitigating some of the sun's growing intensity.

'I thought you said you'd touched nothing.'

'I did indeed.'

'What's that then over the head?'

It was a scarf which I'd brought from the Fiesta and placed on Amy's face. 'She's pretty messed up,' I said. 'I put it there to give her some dignity.'

Pointedly, the female cop said nothing and turned her back on me before grabbing her colleague by the arm and drawing him away. What followed was a short exchange after which the male cop hurried back the way we'd come.

'Well?' I called across to her.

She slowly turned to face me. 'Well, what?'

'I guess you're calling for back-up,' I said.

She didn't answer at once but slowly walked towards me, her right hand undoing the catch over her holstered pistol. 'What I've done or not done isn't any of your damned business,' she said. 'In the meantime, you stay where I can see you. You understand?'

'Yes, ma'am.'

CHAPTER TEN

Sergeant Naidu of the Detective Service took pride in his attire which was not to say he was expensively dressed. I guessed he did most of his clothes shopping at the likes of Mr. Price and Edgars as salaries paid by SAPS to its lower echelons precluded extravagance. I knew because I'd been in the same situation for years.

But Naidu was doing well on whatever budget he set himself. He was wearing a salmon pink shirt with a button-down collar open at the neck, sand-coloured chinos held up by a wide black belt with a fancy silver buckle, and matching black shoes polished so bright they would have put even burnished scales of justice to shame.

The Sergeant found me sitting in the shade of one of the cabbage trees at the side of the house. He'd passed up and down on a couple of occasions after his arrival but beyond providing a brief account of my involvement and what had happened, we hadn't spoken at length. I had though given him the keys to the Fiesta so he could retrieve Amy's cell.

'My thanks for waiting, Mr. Nemo,' he said, his tone cooler than it had been earlier.

I got to my feet and mirrored his facial expression. 'I'm not sure I had a choice.'

'You're right, you didn't.'

Naidu's manner certainly had changed from a couple of hours earlier because his bearing was now stiff and formal. 'Let's start over,' he said. 'What *exactly* was your connection to the deceased?'

Again, I reminded myself that three days had passed since I'd met Moti. It seemed a lot longer than that as I laid out in detail the chronology of events for Naidu's benefit. It was somewhat slower this time because the detective made jottings in a notebook he produced from his back pocket. We were left undisturbed except by a SAPS photographer who needed directing. The rest of the forensics team, with all their gear and herded by the uniforms, had passed by earlier.

When I'd finished, Naidu cast his eyes back over the notes he'd taken. 'There are things I'm not clear about,' he said thoughtfully.

'OK.'

'She told you this was her sister's place, but it's not clear how she got in.'

'No key?'

The Sergeant shook his head. 'There were items of clothing in a holdall that's all. There's nothing that identifies her. No purse or wallet, no documents and certainly no keys.'

'She'd have had stuff like that with her. She told me she'd packed a bag when she left Central. And she would have needed money to get here.'

'No car then?'

'Amy told me that disappeared at the same time as Anton.'

'So maybe a bus or a taxi?'

'I believe she told me she took a taxi.'

Naidu looked at me as though he expected something more. When I said nothing, he changed tack. 'What's your view of the break-in?'

'In what way?'

'I'm asking your opinion.'

'It was done by a pro,' I said. 'I don't remember too many burglars using glass cutting tools.'

'My sentiments exactly,' said Naidu fixing me with a hard stare. 'Are you sure you didn't go inside the house?'

Suddenly, I didn't like his line of questioning. 'Yeah, I'm real sure,' I said.

'So, you won't mind if we take your prints, will you?'

'Of course not. You'll need them anyway for elimination.'

Naidu smiled thinly. 'That's very obliging of you. It will at least deal with one of the issues outstanding.'

'Issues?' I queried.

'I've had enquiries made up and down the street and no one recalls seeing your car arrive here at the time you stated.'

I looked at him incredulously. 'So what?-The car's about as distinctive as a Pick n Pay trolley.'

But Naidu wasn't listening. 'Furthermore, we've got a witness saying a vehicle like yours was parked along the street. That was around one o'clock this morning.'

'Same answer,' I snapped. 'I wasn't here overnight because I only left home early this morning.'

'But you've nobody who can verify that fact, have you?'

'A point I made to you before you even raised the subject,' I snarled. 'And on what basis would I call this in if, as seems to be your view, I was somehow implicated?'

Naidu had retreated half a step under my onslaught, but he wasn't giving way. 'I don't speculate about people's behaviour. All I know is it exists.' Angrily, he drew himself up to his full height. 'In this case,' he went on, 'I've got a young woman who was pregnant and is now dead in an empty swimming pool. When we turned her over, we found extensive cigarette burns to her torso. In short, she'd been tortured. We think it was done inside the house. Somehow, she got away across the garden. There's a heel print we think is hers in a damp area. It's deep and well marked. Our best view as of now is she ran away terrified and fell headlong...'

Naidu stopped talking because he'd run out of breath. He was clearly upset as his face was hot and flushed.

'And you believe,' I asked in a quiet voice, 'that I could be the sort of sick bastard capable of something like that?'

'Right now, I'm not saying anything. All I've got is a lot of questions.'

'And you've got me standing here. But that doesn't mean I'm involved.'

'Time will tell.'

'What does that mean?'

'It means I'm holding you until I've a better idea as to how and where you fit in.'

'This is bullshit!' I raged.

'Not quite,' countered Naidu. 'You told me all this started with Mr. Matsunyane. You said he retained you to find his missing son-in-law.'

'What of it?'

'I spoke to Mr. Matsunyane half an hour ago. He agrees he contacted you and a meeting was arranged. But he says you failed to show up. He was very disappointed as you'd come highly recommended. So, Mr. Nemo, I ask you again: What *exactly* is your connection to the deceased?'

CHAPTER ELEVEN

I well knew police lockups from the other side of their barred doors. The other side where you could choose to walk out into the light of day and talk to a friend, or buy something in a shop, or let the sun massage your face. Or you could decide to do none of these things because you wanted to do something else instead.

We call it freedom and, like so much else that's worth having, we don't value it until it's gone.

The place they put me in was a single unit. It had a solitary window high up that admitted as much daylight as a candle stub seen from behind a pane of clouded glass. There was a metal toilet, a mat to sleep on and a stone bench on which to sit and watch the world go by. In my case, the only world to watch was the stately progress of an elderly rain spider as it made its way laboriously up the cement wall facing me. It eventually disappeared leaving me alone except for the faint but pervasive smell of excrement.

On arrival, they'd processed me in the usual way.

First, I was duly informed I would likely be charged with conspiracy with persons as yet unknown to commit a range of offences as yet unspecified. But there was also a specific charge under the Trespass Act 1959 relating to my illegal entry onto land surrounding a bungalow located in Manor Heights. This last was at least innovative and met the requirements of the Criminal Procedure Act. That said, the charges to my mind were about as likely to support the burden of proof as an old and very tired cobweb. It did though enable them to hold me for up to 48 hours after which the law said I should be brought before a magistrate.

I use two firms of attorneys in PE. There was Grunewald in the Cape Road and one other located in Bird Street within calling distance of the law courts. My experience of attorneys was such that, it seemed every time you needed one, they were unavailable at your convenience. The usual excuses were that they were in court, in conference, or just *incommunicado* for reasons which you couldn't possibly understand and so shouldn't question.

South African law gives you the right to make a call to an attorney. Given the vagaries of effecting contact, I called Effie but got the answerphone. I left her a detailed message and asked her to make urgent approaches to secure me representation.

After that, I was deprived of everything I possessed but saw it listed in an inventory I signed. Next, they took my prints, seizing each finger in a painful grip and forcing it down onto an inkpad before rolling it across a record sheet. Lastly, their photographer did his best to capture my likeness accurately but my opinion as to the extent to which he succeeded wasn't sought.

I was then locked up along with four or five copies of The Herald which were at least a month old. This was all they were able to provide by way of reading material to fulfil another legal requirement under the penal code.

Frankly, I couldn't recall spending a worse night anywhere at any time. Fact is I don't like small spaces, and this one was very small. Light leaked from the corridor into the cell beneath the metal door sufficient only for me to discern the severe limits of my confinement. Trying to read in those circumstances was a waste of time. Besides, there was noise aplenty from adjoining cells which took the form of periodic singing and shouting, jeering and name-calling punctuated by occasional screams and violent altercations. When it became particularly bad, I heard the voice of authority from the main door of the detention wing bellowing obscenities. It was always preceded by the repeated banging of a police baton to get attention, the din of which was probably audible in Jo'burg.

This incarceration did nothing too for my monophobia. It increased my anxiety levels exponentially and left me struggling to avert full-scale panic attacks. Initially, I worked on it by regulating my breathing and doing no more than focusing my attention on the inhalation and exhalation of air from my lungs. But this proved inadequate in dealing with the morbid flights of fancy and dark places to which my mind skittered, often in no more time than the blink of an eye.

I hit upon the idea of exercise as a more effective distraction. There wasn't the room to pace up and down, but I could run on the spot. I started slowly as the night air had become chill and my body with it. Then, as my muscles warmed to the task set them, I ran faster and faster, my arms and legs pumping increasingly hard. I ran until my limbs ached. I ran until I was out of breath and winded. I ran until I was exhausted and could do no more than collapse onto the mat on the floor. At that point, I was as helpless as a landed fish with all my attention directed towards sucking enough oxygen into my lungs to sustain my existence. Once I recovered, the exercise was repeated over and over.

Even so, it was a very long night, and the dawn found me curled up in a state of semi-wakefulness on the mat. Its thin padding and my exertions during the night meant most of my muscles were sore.

They brought breakfast, I guessed, not long after seven, but I wasn't hungry and so only picked at the plate of white maize and sugar beans they served with a mug of water in a new enamel mug. After that, I sat on the stone bench and looked out for the reappearance of the rain spider. It seemed though he was gone for good, a situation confirmed by the way in which the temperature rose in the dry air as the morning wore on.

Small relief was given me later when I was asked to make a written statement. For that purpose, I was escorted back into the main station and introduced to an interview room that was the same size as the cell I'd just vacated. At least the room had a window, but it was heavily barred and looked out over a mass of bushes so thick the view beyond was obscured.

It took a couple of hours for the statement to be reduced to writing during which I half-expected some intervention from one or other of my retained attorneys. Nothing in that regard transpired and I was quickly bundled back into my cell when matters were done. It was then I discovered how poor the ventilation was for the lockup had become as hot as a Durban curry.

Lunch came and went. The afternoon came and went. The evening came and almost went before I heard a key being turned in the lock. The bespectacled woman who opened my cell door simply beckoned to me. Dumbly I followed her wondering what was up.

We went as far as the main desk at the station entrance where, in response to my questioning gaze, she announced, 'You're free to go.'

So unexpected was this turn of events that for a few seconds I was lost for words. I left it that way and satisfied myself with an expectant look.

'You'll be wanting your personal items,' she said.

I agreed I would and watched as she retrieved a sealed envelope from under the counter and opened it in front of me. The contents spilled onto the pitted and pockmarked surface and quickly I retrieved my billfold, keys, loose change, smart phone, bracelet and watch.

But there was a problem with the watch. 'This isn't mine,' I said pointedly.

'It's with your things,' she retorted.

'That's as maybe, but this isn't the watch that was taken from me.'

'So, whose watch is it?' she asked stupidly.

'I've no idea, but it's not mine. Mine was an Omega with a blue face.'

The policewoman grew defensive. 'Inventory says one watch with blue face. It doesn't say anything else. And that's what we're giving back to you.'

What they were giving back to me was a piece of junk you could buy in Greenacres for 150 bucks. The Omega was worth a tad more.

I reasoned what to do next and concluded what to do was nothing. This wasn't the time or the place to try and call the shots. 'I'll sign the inventory,' I said, 'but I'll make a note about my watch. I suggest you put the discharge form and the watch together and pass it along. I'll be in touch in due course.'

'Suit yourself,' she said, indifference written all over her face.

Minutes later, I got the Tomcat back, but minus the ammunition clip, and the Fiesta plus a deal of fingerprint powder inside and out.

When I drove away from the station I'd been out of circulation for 28 hours. It felt like 28 months. With something approaching gladness in my heart, I opened the driver's window and breathed in the cool, clean, night air, before seeking out the road that would lead me home.

CHAPTER TWELVE

The balcony on the floor below my roof garden was adjacent to the work area reserved to Nemo Investigations. There was a circular metal table and four metal chairs with brightly patterned seat covers, a beach umbrella set in a stone base depicting the South African flag and an ice box standing alongside and colour-matched to the day's cloudless sky. The view was out towards the ocean and the links course at Humewood, each of its fairways picked out in emerald green against a backdrop of tawny browns. The sight of it reminded me of van Zyl's reported love of golf.

I found Effie sitting under the umbrella with her head buried in a book. She was surrounded by lever-arch files and several tomes, each of sufficient weight to make it a lethal weapon in the wrong hands.

'Mind if I join you?' I asked, sipping strong black coffee though it was long past breakfast.

She inclined her head of short frizzy hair and smiled stretching thick lips to expose prominent front teeth. 'You really don't have to ask,' she said.

'Course I do. I'm invading your space, and you look like you're busy.' I settled myself into a chair opposite her, but not before removing a large volume with the captivating title Shipping Law and Admiralty Jurisdiction in South Africa. 'How's it going, Effie?'

'It's going fine, Sol.' A look of concern came into her dark eyes. 'Not so good for you, I guess.'

'I'm A-OK.' Effie looked doubtful. 'Really, I am,' I said. 'Look, I wanted to thank you for yesterday. Which of our legal eagles came through?'

Effie shook her head and smiled. 'I didn't contact either of them.'

Startled, I almost spilled my coffee. 'How's that?' I asked sharply.

'You'll recall you left me a detailed voicemail summarising your situation. You specifically said you had no alibi.'

'That's right.'

'There are cameras at reception on the ground floor, Sol, and in each of the lifts.'

I shook my head. 'They were disconnected months ago. There was a row with the management company when some of our more dubious residents objected to the fact that some of their equally dubious visitors might be captured on tape. I read the minutes of the meeting afterwards.'

'They're still recording,' said Effie flatly.

'How do you know?'

'Joseph told me.'

'Joseph?' I had to think who Joseph was. Then it came to me. 'You mean the guy on reception?' Effie nodded. 'Really. Just like that, he told you?'

'Not exactly. We were having a discussion one night a while back and…' She broke off when she noticed my widening smile. 'It's not like that,' Effie said quickly. 'Sometimes I sit with him for an hour or two. He's a law student like me. We were discussing the constitutional right to privacy and from that we got onto the subject of video surveillance.'

To have that sort of a discussion, I thought, took a particular type of individual and a particular type of mindset. But then I'm not a student of law. 'So, what did you do?' I asked.

'Joseph was here on the night before last. I talked to him and explained everything. We went through the tapes and found the relevant ones. After that, I contacted SAPS, and a plain clothes guy came over yesterday morning. He looked at the tapes and logged your times: 5.32p.m. in and 5.41a.m out the following morning. There was no way you could have been in Despatch overnight.'

'Unless I used the emergency stairs,' I said, mischievously playing devil's advocate.

Effie shook her head slowly. 'That's what SAPS said so we checked.'

'And?' I asked surprised.

'The emergency door on this floor doesn't open. There's some sort of blockage behind it.'

'You're joking. It must have been there since the place was built. But then I've never used the stairs. Who was the guy from SAPS?'

'Sergeant somebody…Nadal…'

'Naidu?'

'That's it. Do you know him?'

'Yeah, I know him. When I called SAPS out, he was the guy who showed up. We had a bust-up as to what he should do about me. I ended up getting the worst of it.'

'Why didn't anybody tell you what was going on, Sol? I said to them more than once they needed to keep you informed.'

'You recall what we had to do to get Xavier out,' I said soberly. 'SAPS sometimes aren't great on procedural niceties. Ergo, observance of the law can be rather flexible. Without you, I'd have been in there another day at least. I owe you, Effie.'

'Ach, Sol, you don't owe me anything. Rather it's round the other way. I got a great place to live.' Effie spread her arm to take in the view. 'And what's more it's within walking distance of the campus.'

I was pleased she was happy. What's anything about unless you're spreading a little sweetness and light?

What I said next though conveyed neither sweetness nor light. 'Going forward, I think we need to be careful,' I said, changing the subject

Effie slowly mirrored my set expression. 'You mean,' she said hesitantly, 'how did the people who killed Amy know where to find her?'

'Exactly. Amy texted me her sister's address. I don't think she'd have been telling anybody else at that time of night.'

'Are you ruling van Zyl out?'

I nodded my head. 'I've nothing much to base it on, but I don't think it was him. The guy's well out of the picture now.' I paused. 'Look, I'm sorry to have to tell you this, but Amy was tortured.'

Effie gasped and shock flooded her face. 'I-I didn't know that. Was this about van Zyl?'

'That would be my guess. Or they thought she knew where whatever it is they're looking for could be found. Either way, I don't believe she was able to help them.'

Effie was quiet for a long moment. 'What happens now Sol?' she asked at last.

I turned my mind back to practicalities. 'They've done the tyres on my car so that's my first port of call. After that, I'm going to visit a golf club. Some of these golf nuts share stuff with each other they wouldn't tell a priest on their death beds.'

Effie smiled. 'Shall I chase up the IT guy?-I left a message day before yesterday.'

'Good idea. And while I think of it there's a database of people I sometimes contact to get some eyes out around the city. I'm not hopeful but it's worth a shot. Do you think you could send a screenshot of van Zyl's photo and ask if anyone's seen him? Tell them the offer's open for seven days with the usual terms. Some of them can get carried away so stress they should be careful before getting back to you.'

'And if I need to contact you?'

'I'll call in from a landline or internet café if I can.'

'Are you sure?'

I nodded. 'Moti's one of the most powerful people in the Eastern Cape,' I said. 'And I reckon he's up to his neck in all this. As soon as he told SAPS we'd never met my hunch about him morphed into something much more disturbing. And don't forget he lied to me about his daughter.'

CHAPTER THIRTEEN

They were hills, but the description that they were *merry* was a misnomer. Fact was they were brown and dry and barren but for scrub. One area in the distance as I followed the dusty track to the Merryhills Golf Club was burnt out, leaving behind only the twisted and blackened skeletons of thorn bushes.

I pulled the Mustang into a space between a BMW M5 and a white Jaguar. Scent from lavender bushes hung heavy in the air as I walked across the baked asphalt towards the clubhouse. I was less than ten kms from the centre of PE but there wasn't a breath of wind and that meant the air temperature was several degrees higher than that at the coast.

Whence Merryhills had derived its name was answered by the commemorative plaque I noticed adjacent to the clubhouse entrance. It told me that Jonny Merryhills had founded the place in 1978. I figured he couldn't still be out there striding the fairways and swearing because of his errant tee shots. Or could he?-Maybe old golfers are like old soldiers.

The dining room with a vaulted ceiling, high as a barn, had a view over a wide patio to the 18th green. Access to it lay through a set of doors that stood open to the elements. But whatever light intruded through these and the tall windows was diminished by the heavy mahogany panelling that lined the walls. A bar ran the length of the back and the space before it was occupied by a sea of circular, dark-stained tables and club chairs covered in *faux* leather. The place was quiet and almost empty, so I distinctly heard the grandfather clock in one corner tinkle the quarter-hour.

I asked about my quarry at the bar and was uncertainly directed to three old guys sitting sprawled around a table whose top was littered with empty bottles of Castle. From what I could see they were napping. That or they were contemplating some knotty existential conundrum requiring closed-up eyes and slow but rhythmic breathing.

But as I approached, one of them in whose line of sight I happened to be, suddenly raised his head and glared.' We want more drinks, we'll call,' he growled.

Perhaps I looked like bar staff. More like he got no further than registering the colour of my skin. 'I'm after information,' I said.

'Information?'

'Yeah, that's right.'

'Maybe, I can help you there,' he said indistinctly. Then with a lopsided grin at his companions, he went on: 'For instance, I can direct you to the head green keeper's office. He might have some casual work. Some of the beds out front could do with tidying up. Or if it's the toilets you're after, you'll need to find our cleaning supervisor.'

I kept my temper with difficulty. 'I'm a private investigator,' I snapped. 'I'm looking for someone who went missing several weeks ago. You understand what I'm saying to you?'

That made the guy struggle to sit up straight. He glowered at me. 'I don't care for your tone.'

I was about to say something more when one of his companions intervened. 'Can it, Joost. This is interesting. Let the man speak.' He inclined his head in my direction. 'How can we help you, son?'

I excused the condescension because of his age. 'I'm looking for a party by the name of Anton van Zyl,' I said. 'Apparently, he's a member here.'

'Can't say I've come across him. Maybe he only plays at…'

'I know Anton,' another voice cut in abruptly. It was the last member of the trio who was well out of it when the altercation with Joost had started. 'And you're quite right, Hans' he added, 'he only plays at weekends.'

'When did you last see him?' I asked.

'Three, maybe four months ago. They'd give you a more precise date in the office. He enters a lot of competitions.' He looked at me out of blue eyes set beneath brows that must have been in rebellion for decades. 'What's this all about?'

I'd barely embarked on an explanation before Joost stumbled to his feet and with an infuriated nod to his companions headed for the door.

'Better go after him, Hans. I was watching what he was drinking, and he's had way too much.'

Hans stood up. 'Sorry, I wasn't able to help,' he said to me with a smile. 'I'll call you in the next day or two, Richie.'

Richie and I watched Hans hurry away. After that, he invited me to sit down.

'I'm sorry about Joost,' Richie said, looking at me across the bottle-strewn tabletop. 'That was inexcusable. Inexcusable until you know he lost his wife last month. Cancer. Took her off within weeks. Difficult to know what to do. I pray for him.'

'I guess,' I said.

'Now where were we, Mr...?

'Nemo. My name's Sol Nemo.' I sat back and crossed my legs before telling Richie as much as he needed to know. 'I'm working my way through a number of leads,' I concluded, 'but I've been at this nearly a week and I can't say I'm making a whole lot of progress.'

'I played golf with him, that's all. I wasn't connected to any other part of his life.'

'Fine, but you must have gained some insight into his personality and lifestyle.'

Richie looked at me uncertainly. 'He's a great golfer.'

'And?'

'Handicap of five last season. He said he used to play at scratch.'

I made to interrupt, but Richie beat me to it. 'Of course, you could never be sure about what he told you.'

'How come?'

'Anton made a lot of claims. How many were true was another matter.'

'For instance.'

'He always gave the impression he had money, but you only had to look at the car he drove to know that wasn't true.'

This piqued my interest. 'What sort of car?'

'Fiat, I think. It had two doors, so he struggled getting his clubs in. Some of the others made fun of him behind his back.'

'Because of his stories?'

'That and probably jealousy as well.' My surprise at this must have shown because Richie smiled knowingly. 'Anton was very attracted to women. And, if the truth be known, they to him. He seemed to give off something that made them come running. You had to see it to believe it. If he could bottle it, he'd make a fortune.'

'Was there anyone in particular?'

'Here?' I nodded. 'No, but he did tell me he was living with someone.

Had been for a few months. He told me she was expecting a baby so she must have been much younger than him. I could tell he was excited about it. He said he had no children from his marriage.'

I assumed he was referring to Amy, but I had to check. Unfortunately, Richie didn't know her name. 'Did he say where he was living?' I went on.

'Somewhere in the city. I think he mentioned Central.'

Now that had to be Amy which dispelled any notion he might have more than one woman in tow. 'Did you notice any changes? - In his behaviour I mean.'

Richie had to ponder that one. 'His game was off,' he said at last. 'Five or six shots a round now I come to think of it. That took him from being our number one player to being no more than good club standard.'

'Did that affect him?' I asked, though I wasn't really interested.

'No, Anton was a relaxed sort of guy. Mostly he took everything in his stride.'

'Mostly?' I persisted, but I could see Richie was getting edgy. Too many questions from a party he'd never seen before who'd blown in unannounced and disrupted his afternoon. 'It could be important.' I added.

The old golfer concentrated. 'There was one incident a week or two before he stopped coming,' he began. 'We were on the fourth green… Or was it the fifth?-Ach, it's not important. Anton took a call. That was unusual. And whoever it was he spoke to upset him.'

'Any idea who it was?'

Richie shook his head. 'None, I'm afraid. What I can tell you is he double bogeyed the next hole and then walked off pleading a migraine.'

'Did he say anything about it subsequently?'

'Brushed it off as though it hadn't happened.' Richie looked pointedly at his watch. 'Look, I'm really going to have to make a move.'

'Of course.'

I watched Richie rise stiffly to his feet after which I followed suit. What he'd told me had me intrigued while not advancing matters much. Nevertheless, I thanked him for his time, perhaps more effusively than was justified. But I saw the gesture rewarded when, as he neared the door out of the dining room, he turned and called me over.

'There was one other thing,' he said apologetically. 'I don't know whether it helps but Anton used to keep a caravan down on the Sundays River.'

'When was this?' I asked sharply.

'I'm going back a couple of years or more. That's the last time he spoke about it. Of course, anything could have happened since.' Spontaneously, he stuck out his hand and we shook. 'I hope you find him,' he said. 'I rather liked the fellow.'

CHAPTER FOURTEEN

I've met fat people whose minds are as sharp as whetted knives. The site agent sitting in front of me wasn't one of them. Either there was sand in the gearbox of his brain or a cog or two was missing. Right now, he was looking at me with indecision written all over his podgy face.

It was too painful to watch so I advised him to take his time before turning away and looking out through the office window. The park was as busy as a kicked anthill with an array of caravans, motor homes and large SUVs dotting the landscape. Between them people moved with apparently little purpose or sat in small groups around *braais* that streamed rich blue smoke into the still air, and often into their faces. Beyond were the fast-flowing waters of the Sundays River and on the far side of it the high banks favoured by sand boarders.

'Let me get this straight,' said a voice behind me at last.

'OK,' I said, turning back and painting a smile on my face.

'You're trying to buy me, aren't you?'

'I wouldn't put it quite like that.'

'How would you put it?' His pouchy eyes nailed me with a stare.

'What I'm suggesting is a trade. For letting me look at your records, you'll receive a payment. In my world, it's called a commercial transaction.'

He considered this for a long moment but the question he then asked showed he was not averse to the idea of payment.

'A thousand bucks,' I countered.

Evidently, he considered the offer too low. 'I could lose my job,' he said indignantly.

'Unlikely,' I said. 'If we agree a story, there's no risk to you at all.'

'Story?-What do you mean a story?'

'If your manager comes in, you say I'm from SAPS conducting an undercover inquiry. Of course, I'd back you up with some appropriate details.'

'But you're not in uniform.'

This needed the patience of Job. 'I'm undercover,' I reminded him.

He got that message, eventually. 'How's about ten grand?' he suggested.

I shook my head. 'I don't carry that sort of dough. And besides the client's not gonna OK it as expenses. Sorry.'

I made a hard face and stared him out until he came back with a reduced figure. Eventually, we settled on 2,000 bucks which I passed over to him. Then I let him explain how their systems worked but only until he was called out to investigate a water leak in the shower block. He said, he'd be gone no more than a half hour.

There was much more than half an hour's work to be done. What quickly emerged was that the company's records were in a mess. I suspected this was down to the fact that my fat friend was more proficient with adjustable spanners and pipe wrenches than he was with bookkeeping and orderly filing. To get the information I wanted required various sources of information to be cross-referenced which wasn't easy as at one point, three years back, they'd had a makeover and started doing things differently.

I got there in the end, but it took the rest of the morning. What I found was that one Mr. van Zyl had paid for a pitch for a period of almost five years. The problem was it had been vacated ten months earlier leaving behind only the sort code and account number of a branch of ABSA and an address for mail which was that of Anton's marital home in Sunridge Park.

'What happens when people give up their plots?' I asked.

'They transfer elsewhere or sell up'.

'If they sell, would they use your company as their agent?'

'Most times they do.'

'Do you know what happened in this case?'

'There's a sales file I can consult.' He gave me what passed for a meaningful look leaving me depressed as to the unexpected improvement in his uptake.

'How much?' I asked.

'Two grand.'

This time he wouldn't negotiate. I reckoned it had dawned on him that my spending so much time rummaging amongst the company's paperwork in a hot and cramped office meant my quest was important.

The sales file when consulted yielded the information that attempts had been made to sell a Jurgens Exclusive twin-axle caravan for a period of four months without success. After that, it had been towed away from its plot and its current whereabouts were unknown.

CHAPTER FIFTEEN

Crime writers peddle a lot of *kak* about police work. Their readers are frequently left with the impression that one event leads seamlessly to another, and to another, which remorselessly closes the gap between the start of an investigation and its successful outcome. It's the reason why most crime writers would be unsuited to police work and why most police officers don't read crime fiction.

The fact of the matter is that most investigations are messy with open-ended timescales and no guarantees of success. Often, they stall and in a world of ever-shifting priorities they can be sidelined or sometimes abandoned altogether. And if you worked for a police force like SAPS you often had to contend with organisational ineptitude, administrative bungling, political interference, and a level of ongoing corruption likely to dog your footsteps at every second turn.

I didn't have any of those excuses. Nor were there other things crowding me in and, even if there had been, this case would have remained my priority. It was for the reason I dislike leaving things undone but also because a dawning realisation had taken hold of me.

Simply put, I considered myself now working for a posthumous client by the name of Amy Smit. When I met her in the apartment in Central, she asked my help in finding her lover. I remembered saying I would and when she asked whether I got results she received a positive answer. Fact was I owed her because a profound sense of guilt possessed me after what had happened. Sometimes, it overwhelmed me. If I'd got to her that night, maybe I'd have made the difference. Maybe not. Whatever the outcome now, I would at least have tried my best for her. History couldn't be rewritten, but I might at least try to atone.

The rest of the day was spent in the Sundays River Valley trailing from one tourist spot to another. I was looking for a Jurgens Exclusive caravan which, if I was lucky, would disgorge the missing Anton van Zyl at my bidding.

Achieving the first part of my objective wasn't difficult. There were a few caravans which fitted the description and each time I saw one my heart leapt. But not for long as it soon crashed back to earth in the face of yet another dead-end.

I wound up at the end of the day back on the site where I'd started that morning. It was only because the Mustang needed filling up before driving back to PE. By the petrol station was a small supermarket and a café, the smell of food reminding me I'd not eaten. I bought a Gatsby with a bottle of sparkling water and settled myself outside at a bench-style table loaded with debris from the day's trading. I wondered if it had been left as testimony to the success of the place, or maybe they were short-staffed.

I was hot and tired, but the bread roll filled with fish, chips and *piri-piri* sauce made me forget my fatigue. Around me, the light began to leak away and as it did the glow of cigarette tips from an adjacent table became brighter. The smokers were white kids drinking bottled beer and loudly exchanging mock insults that flew between them fast as meteorites.

I envied them their youth and careless ways only until someone emerged from the gloom and told them to put out their cigarettes. This was greeted by catcalls followed by an altercation that was drowned out by an unexpected uproar.

The source of the clamour lay in a car park thirty metres away across a strip of yellowed grass and beyond an open-railed fence. It was made by a *bakkie* with defective baffles that pulled out suddenly and accelerated away into the gloom. Before it did, its headlights picked out the rounded shape of a small blue car parked alongside and the figure of a tall man wearing glasses. As I stared, the man opened the driver's door and climbed in. Seconds later, the car's engine fired up and it started to move off.

By that time, I was on my feet and dashing across the grass to the fence. Half-vaulting, half-falling over it, I landed on my knees. Looking up, I was in time to confirm the car was a Fiat and for me to suspect it was van Zyl at the wheel. He wasn't driving quickly but, even as I started running, I knew I couldn't keep up. Winded, I halted and watched as the car's tail lights receded into the distance, the track between the trees running straight for several hundred metres.

After that, van Zyl indicated left and abruptly vanished. I couldn't recall a turn at the spot where he disappeared. It didn't matter. I needed my car and sprinted for it. Executing a tight three-point turn, I gunned the engine and hurtled after him.

I missed the turn by a margin and had to back up. It descended through a narrow defile after which it climbed barren ground. I killed the lights and with a gentle throttle ascended at little more than walking pace. At the top of the rise, I applied the brakes and looked out through the screen. I discerned nothing until I saw a speck of brightness away to my left. I ran the Mustang forward a short distance, braked and switched off.

The light came from a window set into the end wall of a small dwelling. It looked like nothing more from the outside than a large shed. At one side, as my eyes adjusted to the darkness, I spotted the Fiat.

I wondered what to do. I stretched the wondering into a long minute. After that, I transferred the Glock to my right hand. Automatically, I slipped the safety off.

There was a door to the place but no knocker. I rapped with my bare knuckles on grainy wood. But the door was stout and there was no echo. I tried again with the same result. I was about to give it a third try when I heard a voice. I couldn't make out what was being said so I rapped again.

'What do you want?' The man's voice was louder but neutral, conveying neither fear nor anger.

'Need to speak with you,' I said.

'What about?'

'Amy sent me.'

'Amy?' Now there was surprise in the tone.

'Yeah, that's right. You think you could open up?'

'Who are you?'

'The name's Nemo. I'm a private investigator.'

There was silence from inside, a silence that made me acutely aware of the racket made by cicadas in a stand of trees close by.

I was about to knock again when I heard a bolt being drawn back. After that, the door squeaked on rusty hinges as it was opened a fraction. In the gap between door and frame, I saw a bespectacled dome of a head. It was lit softly from behind.

'Did you say Nemo?'

'Sol Nemo. I'm a PI in the city.'

'And you've come from Amy?'

I hedged. 'In a manner of speaking.' I flashed one of my icebreaker smiles. 'Do you think you could let me in?'

With only slight hesitation, the door opened to reveal a tall, slim man who appraised me critically. He was dressed in black shorts with white stripes on the sides and a T shirt depicting a springbok and a protea. 'Come in,' he said at last, standing aside. 'Go straight through,' he advised as he let me past.

I walked into a single living-cum-dining room with no more than a few sticks of furniture set out upon a threadbare oatmeal mat. Light was cast by a single, old-fashioned standard lamp with a faded red shade. At the back was a closed door. Surreptitiously, I put the safety back on the Glock, before slipping the weapon into the waistband of my shorts.

When I turned round, Anton was looking at me, the expression on his face watchful. Behind heavy, black-framed glasses, his eyes searched my face. 'How did you find me?' he asked.

'With some very considerable difficulty.'

For the first time, Anton smiled. 'That's good to know. But *how* did you find me?'

'I discovered the lease for the place in Central. Look, I need…'

'Where?' he interrupted.

'It was buried in a pile of bank statements. I'm sorry but I've…'

I got no further for at that moment there was a crash of breaking glass. Something black and heavy came through the window and landed between us. Slowly, it rolled away and was lost under a heavy armchair. Next, there was a blinding flash and a deafening explosion, the sort made by a stun grenade. It sent me reeling and I cannoned hard into the lamp before falling. With singular presence of mind, I managed to rip the wire flex out of its socket. The intense pulse of light now gone, the room was plunged into darkness.

Momentarily, I saw nothing and heard less. But pain registered all right when Anton stepped on my leg as he hurried across the room. Next, fire caught hold in the fabric beneath the armchair. Flames fanned outwards from the base and started to make smoke. But it wasn't this that so much grabbed my attention as the torch beam I saw at the front door. Whoever had attacked the house had managed to gain entry.

I turned on my side and fumbled the gun out of my shorts. Raising it, I fired twice at the beam. At once, it vanished but I knew no more than that because I'd been deafened by the grenade. In front of me, the armchair fire was now licking towards the roof. Choking black smoke spread its tendrils ever wider and made me cough. I had to move and fast.

Crawling on my stomach, I found the door at the back of the room. It now stood open. I guessed it was the way Anton had escaped. Lit by the flames behind me I discerned a short passage with a room on either side. I went left which I figured was at the rear of the house. Keeping low, I crawled past a bed. Then I felt a gentle breeze on my face from an open window. I positioned myself under it and took stock.

Fire from the living room grew ever brighter but I could barely hear it. It was like my ears were filled with wax. My loss of hearing distressed me, but the feeling was made worse because I'd no idea what was happening outside. To do that, I needed to put my head above the window sill. That seemed to me to carry with it a considerable risk.

But I couldn't stay where I was. Smoke was now billowing into the bedroom. Even at ground level I was struggling to breathe. Panicking, I took a tissue from my pocket. I held it over my mouth and nose.

After that, I moved to one side of the window. Protected by the wall, I stood up. There was a sharp pain in my leg but it hardly registered. Cautiously, I peered out.

I was much reassured by what I saw. There was darkness and no moon. The overcast made the landscape a canvas of greys and blacks.

Behind my back, I felt the heat of the fire. It was becoming impossible to breathe. There was nothing more to be thought about. I thrust the window wide and got up onto the sill. I didn't linger but dropped to the ground.

I fell into a thorn bush. It scratched my arms and legs and lacerated my face. With difficulty, I extricated myself but at the expense of a torn T shirt. Then, in a crouching run, I sprinted a couple of hundred metres away from the house.

When I did stop and breathlessly look back, it was from a shallow ridge. Below me, the house was well-ablaze with flames leaping high above the roof line and a plume of oily smoke drifting in the still air. On the far side, where the Mustang was parked, a group of people were gathering as the fire raged out of control.

I gave the onlookers a wide berth and approached my car by a circuitous route. Nobody paid me any attention as I slipped the Mustang into Drive. It was only when I pulled over a minute or two later to let a fire engine through that I found myself profoundly deaf.

CHAPTER SIXTEEN

I drove the distance to a truck stop on the Grahamstown Road. It offered a place of safety as its range of services included guarded parking. More used to keeping a beady camera eye on high-value loads travelling inter-city in three-axle artics, the attendant who exchanged a room key for money looked at me askance and then spoke. As I couldn't hear what he was saying, I did no more than smile and turn away. Halfway across the floor though, he tapped me on the shoulder and offered me a half empty bottle of Dettol. Mystified, I took it and smiled again.

The overnight accommodation was in two lines of single storey units divided by a concrete causeway. They didn't look like much from the outside and they didn't look like much from the inside either. But they were clean and tidy and would meet my needs for the remaining hours of the night.

I took the holdall containing a change of clothes I carry from the car and found my room. After locking the door and leaving the Glock within easy reach, I discarded my torn T shirt and examined myself in the bathroom mirror. The reason for the antiseptic became clear when I noticed a long gash to the side of my neck.

The Dettol stung like fire as I used a tissue to remove congealed blood and clean up. Other lacerations were similarly attended to but my mind, in truth, was soon somewhere else.

What the hell had gone wrong?

Clearly, I'd been followed to van Zyl's hideaway but how? I thought back over the events of the day and recalled all the places in the Valley where I'd stopped. There must have been half a dozen or more where I'd pulled up, left the car and walked round looking for that twin-axle caravan. I'd been amongst all those visitors at the height of a South African summer: retired couples in let-it-all-hang-out dress mode; parents with young children in tow; groups of loud and cheerful students; and foreign tourists.

I'd spotted nobody with the lean and hungry look of a pursuer. I thought I'd kept my wits about me; thought I'd been aware of who was around and what they were doing; thought I was safe and secure.

It was chilling to think that hadn't been the case.

And that brought with it another thought. If they'd got me taped, they could have taken me out at any time. More than that, they could have ended it at van Zyl's place by lobbing a hand grenade rather than a thunderflash. They had us both cold and the fact they'd not sought to exploit the situation meant they wanted van Zyl alive; I wasn't in doubt that once he'd been caught, I'd probably have been toast. Letting him live meant he had something or knew something they wanted to get their hands on.

But had he got away? He had a head start on me of at least a couple of minutes. I was sure he'd left the house the same way I did. Nobody had been waiting outside for me so was it safe to assume he too had got clear?

I slept fitfully and awoke before six when light pierced a gap in the curtains and shone onto the bedspread. I got up and turned on the shower. The previous night the water had streamed silently, now I heard a distant cascade. It was the same when I brushed my teeth and washed my hands under the tap.

Glancing out of the bathroom window, I was in time to see metal shutters being rolled up on the far side of an empty expanse of concrete. As I watched, a middle-aged coloured guy with a black moustache and dressed in stained overalls emerged into the sunshine and stretched. He had the look of a proprietor about him as he carelessly threw the contents of a china mug down on the ground. Behind him, I saw the interior of a workshop with a four-post lift at the back. It was in a raised position with a white delivery van mounted on it. The sight of the vehicle put something into my mind that I had to act on.

Moments later, I retrieved the Mustang and drove across to the workshop, parking inside adjacent to a small office. The burble from the engine before I cut it was so muted it wouldn't have disturbed a napping cat.

I found the proprietor sitting behind a paper-strewn desk in the office. He didn't look pleased to see me and when asked if he could help me, I didn't hear his answer.

'Come again,' I said.

The guy lifted his arm and showed me the face of his watch. 'Sorry, come back in a couple of hours. I'm catching up on my accounts.' He pointed to the mess on his desk.

Catching his drift, I said pointedly, 'I can help with that.'

'How?'

'With your cash flow. I need access to your lift.'

'What's the problem?' he shouted back at me, now deducing I was hard of hearing.

I shrugged. 'Not sure. That's why I want to look.'

The guy got to his feet and crossed over. For someone in his line of work, his fingernails were remarkably clean but close up he exuded a strong smell of oil. 'Cost you a thousand bucks,' he yelled.

'Whatever.'

The money paid, he took the wheel of the Mustang and turned it to face a lift at one end of his workshop. This was ideal because it couldn't be seen from the entrance. I watched as he manoeuvred the car onto the lift after which he hoisted it using an electric button pad.

Overcoming an irrational thought that the lift would collapse and crush me, I stood beneath the raised vehicle. Using a powerful torch, I examined the underside from end to end amongst a deal of road dirt and caked mud. Nevertheless, I found the tracking device in less than five minutes. It was about the size of a pack of cigarettes and had two silver magnets on its side.

But I didn't stop the search and that proved the right thing to do. There was a second device wedged into a space hidden from view by a branch of the twin-exhausts. I took both trackers and placed them inside the Mustang's cabin.

Figuring what to do with them was the next problem. Assuming my car was being eyeballed much of the time, it seemed to me I needed to put some distance between where I was now and wherever I was going before dumping the devices. And doing it in such a way it was thought they were still attached to the car was important.

I pondered that one over a quick breakfast of French toast and black coffee before getting my things together and heading off on the N2.

I booted it the 300kms to East London. It took me under two and a half hours. Of course, I knew they'd follow me, but they had no need to be hot on my heels as the trackers provided ongoing reassurance as to my whereabouts.

Exiting the motorway on the east side of the Nahoon River, I passed through Beaconhurst and wound up in Blue Bend in the vicinity of a cluster of B&Bs. It wasn't them though that caught my attention so much as the gated estate a few metres along the road. Leaving my car, I took the trackers and approached the entrance in time to see a large, unmarked panel van stop and wait for the gates to open. Swiftly, I crossed to it and fixed the trackers inside the nearside rear wheel arch. My actions went unobserved except by a group of guinea fowl, but I reckoned they were too busy foraging to have the energy to tell tales.

Whether my initiative sorted the problem needed me to stick around. I moved the car down the road and parked in the deep shade of a group of palms. Locking up, I jogged back the way I'd come and then walked into the grounds of one of the B&Bs. They were still serving late breakfast on the first floor, and, with all the self-assurance of a paying guest, I helped myself to a coffee from their hospitality tray and strolled over to a small table by a large picture window. It had a view over the entrance of the gated estate where the guinea fowl continued to peck at the verge.

A long ten minutes passed before anyone showed up. By then I was enjoying a second drink and wondering how long it would be before someone asked who I was.

I ceased to worry about that though when a large dark car appeared and halted outside the estate. It was a black Mercedes saloon with polished alloys. As I watched, the driver's window slid down and I saw the guy inside light a cigarette, draw on it deeply and exhale a stream of blue smoke into the listless air.

He was joined a few minutes later by another car that parked nose to nose with him. Its two occupants climbed out and joined the smoker on the verge. An animated discussion ensued that I guessed centred on the impasse created by their quarry being on the other side of security gates and just how long he might remain there.

As far as I was concerned, they could wait until the crack of doom and that fact alone brought a grin to my face. It became wider as soon as I realised their presence could only mean van Zyl had eluded capture.

CHAPTER SEVENTEEN

I didn't linger after that. I left the B&B via a back way that faced out over the river. From there, I returned by a circuitous route to the Mustang and left East London passing the airport on my right. It was only when I was well to the west that I picked up the N2 again and drove home.

I'd forgotten Effie was away for a few days attending a Law of the Sea conference in Pretoria. After that, she was spending some time with cousins who lived west of Nelspruit. It didn't matter though as she had left me notes summarising her efforts since I last saw her.

The IT guy had worked his alchemy in respect of Anton's laptop and revealed its secrets. Whether they'd prove worth knowing seemed to me an open question. There was email traffic but it was more than five years' old so I couldn't feel excited. It consisted of the usual mix of personal stuff from friends and/or acquaintances, exchanges with third parties over household and related matters, plus junk mail from a diverse group of organisations selling everything from transcendental meditation to discounted golf balls.

I compiled a list of the friends and acquaintances and sent them all an email explaining my role and why I was seeking van Zyl. But I knew five years was a long time and that many of the people may have dropped away to be replaced by more recent associations of which I knew nothing.

There was a Documents section, and I appraised what I found there. Not much held my attention though except a series of articles on South African labour law. These came from various sources and had been scanned into the database. Intriguingly, this work had been done in the last six months and, as far as I could see, was the most recent of any of the material held on the computer.

I broke off at that point and walked out into the roof garden. The day was bright, but the wind had gained in strength making the flags outside the Radisson Blu far below flail and snap.

It wasn't comfortable to sit out, so I walked back in and viewed the material that Effie collated from my eyes and ears out in the city. As ever, there was an anxiety to please, driven by the prospect of a cash bonus for confirmed sightings. Despite viewing all the pictures and videos closely, along with the tags which identified the time and location of each, I couldn't see any matches. After all, I'd eyeballed van Zyl less than 24 hours earlier and been able to commit to memory the cast of his features and the way in which he moved and held himself.

At that point I took stock. It seemed a crossroads had been reached. I could call a halt and give up or work with what was available and press on. I'd told Amy I'd find van Zyl for her. That objective was now redundant, and nobody would think the worse of me should I choose to quit.

Against that had to be weighed the fact that Amy appeared to have died because of her lover. I'm kinda old-fashioned and to my way of thinking her death ought to be avenged and, even if that proved impossible, it should at least be understood. I didn't see anybody but me attempting that. Also, there was a mystery to be solved and I'm a curious sort of a guy.

These thoughts ran through my head for the rest of the day as I grew increasingly restless. Idleness doesn't suit me and the silence in the apartment began to play on my nerves. It's difficult to describe a fear of being alone if you've never experienced it. But then it's no different from the fear that someone else will experience of open spaces; or of flying; or of dogs. It's how the mind tyrannises the body and seeks to gain mastery.

It started as a distraction, something to keep me busy and channel a negative mindset along a productive path. I got better at it with each call I made. Most of them went something like: ...*Yeah, hi to you too. Look, I'm calling from the DMU at the Department of Health...No, not many people have but we're part of the Stats Section in Pretoria. DMU stands for Data Migration Unit. I'm trying to trace some people whose files have been corrupted...Yeah, we've lost everything except the names. They're part of a cohort we've been monitoring remotely...I wish I could tell you, but I can't. Can I give you the names anyway?... That's much appreciated. They're Stolz, Grobbelaar, Wise, van Zyl, and Hermanus. Are any of them residents of yours?... No?-OK, I'm sorry to have bothered you...Yeah, you have a great day too.*

It took a while as I had to make a considerable number of calls but, in the end, I knew where in the Northern Cape, van Zyl's wife, Namzano, was to be found.

CHAPTER EIGHTEEN

The following day, I took an early flight to Cape Town and hired a car. My destination was the Namaqualand region straddling the Namibian border and it can be reached via the N7. It isn't the most remote place in South Africa, but it's right up there with the contenders.

I drove almost as far as Port Nolloth which constitutes part of the Diamond Coast. The area's well-named as its climate is as hard and unyielding as the gemstone and when the wind blows it's about as appealing as the dark side of the moon.

The Sanctum though belied its surroundings for it lay at the end of an asphalt road and in a hollow replete with camel thorns. From where these got water wasn't apparent, but they stood tall and cast welcome shade over the grounds of a two-storey Victorian building painted white with blue shutters. A verandah wrapped itself around the ground floor of the property and accommodated a few easy chairs made of cane with fat cushions.

With its rough and deeply grooved trunk, I drew up in the shade of one of the thorns. Even so, I was reluctant to step out of the car. Charcoal grey flannel, even if it was in cotton, was the wrong material and colour to cope with the sun and besides the long pants I was wearing were too tight. I should have disinterred them from the suit carrier back in PE and tried them on, but I was sure my measurements hadn't changed. Only it was apparent they had and consequently I felt pinched at the waist. Releasing a notch on my black crocodile belt with its flat buckle didn't assist matters much but at least it matched my black shoes. It was all part of the rig helping me look the part I was about to play, my white shirt with its button-down collar and cowhide attaché case complementing the picture perfectly.

With the pants sticking uncomfortably to my legs, I walked across to the house and let myself into a capacious vestibule. Looking around, it seemed time had stood still, probably from the date Cecil Rhodes became the founding Chairman of De Beers. Heavy wood panels encased the walls and above them expanses of tired cream paint were unrelieved except by a series of prints in glass-fronted frames. What these depicted was anybody's guess for natural light was in short supply and the glimmers cast by a single chandelier hung on a long chain did little to illuminate matters.

I crossed the room past a round oak table littered with old magazines and a crystal vase full of imitation agapanthus. The place was as quiet as a nun observing vows of silence; quiet that is until I heard snuffling. It came from an alcove beneath the grand staircase, and I directed my steps towards it.

The recess housed a small reception desk and behind it sat a man in a nurse's white uniform. He was slumped and asleep in an upright chair, arms folded over a massive stomach and short legs extended in an attitude of carefree relaxation. The snuffling came from him or more precisely from nostrils the size of gun barrels set in a wide flat nose. I contemplated this only until my eyes alighted on a brass bell. Tempted to thump it, I desisted as this was an occasion where cooperation, not confrontation, had to be my mantra.

Instead, I crept back to the front door, opened it and then slammed it shut. After that, I sauntered the long way back to reception.

By that time, the nurse had woken up and I caught him in the act of knuckling his newly opened eyes. When he finished, he stared at me with something a distance short of interest.

'*My god dit ist warm,*' I said conversationally giving him a wide smile.

He didn't comment on the state of the weather, but remarked sourly: 'Gives some folk's an idea where they're likely heading. That's if they don't mend their ways.'

I let that go and, as he ventured nothing further, I pressed on: 'I'm here to see Mrs. van Zyl.'

The nurse shifted ponderously in his chair and wiped his forehead with the back of his hand. He seemed unaware of the line of moisture that ran the length of his fat upper lip as he consulted the desk diary in front of him. 'Got no appointments listed here,' he said. 'It's like that most days. No appointments for Mrs. van Zyl. None for any of the residents.'

I anticipated this. 'I understand the arrangement was made a couple of weeks ago by my office in Port Elizabeth. It was at the request of Mrs. van Zyl's father, Mr. Matsunyane. No doubt you've heard of him?'

But his look told me that however big a wheel Moti might be in the Eastern Cape his writ didn't run here. That was fine with me as I didn't want an encounter with someone having a hot line to the big wheel's personal cell.

'My name's Jake Ahmed,' I went on smoothly. 'I work for attorneys called Stein and Partners in Port Elizabeth. You can call them if you like. They'll confirm who I am.' I relayed all this with authority as it was information reproduced on the business card in my wallet, should I need to produce it. The downside was that Effie wasn't around in the apartment to answer any call made to the landline number on the card. I'd have to deal with that if the necessity arose. For the moment, it was slowly, slowly, catchy monkey.

But the nurse was in no rush to do anything but simply look me up and down as he stifled a yawn. 'You come all the way from Port Elizabeth?' he asked finally. 'Must be important.'

I shrugged. 'I drew the short straw and some. Didn't realise how far north you are. Seems an odd location for a place like this.'

'People put folks here so they can say they done the right thing,' opined the nurse. 'Every care and attention guaranteed. No expense spared. All that *kak*. Once these people's done the right thing they can walk away with a clear conscience. And they don't visit neither because it's too far and of course they got no time.'

'I never thought about it,' I said, 'but I guess you're right.'

'Being right don't count for much it seems to me. What's your business with Mrs. van Zyl?'

'I need to assess whether she's *compos mentis*.'

'You a psychiatrist as well as a lawyer?'

I laughed at that, but the nurse kept a straight face, and a questioning look in his eyes. 'I think maybe you misunderstand,' I said. 'The test of mental capacity is no more than my determining whether she's aware of her surroundings and something of what's happening in the world. I also need to be sure she understands what's said to her and that she can express herself in a way that makes sense.'

'And what's it all for?'

'As I understand it,' I said, with as much confidence as I could muster, 'Mrs. van Zyl's affairs are currently managed informally. But Mr. Matsunyane isn't getting any younger and wants appropriate provisions in place to safeguard her care and welfare going forward, should such be deemed necessary. That would need the authority of the High Court. What I'm doing is no more than taking a first step in that process.'

The nurse heard me out without expression. 'OK, I can take you to her,' he said. 'It won't be for long as she gets agitated, and I can't leave her alone with you for safety reasons.'

'Mine or hers?'

'Both,' retorted the nurse soberly.

CHAPTER NINETEEN

Abandoning his post didn't seem to give the nurse, who told me his name was Joseph, any qualms as he placed a small notice in Afrikaans by the brass bell. It read: *In the event you get no response, please dial Ext. 12. We will attend to you directly.*

After that, he took me through to the back of the house where it connected with a short passage of contemporary construction. At the end of this was a locked steel door that he opened with a large key.

The far side was a revelation for I found myself looking across a corridor and out through a large picture window to a rectangular courtyard. The building surrounding this open space was single storey with access doors from it giving on to a garden with shady nooks.

Joseph noticed my surprised expression. 'This is our High Care Unit,' he said. 'They built it a few years back. The old house is now just staff rooms and admin.'

'How many people can you accommodate?'

'Seventeen all told. There's a small max security facility at the far end.'

'How long's Mrs. van Zyl lived here?'

'Namzano's one of our oldest residents, but she's not been here all the time. Sometimes, she's gone home.'

'Recently?'

The nurse shook his head before acknowledging a colleague who was accompanying a young white man in jogging bottoms.

I couldn't ask further questions because Joseph turned heavily on his heel and moved away. I went after him along a corridor hung with photographs of bucolic landscapes and sunlit seascapes; of furry animals and brightly plumed birds; and of people, all races of people, with crinkly smiles and kindly eyes. They say all the world's a stage, but this parade had about it as much reality as a costume drama depicting elves and fairies.

Joseph halted at last before a steel door, knocked softly and, without waiting for a reply, pushed his way in. I followed and was at once struck by two things. The first was the subdued hum from air-conditioning and the second was the smell of sandalwood. It wasn't possible to detect the source of the incense because the room was in shadow, the drapes being partially drawn.

Joseph navigated his way past a sofa and some sticks of furniture plus a TV turned so it faced the wall. He noticed how it drew my gaze and whispered: 'Namzano hears voices.'

'Voices?'

'From the TV. They make comments. Sometimes they order her about.'

I made no response and watched Joseph approach another door on the far side. It stood slightly ajar allowing a shaft of sunlight to pierce the carpet.

'Give me a minute to talk to her,' he said, before disappearing and closing up behind him.

I waited in the renewed gloom, my gaze repeatedly returning to the incongruous sight of the TV's back panel. Eventually, I set down the heavy attaché case and flexed the fingers of a hand grown stiff. In the filtered air, the flannel of my pants gradually unstuck itself from my thighs.

The minutes passed as muffled voices from inside the other room droned on. I had the impression something was being negotiated, that some favour or dispensation was being sought. It was only then it occurred to me that Namzano had every right to refuse to see me. I chewed that over in a negative state of mind until my eyes came to rest on the far corner of the room.

There was a sideboard there and something lying on top gleamed intermittently. Curious, I stepped over to it and discovered a small box. It was made of olive wood and its opened lid displayed silver hinges. These glinted sporadically as the flame from an incense burner, half-hidden behind a bone china vase, danced in fickle currents of air and teased the metal's polished surfaces.

I don't remember the quotation in italics glued on a thin laminate beneath the hinges. It was something taken from one of the Old Testament gospels. It encouraged strength and courage because God was with you wherever you went. More, my attention was caught by a plain card that lay inside the box. It wished Namzano well on her birthday and was signed in a very shaky hand by someone called Grace. Underneath was printed the words: *Church of Redemption, Port Elizabeth*. They appeared adjacent to an embossed crucifix.

At that point, Joseph called to me from the open door, his huge figure framed in sunlight. I moved towards him retrieving the attaché case on my way.

'Just keep it simple,' he hissed when I was close enough to hear. Intrigued, I followed him into the room.

The space was larger than I expected and had double aspect windows each barred on the inside. Judging by the single bed in the back of the room its original purpose was as a place to sleep but that now was subservient to the artist's studio it had become.

An easel stood between the windows and nearby was a low table covered in an untidy mess of paint pots of all sizes and jars of turpentine with brushes sprouting from them. Beneath the table was a stack of picture frames, some staves from a broken barrel and a selection of tools including an electric drill, a hammer and a quantity of palette knives. On the wall facing me a few pencil sketches had been crudely stuck up at various angles. Each depicted a human head with some aspect of the features grossly distorted thus creating a series of bizarre images.

The originator of this artwork had her back to me as she faced towards the easel. In one hand she held a board and in the other a knife with which she transferred dollops of flesh-coloured pigment onto a stretched canvas. She was wearing a light green T shirt and khaki shorts both liberally stained with paint. Her uncombed hair was jet black and almost matched the colour of her legs and bare feet. The rug beneath those feet was splashed with colour as was the upright chair standing off to one side. What could still be seen of its plush red seat provided a convenient resting place for an overflowing ashtray, a pack of Dunhill cigarettes plus a lighter and a mug on which was stencilled the message I'M FABULOUS.

'Namzano,' called Joseph.

There was no reply, so he called again. At that, and like some skittish yearling, Namzano raised her head and without warning spun round. When she saw me, the arm holding the palette knife extended itself in my direction and her hand tightened its grip.

'Easy, Namzano, easy,' soothed Joseph. 'This is the guy I was telling you about.'

'I don't like lawyers,' she said vehemently.

'As you said, but Jake Ahmed here's come a long way to see you.'

'I need a few minutes of your time that's all,' I added giving her the benefit of my pearly whites.

In response, she nailed me with a hostile stare out of a chiselled face with sunken cheeks. 'You work for my father, don't you?'

'Rather for the-er-beneficial trusts and financial vehicles that administer his assets,' I replied trying to sound authoritative.

'Fucking lawyer speak!' she spat back. 'What does the old bastard want this time?'

Verbal aggression doesn't faze me. It comes with the territory I inhabit along with much else. But I guessed for Jake Ahmed it might be a problem, so I retreated a step or two. Joseph, who was standing to one side between us, flashed me a look of sympathy. 'T-There are some dispositions he wants to make for your-um-future,' I said.

'What the fuck does that mean?-Can't you talk English? I'm guessing Zulu is quite beyond your tiny brain.'

'Well, the thing is…,' I began before I suddenly lost my train of thought. The cause was Namzano's bending to put down the board and palette. Her moving exposed to my gaze the canvas on which she'd been working.

Like the pencil sketches on the wall, the image depicted was of a human head. Unlike the sketches, this was done in oils, the predominating pigment being flesh-coloured to create the contours of a face. But those contours, the shape of the nose, the cast of the cheekbones, the line of the jaw and the size and angle of the forehead were as nothing to that of the single eye horrifically set into one side of the face.

The eye was oversized and wide open. Its pupil was dilated and painted a fiery red. The white of the eye was shot through with an exaggerated tracery of veins of the same fiery red so their appearance resembled flashes of lightning in an angry night sky. Droplets of blood fell from the tear duct and formed a thin stream that trailed down the neck.

'Do you like it?' Namzano asked giving me a hard stare.

'V-Very much,' I said much too quickly.

'Why?'

'Well, it's-er-an extraordinarily powerful image.'

'And?'

'I'd want to give that more thought,' I said slowly, but noticed the look of scepticism beginning to creep into Namzano's eyes.

I regrouped and pressed on with no real idea where this was taking me except further along Bullshit Alley. 'I see the eye though as a metaphor,' I went on slowly. 'A metaphor perhaps for the bloody times in which we live. It seems to me to be a significant statement for this society at this time given the levels of violence we experience.' I stopped out of breath and grabbing the initiative asked: 'Can you share with me *your* vision as regards the work?'

Namzano's face had softened somewhat in response to my words and for the first time she smiled revealing heavily stained teeth. Then, in one fluid movement, she lifted the pack of Dunhill and the lighter. Selecting a cigarette, she fired up and, with smoke cascading from her mouth, said, 'You've identified one aspect but there are others. The eye's also a metaphor for the surveillance society in which we must live. You know, Big Brother's watching you. More than that, the bastard's recording everything you say and do.'

Joseph had remained silent throughout this exchange with a bemused expression on his face. Now he felt he had to say something. 'Come on, Namzano. By saying that you're criticising this place and no ways what you're saying is true. No one's watching you and no one's recording anything.'

'You've got fucking cameras everywhere and you send the stuff to my father. That's why he never comes to see me.'

'We've talked about this before, Namzano.' Joseph spoke quietly and patiently. 'You're getting yourself all hung up for no reason.'

But she wasn't so easily appeased. Furiously, she threw the cigarette on the floor and stamped it out with her bare foot. If she experienced any pain, it wasn't apparent but then her face was contorted with rage and her black eyes were wild and staring.

I watched her for a few seconds and went to say something, but Joseph put up a restraining hand and shook his head.

We waited a couple of minutes and sure enough Namzano lowered her gaze, and the tension ebbed from her body. After that, and seemingly exhausted, she stepped back against the table and used it as a prop to keep herself upright.

Joseph signalled it might be time to leave. I bent down and picked up my case but as I turned to go her voice reached me. 'When will you next see my father?' she asked in a voice strangled with emotion.

I hedged. 'I'm not sure. Maybe in the next few days.'

'You tell him when you see him, I know stuff.'

I pricked up my ears. 'Stuff?' I asked.

It was though she'd not heard me. 'Anton told me things when he was here last time.'

'What sort of things?'

'You just tell him to get himself here so we can talk. He needs to know I can hurt him. You got that clear?'

There was enough time for me to say I was clear before Joseph made it equally clear I should be gone. 'Wait for me outside,' he ordered.

I let myself out and stood in the corridor outside the room. An adjacent picture window gave me another view of the garden. Under a canopy of thick greenery, a man-made stream ran through the middle and could be crossed by a narrow bridge made of pine. Matching benches stood close by, one of which was occupied by the nurse and young man I'd seen earlier. They sat with their heads close together like a couple of conspirators, only their plotting I guessed had the goal of healing. Silently, I wished them luck or the blessing of whatever god they might perhaps be invoking.

It was a few moments before Joseph tapped me on my shoulder. As I turned to face him, he asked, 'Did that help you?'

'Some,' I said. 'Is she always so mercurial?'

'If she flushes her meds.'

'And if she's cooperative?'

'It's easier,' he admitted. 'By the way, in case you understood different, she lives here voluntarily. This is the best place for her because of all we got. But, if she wants, she can hightail out the place any time.'

'But where would she go?'

Joseph shrugged. 'That's the problem. She needs ongoing specialist support, and her father don't want her with him.'

'What about her husband?'

'They ain't an item. Used to be, but not now.'

'Though he visits?'

'You sure ask a lot of questions, Jake.'

I smiled. 'Remember, I'm a lawyer.' But Joseph's eyes told me this wasn't cutting it. 'Mr. Matsunyane's not too forthcoming about his son-in-law,' I added. 'I'm trying to figure out where Anton might fit in. From a financial standpoint I mean. As I understand it, they're separated but not divorced.'

'You understand right.'

'But he visits her?' I persisted.

'Has done. From time to time.'

'When was the last time?'

'Six months I reckon.'

'Do you think he might have told her something that could affect her father?'

Joseph drew himself up to his full height. 'You mind if I give you some advice?'

I smiled again. 'Go for it.'

'Have you met Anton?'

'No,' I lied.

'Your loss. He's a real nice guy.' Joseph paused and pursed his lips. 'Namzano's damaged,' he began. 'She's a history of psych problems going back forever. As I heard it, Anton stuck around for a lot of years till he gave up on her. You saw how she is. I doubt Anton would have told her anything that might play on her mind. One thing you learn real fast with Namzano is to cross-check anything she tells you.' Joseph paused again before clapping me on the shoulder and smiling bleakly. 'I guess that don't help you much deciding whether she's playing with a full deck,' he said, 'but I reckon that's why you guys get paid so much.'

CHAPTER TWENTY

I could have been sharper.

My excuse was that having driven 650 kms up the N7 in the morning, I was finding it a tad tiring making the return trip through an empty landscape in the heat of the afternoon.

What happened was that a long-wheelbase white *bakkie* powered past me without fanfare. But instead of racing off, it held a position a hundred metres ahead. Distracted, it took me a second or two to register that the large dark saloon, which had come up behind me, was now sitting on my tail. By the time I shifted my eyes again, the *bakkie* had braked heavily and was displaying a neon Stop! sign.

I stopped and then pulled over because I didn't have a choice. Besides, kidnappers and carjackers don't generally display neon signs in the rear windows of their vehicles. Particularly, ones featuring the gold, eight-pointed rayed star of the South African Police Service.

I wasn't complacent though. Fumbling the Glock from the cubbyhole, and with my heart starting to pound, I placed it on the passenger seat with its butt facing me. SAPS has some rogue cops who interpret the pledge to work for a safe and secure South Africa as an invite to pursue a campaign of income redistribution.

I checked out the car behind but there was no movement. I saw two heads that appeared to be talking and one of them, bent forward, was fiddling with something on the dash.

Up ahead, a door opened, and a young man stepped out. He was dressed, like me, in a white shirt and dark pants, the top half of his face obscured by reflective sunglasses with gold frames. Crossing the distance towards me, his stride was purposeful and the anti-clockwise motion with the finger of one hand unequivocal.

I slid the window down about ten centimetres. 'Hi,' I said looking up.

The guy carefully removed the sunglasses and peered at me. 'Good afternoon, sir. I'd be obliged if you'd step out and follow me.'

I didn't move a muscle, other than those controlling my vocal cords. 'What's this about?' I asked.

'Just a parley. It won't take long.'

'I'm fine here,' I said. 'You speak first.'

He smiled at that. 'Not with me.' He indicated the *bakkie*. 'With my superior.'

Something wasn't right about this. I knew SAPS and this approach was all wrong. For one thing, the guy sounded like he had a lot more education than a Senior Certificate would have provided and for another his demeanour was far removed from the blunt interaction that characterised the typical SAPS officer.

I pushed the envelope. 'Do I have a choice?'

He shrugged. 'I suppose my superior could come and sit with you, but from choice she'd elect otherwise. Besides, it'll be more comfortable in the *bakkie*.'

'OK,' I said making up my mind. 'Let's not trouble the lady. Her place it is.'

I made to open the car door, but the guy was standing too close. 'The gun stays,' he said firmly. 'And the law says it stays out of sight.'

I returned the Glock to the cubby-hole and got out. The car behind was parked less than a metre off my rear bumper. The men inside continued to pay me no mind, their heads angled in the same way as before though one was now using his cell.

Walking over to the *bakkie*, I noticed it rear windows were blacked out and it was long, even for a stretched 4X4. The reason became clear when I was urged to climb inside. The area behind the front seats had been modified to create twin benches in black leather facing each other.

The woman who sat across from me as we settled ourselves down was of Indian origin and indeterminate age. She had cropped hair that matched the colour of her two-piece suit, and her face was devoid of make-up. The only concessions to femininity were expensive pearl earrings set in silver cups and a pearl broach in the shape of a protea adorning her flat chest.

She looked at me out of eyes as cold as a dead fire. 'I appreciate your cooperation,' she said.

'I haven't shown any.'

'I'm thanking you in...'

'Who are you?'

'My name's Lydia Estleman.'

'That's not what I meant.'

She rewarded me with a look of exasperation. 'It'll be quicker if I ask the questions.'

'You're not SAPS, are you?' I persisted.

I wondered too about her origins. We were speaking Afrikaans, but her accent seemed to have become stranded somewhere in mid-Atlantic. She reminded me of a South African I'd met a few years back who'd spent a couple of decades living in California.

'Look, I don't have time for this, Mr. Nemo. I've been...'

I interjected again, 'How the hell do you know my name?'

Lydia Estleman had been sitting forward in her seat but now she leaned back wearily. 'Tell him Paul,' she said, 'and then maybe we can get on with this.'

'From your car's reg. plate,' the guy calling himself Paul said. 'From the plate we ascertained the vehicle's ownership and the lease agreement it has with the car rental company. There are intermediary steps I won't bore you with, but the upshot was you signed it out of Cape Town International at 8.07 this morning. To do that, you produced ID and a credit card. Need I say more?'

'Yeah, I get that,' I said, 'but how come you did it so fast?'

As soon as my mouth was shut, I knew the answer to my own question. This revelation must have shown up in my face for the two of them exchanged glances before Paul said matter-of-factly: 'Give us a week and in the exercise of our legal powers we could sequester your assets. Redress might prove difficult because lawyers generally don't work unless you pay them. Six months after that you could find yourself homeless. And if we were vindictive, you might wake up one day to discover you're stateless.'

'That's why we'd appreciate your cooperation,' added his companion tonelessly.

Choosing your battle grounds is a gift given the wise. 'As a responsible citizen of our Rainbow Nation,' I replied, 'I'd be delighted to help you.' I said it tongue in cheek, but not so they'd notice.

The shadow of a smirk played itself out upon Lydia Estleman's lined face. 'You visited Namzano van Zyl this morning,' she said.

'I did.'

'For what purpose?'

'It was in connection with a case I'm working.'

'Case?-I don't understand.'

'I'm a PI.'

Lydia raised an excuse for an eyebrow. 'Who's retained you?'

'Mrs. van Zyl's father, Mahumapelo Matsunyane.'

'To do what?'

'Locate his missing son-in-law.'

'When was this?'

'About a week ago.'

Lydia had dark brown eyes, but they were as impervious as marbles. 'Give me an account of your investigation to date,' she said slowly. 'And in your shoes, I wouldn't be tempted to leave anything out.'

But I was tempted, and to tell the truth I succumbed. By my reckoning, based on the questions she'd so far asked, Ms. Estleman didn't know too much. Of course, I was keen to avoid any mention of my brief encounter with van Zyl, the fire at the house in the Sundays River Valley, and more particularly my shooting of one of the intruders. I didn't want SAPS, or indeed any other government agency, crawling all over me and asking a lot of awkward questions, such as why I hadn't reported the incident long before now.

So, I gave her what she wanted and provided a snapshot of my activities that was detailed and credible. I saw from the expression on her face I won a modicum of trust. Meanwhile, Paul tapped notes into a laptop and tersely fielded a call that came into his cell.

The inevitable questions followed the conclusion of my monologue.

'I'm not clear as to how you got to meet Namzano,' began Lydia. 'You said yourself her father didn't want you seeing her.'

'I masqueraded as a lawyer seeking to establish whether she was *compos mentis*.'

I got the eyebrow treatment again. 'How very-er-inventive of you,' she said. 'And is she?-*Compos mentis* I mean.'

I shrugged. 'I'm neither a psychologist nor a psychiatrist. The nurse told me she's damaged. The one thing I did discover was van Zyl's not visited her in six months.'

'We know that already.'

'That would be from the person you've got on the inside.'

Lydia blanked me, but I wasn't going to let that put me off. I changed tack. 'What's *your* interest in Anton?' I asked.

'You really expect me to answer that?'

'Yes, I do. Presumably, this discussion ends with you saying that if I find out anything I must bring it to you.'

'Your ongoing cooperation would be much appreciated.'

'So, lift the lid, Ms. Estleman, and let me peek into the pot.'

For some reason, Paul thought this amusing, but his superior cast a disapproving look. After that, she turned back to me and said slowly, 'Van Zyl's a person of interest.'

'Suspected of what?'

'I didn't say that.'

'I know how the term's used,' I snapped. 'Credit me with some intelligence.'

'I can only repeat what I've said already. Your quarry's someone we'd like to liaise with concerning various matters.' I was about to say something more, but she raised a finger to her lips. 'We're done, Mr.Nemo. Apart from one thing.'

'Oh, yes?'

'You'll need to know where to reach us.' Lydia Estleman eyeballed Paul. 'Have you a card?'

Wordlessly, Paul leaned to his left and retrieved a scuffed pigskin wallet from his back pocket. Reaching inside, he produced a business card and passed it to me. It featured nothing but a printed number in italic script on one side.

I looked at it. 'You're a long way from home,' I said. 'Isn't 12 the area code for Pretoria?'

She ignored me. 'Calling that number connects you with a duty manager. Ask for me by name, leave your number and ring off. I'll contact you day or night within 30 minutes. Do you understand?'

'What happens if you're on holiday?' I asked.

She saw the roguish look on my face. 'Goodbye, Mr.Nemo, and don't forget what was said earlier. It'd be a shame if there was any misunderstanding.'

I shrugged and said nothing as, following Paul's lead, I moved away along the bench. As I stepped out of the *bakkie*, I saw the car parked behind mine had slipped away as silent as a shadow.

CHAPTER TWENTY-ONE

Spooks, agents, spies, moles, snoopers.

Whatever you want to call them, every country that believes it has something worth protecting employs them. And quite a few that have nothing worth protecting, other than the advancement of some agenda or other, also participate in this dirty business. From whichever side, they're the men and women who fight covert wars in the name of something that is bigger than they are. And, because so little is known about their activities, they offer fertile ground to those who want to make things up. After all, there's little fear of there ever being credibly contradicted.

In the years I spent with SAPS I never had dealings with the Security Service. As I understood it, their focus in those days was al Qaeda and mercenaries. Neither of these threats was any sort of big deal in South Africa. I guess we should have been thankful for small mercies bearing in mind all the other *kak* that has to be dealt with.

So, what was it that put the spooks on to van Zyl? In what way had he managed to show up as a blip on their radar screens?

It gave me food for thought and I chewed on it for a while on my interrupted journey south, but only until it hit me that it was high time I chewed on something solid.

Instantly, I abandoned any thoughts of flying back to PE that night and instead followed a sign off the N7. It was to one of those places that the tourist guides, desperate for something engaging to say, usually describe as charming or homely or welcoming. But the reality was that it was a one horse *dorp* and straight out of the pages of John Buchan or Arthur Conan Doyle.

This particular place comprised no more than a Post Office, a convenience store, an ATM, a laundry facility, a few Victorian buildings and the inevitable Dutch Reformed Church. It boasted a clock with

Roman numerals that was right a couple of times a day and a spire with peeling paintwork. I passed it as long shadows bathed the street and before the curve of the road took me towards a destination originally signposted when I left the highway.

Five minutes later, I wound up at a modest guesthouse with a green roof looking out over hills. As the sun began to set, I pulled the car onto an area of beaten earth, retrieved my holdall, and walked inside.

If anyone thought I cut an unusual figure in my ill-fitting fancy pants, black shoes, and white shirt with button-down collar, they were too polite to say so. And too polite again to make any comment when I emerged twenty minutes later wearing shorts and a Billabong T shirt.

Providing food, other than breakfast, wasn't part of the offer of service, but I prevailed upon the owner to make me French toast to which she added a generous portion of *boorewurs*.

I ate outside on the verandah sitting on an old three-seat couch covered in taupe and with the food balanced on my lap. The sausage was some of the best I've tasted but my enjoyment of it was marred by the realisation that if the Security Services couldn't find van Zyl, how was I going to?

But, later that night, it came to me as to what I should do next. Accordingly, I booked myself onto the first flight out of Cape Town the following morning. It would mean leaving the guesthouse before dawn but that was unavoidable when I understood that time was of the essence.

CHAPTER TWENTY-TWO

The Church of Redemption lay at the northern end of the street grid of which Sixth and Seventh Avenues in PE are a part. It occupied a corner lot and was sandwiched between a large bungalow with steel entrance gates and a double storey house that, judging by the number of cars parked outside, was in multi-occupation. Or maybe they had a connection to the Church whose own parking was inadequate given the number of vehicles cluttering the length of the street.

Even though it was Sunday, I'd phoned their office but found it closed. There was another line to ring if one was after a word of faith. I figured what I wanted didn't make that grade so driving over was unavoidable.

I took the Mustang because without the tracking devices there was no reason not to. Accepting the same thing might happen again didn't justify mothballing it. Besides, I hammered the car for 50kms out of the city on the N2 before pulling over for a few minutes to see if I had a tail, then turning round and hammering the road back. Tedious for some perhaps but the compensation was enjoying the raw killer power of a cross-plane V8 with near 450bhp on tap

Noise though from the twin exhausts can kinda irritate members of the local populace. Usually, I wasn't around long enough to suffer the backwash but this time I drew the short straw. My manoeuvring into a tight space at a distance from the church didn't go unnoticed. As I stepped out of the cabin, a middle-aged guy with a shock of white hair and broken veins in his face approached carrying a pair of shears.

'You can't park there,' he yelled while he was still a few metres off.
'Why not?'
'Because I say so.'
'Uh-huh.' I pressed the remote and began to walk away.
'I'm expecting visitors.'

I turned back and looked over his shoulder to the driveway of his house. 'You've got enough space to open a used car lot.'

The guy came closer, and my eyes focused on the shears. His grip had tightened, and the sharp end was pointed at my stomach. 'You one of those Joes from along the way?' he asked.

'Joes?' I repeated, puzzled.

'Holy Joes.'

'Ach, right.'

'Well, are you?'

'Just visiting,' I said, making my face adopt a beatific expression. 'This isn't my church, bro, but I've been called today to give the message. I'm sharing with you now in the hope the spirit moves you to attend.'

That left the guy speechless, but walking away I felt the points of those shears in the small of my back.

Close to, I saw building the Church of Redemption hadn't come cheap. It had red brick facings with fancy marble inlays featuring the Christian symbol of the fish and tall glass panels that reached up to heaven. More than that, the large silver cross above my head had come from some place where the price tag hadn't exactly been preying on anyone's mind.

Making my way across a crowded and highly polished linoleum floor, I found myself behind a family done out in their Sunday best. The sight of them made me feel under-dressed but I got over it.

I hadn't taken many more steps before a girl detached herself from a group of people and approached me. She gave me a big smile, which along with some inner light radiating from her blue eyes, illuminated her whole countenance. I couldn't remember the last time I'd seen something like that.

'Welcome,' she said, or I think that was what I heard because a live band suddenly struck up from the adjacent auditorium.

'Hi,' I cried. 'Maybe you can help me. I'm looking for someone by the name of Grace.'

From the girl's response, it was obvious she only caught part of what I'd said. 'Grace is what we all seek,' she yelled back at me. 'It's given us by God because…' I lost the rest because a blast of feedback from amplifiers drowned her out. When it cleared, she went on unperturbed, 'It's the love and mercy given …'

I put up a restraining hand and smiled. 'Sorry, you misunderstand me. I'm looking for *someone* called Grace. I think she's a member of this church.'

The girl was unfazed. 'We have two Graces,' she volunteered. 'What's her surname?'

I shook my head. 'I don't know. But the one I need to talk to has a friend called Namzano van Zyl.'

'I'm sorry, but the name means nothing.' Then visibly brightening, she went on, 'Both Graces though are here today. After the service, I could ask them about Namzano.'

'What time do you finish up?'

'Around 11.30.'

'So, we can meet up then?'

'Why?-Do you have somewhere to go?'

'Not particularly,' I said. 'I can wait outside. It won't be long.'

'Or you could come to the service.'

'Who me?'

'Yes, you,' she said giving me another wide smile. 'There's no entrance fee.'

My recollections of church attendance were buried deep in the experiences of childhood. Vague memories stirred within me of stern-featured elders with disapproving stares; singing, absent of any sentiment or feeling; the droning voice of the minister; and always of proceedings conducted in an environment that was dank and gloomy even at the height of summer. I'd parted company with the whole depressing experience as soon as ever I could and turned my back on it all forever.

But, despite my misgivings, I mirrored her smile and mouthed OK. Words were futile as the band was now in full cry and waves of sound were crashing in upon us like breakers on a stormy beach.

She led me through double doors and down a long aisle between filled rows of seats. Not that anybody was sitting as young and old were on their feet, their bodies swaying, and their arms lifted in supplication to some higher power.

Up ahead, the lead singer stood centre stage flanked by a female backing group and a couple of guys with electric guitars. A drummer at the back, placed between banks of speakers, was on fire for something that they'd surely have told me was God. All I saw was his flailing arms and tapping feet as the sweat poured off him, his green T shirt showing dark stains beneath the armpits and across his chest.

I shifted my gaze to the far side of the stage where there was a line of chairs with high straight backs. One of them was occupied by an old man with olive skin whose remaining hair was as white as the pickguard on the body of the bass player's guitar. He sat bent forward, his hands on his knees and his eyes focused on something at the level of the mezzanine that ran around three sides of the auditorium. He alone was a repository of peace lost in the maelstrom of sound and movement that swirled everywhere else.

At last, the band gave way to a young, fresh-faced man who leapt onto the stage with a mike in his hand. 'This is God's Day,' he shouted to the worshippers. 'And what a beautiful day it is! Aren't you glad you came to church?'

There were cries of affirmation from the assembled throng, but the guy seemed hard of hearing. He asked the question again and was then, like me, deafened by the tumultuous response.

But the main event was the address by the pastor. Invited reverentially to come to the front, the old man rose unsteadily to his feet and tottered forward. He was like a thin bent stick as he moved, his dim gaze scanning the believers spread before him.

A lectern was set up for him at the front of the stage. Personally, I doubted whether he'd make it that far, but when he did finally stretch bony hands towards the pulpit, his grasp on its sides was sure. Then, slowly raising his head towards the ceiling, presumably to invoke the power of heaven, he stood motionless.

He stayed that way for 30 seconds while he waited for the hubbub to die down, waited for every distraction to be dealt with, and waited for all eyes at last to come to rest on him.

'Weeping may endure for a night, but joy comes in the morning,' he said without warning, intoning the words so softly that only those at the front heard him. The rest of his flock were left straining their ears, their impatience to receive the message now manifest in their faces.

It was then I witnessed a transformation.

The pastor rose up before my eyes, his back straightened and his hands, which had grasped the lectern for support, were now raised high towards the heavens.

'Weeping may endure for a night,' he thundered, 'but joy comes in the morning! Do you not understand?–Joy comes in the morning! Think of it: Night is when the powers of darkness flourish. Night is when wickedness tries to hold us captive. But, as Christians, we have the assurance each morning of a new day! Trust in it brothers and sisters: A new morning every day of our lives! Our Holy Father didn't ordain that any night...'

I heard him out.

His was a message about faith. It always is. It's the faith that moves mountains; that makes possible the impossible...

But, in a world of cynics, it's easy to dismiss the notion of faith. And if there was some supernatural presence in the place, I can't say it touched me.

What I was left with though was the physical transformation I'd observed. It wasn't something I could wave away, particularly as the pastor shrank before everyone's eyes when he finished speaking and took on once more the mantle of a burned-out husk.

Bemused, and amongst a slow-moving stream of people, I left the auditorium. It was then I felt a touch at my elbow. I turned and looked down to see a white woman in a motorised wheelchair.

'I understand you want to talk,' she said. When I didn't answer, she added impatiently 'About Namzano?–I'm Grace.'

Moving out of the stream, I did a double take. She was around 60 and at a guess suffered with Parkinson's disease or something related. At least that was what I concluded because there was a tremor in her thighs and lower trunk that meant her body performed a slow and intermittent rumba. It was serious enough for her to be wearing a loose seat belt to prevent her falling from her seat.

I smiled. 'My name's Sol. I'm surprised you found me in this crush.'

'You were pointed out. Besides, this church doesn't have many coloureds.'

I didn't know how to respond to this. Looking about me, what she said was true, but I'd never been colour-matched in that way before. Not unless you counted experiences I'd had at school.

'I'd like tea,' said Grace. '*Rooibos* with a little milk and two spoons of sugar. And please ask for a closed beaker. You do that and I'll find us a table.'

With that she left me and threaded her wheelchair across the floor to a side area filled with tables and chairs. Adjacent to it was a counter where there was a selection of hot and cold drinks served by volunteers. I made for it and joined a long line of thirsty worshippers.

The beaker proved a problem, and I had to wait. Eventually though I returned to Grace with her tea in one hand and a bottle of water in the other.

She'd parked her wheelchair awkwardly between two circular tables, both occupied by family groups. That there was a lack of rapport was apparent as neither had eye contact with her. The reason for this became clear when she spotted me walking towards her.

'My friend's arrived,' she declared loudly. 'Somebody will have to move and make way. We have highly confidential matters to discuss.'

I stood there and grimaced as one family looked from Grace to me and back again before deciding enough was enough. They got up and filed past giving me looks I considered kinda lacking in Christian charity.

I took a vacated seat alongside her. 'You didn't have to do that,' I said softly.

'Why not?-They've got legs, haven't they?'

I changed the subject. 'Would you like to try your tea?' I asked.

'You'll have to help me,' she snapped.

I followed her gaze to hands which were trembling. 'Any way I can,' I said with a smile. 'It may be best if I hold the beaker for you.'

It *was* best, but then she complained the tea was too sweet. I let that go and contented myself with taking a long pull from the bottle of water.

'So, what is it you want?' she asked pointedly.

'Information,' I said. 'I work as a private investigator. I'm looking into the disappearance of Namzano's husband.'

'Anton?'

'Yes.'

'Haven't seen him in years.' Grace put her hands together in her lap to curb their shaking. 'How did you find me?'

'You sent Namzano a birthday card and the church's name was printed on it.'

She was surprised. 'You've seen her?'

'I have.'

'How is she?'

I hesitated. 'I only met her briefly but…'

'She's as mad as a hippo with gut ache,' interrupted Grace, before smiling for the first time.

I recoiled at this: it was like calling someone with palsy a spastic. 'Was she always that way?' I asked coldly.

'Not always, but that was in another time. It was before I got sick and a while before she got sent away.'

'Sent away?'

'Her behaviour embarrassed her father once too often.'

'You mean Moti?'

'Yes Moti. Who else would I mean? That jumped-up *kaffir* has a lot to answer for.'

Grace hadn't spoken loudly but it was loud enough to carry. I felt a ripple of disapproval wash over me even though the numbers of people sitting around us had diminished.

'What did Anton think about this?' I asked.

'He accepted it. He didn't have the money to pay the bills for the care she needed. And by that time, he'd had years trying to cope with Namzano's bizarre behaviour.'

This was all very interesting, but it wasn't gaining me much ground. I decided on a new tack. 'Can I ask how you first met Namzano?'

'You can, but first I need another drink.'

The hospitality area had closed so there was no chance of getting fresh tea. 'Do you want water?' I asked.

'No, I want tea.'

'But you said it was too sweet.'

'I've changed my mind.'

I shrugged, stood up and helped her drink again from the covered beaker. She put her hands around mine as she did so, and I noticed how hot they were.

When she finished, she said, 'Namzano and I used to work together. She brought me to the church originally.'

'And what about Anton?'

'He came for a while, but it wasn't his thing. For him attending church was a waste of effort. If he had spare time, he wanted to help people.'

I remembered what I'd been told by Amy. It seemed like months since our conversation. 'I heard he did charity work,' I ventured.

Grace nodded. 'At that time, the church had various outreach programmes.'

'But not now?'

'We still have them, but they've changed over the years.'

'What exactly did Anton do?'

'He was with a programme that helped people get work experience.'

'How did things pan out?'

Grace didn't answer immediately because a spasm shook her left thigh violently. Embarrassed, she put her hands down to try and control it, but the attempt was futile. It was the same when she tried again.

'To hell with this!' she exploded. Then, staring at me angrily: 'You know I only come here now to pray for a miracle! But it's been six years, and it isn't getting better. In fact, it's getting worse.'

I mumbled something ineffectual and inadequate because there are no right words. No words that don't sound like a cliché that insults the intelligence or the sort of bullshit you hear trotted out when there's been a disaster some place and somebody has to say something so we can all feel better about ourselves.

I waited for Grace to calm herself and, when she didn't, I went and found the lady she told me had brought her to church. When she came over and began to console her, I took it upon myself to hunt down the means of making fresh tea. As a response to her distress, it was no more than a gesture, but it was all I had to offer.

On my return with a recharged beaker, I found Grace alone once again and sitting amongst a sea of empty tables and chairs. Raising a tear-stained face to mine, she said: 'I've only got a few minutes. Then I'm being driven home.'

'Are you sure you're up to this?' I said, sitting down next to her once more. 'Maybe we could talk another time.'

'You told me you wanted information.'

'OK,' I said, registering the determination in her eyes. 'What else can you tell me?'

'Anton was attached to a programme called Redeemed Youth or RY,' Grace began. 'The idea was to use church members to generate work opportunities. It was for the benefit of young people in the locations. Anton contributed by doing some of the accounts and admin work for them.'

'Was it successful?'

'The church had some very wealthy members who were also well-connected. It focused minds on what was a fresh initiative, and it soon gained momentum.'

'What happened?'

'The municipality is what happened. They heard about RY's success and offered to put money in. Some people in the church thought that a good idea but there were more who didn't.'

'I'm guessing there was a bust-up.'

'Not exactly. But there was a debate about God and Mammon.'

'How did that play out?'

'The church's view was that the municipality was corrupt. Even if it hadn't been, it was unhappy about its reduced ability to promote the ideals that directed its charitable giving.'

'But money talked?'

'Yes, but not at once. It was only later that the church gradually pulled away until it withdrew its support altogether.'

'And what did Anton do when that happened?'

'I have no idea,' said Grace, evidently surprised at my question. 'As I told you from the outset, I haven't seen Anton in years.'

'But didn't the subject ever come up when you were in touch with Namzano?'

Grace shook her head. 'Conversations with Namzano tended to concentrate on one thing and that was Namzano. Still do which is why we don't speak too often. I'm sorry I can't be more useful, but you can help me take another drink before you go. After all, you made fresh tea. I just hope this time it's drinkable.'

CHAPTER TWENTY-THREE

Reflecting on how my investigation stood, I concluded I might be chasing a will o' the wisp. You know: one of those atmospheric ghost lights seen by travellers at night that recedes farther and farther into the distance as you draw closer.

Finding van Zyl had brought me to a point where there wasn't much to go on except a single lead as regards his charitable work. The consolation might be that, from what Amy had told me, it was an activity he'd been pursuing up until recently. And it was also work he'd been undertaking in the PE area.

Redeeming Youth had been the name of the charity established by the Church of Redemption all those years ago. But, once its charitable objectives had been redefined in secular rather than spiritual terms, I guessed its name might have changed as well. Nonetheless, I had to try and find it.

I visited the Nelson Mandela Bay Municipality website. There was no Redeeming Youth listed amongst the charities with which they were involved or which they endorsed regarding volunteering. In fact, none of those mentioned was concerned with helping people into employment. Perhaps this wasn't surprising given that the workless in our Rainbow Nation are not much less numerous than the grains of sand found on any one of our magnificent beaches.

I rang the Municipality the following day to see if there was further information to be gleaned. Making calls to government offices is an occupation best suited to people with a lot of time on their hands, a high threshold of boredom, and expectations regarding outcomes lower than the line of sight of a pygmy mouse. Consequently, I wasn't fazed when I was passed from one person to another before ending up talking to some lady in their archives section. As she was prone to sneezing, I assumed her location to be in the bowels of City Hall, no doubt surrounded by shelves creaking under the weight of dusty documents and mouldering files.

Early on, she left me hanging for a long while with nothing to pass the time but a road test I was reading on the Mustang Bullitt. The car was a special edition in dark highland green with black painted wheels commemorating the eponymous Steve McQueen film. It looked like a real beast and ticked a lot of boxes.

At last, the archivist broke in on my thoughts.' We do have a file,' she said.

'Right.'.

'There's not much information in it.'

'You don't say.'

'Forgive me, but you don't seem surprised.'

'Expressing surprise is something I dispensed with decades ago. What have you got?'

'Well, there's some corr…corr…' Her voice was hijacked by a gargantuan sneeze that nearly blew my eardrums into the next room.

'*Gesundheit*,' I said.

'Pardon?'

'Good health. Now, tell me what you've got.'

What she'd got amounted to letters that had passed backwards and forwards between the church and the municipality; some committee agendas and minutes; two sets of accounts; and a certificate of re-registration under the Nonprofit Organisations Act when the charity had changed its name to Project Hope.

'And?' I asked when she finished speaking and the silence became unbearable.

'If you mean is there anything else, the answer's no.'

'But what happened to the project?'

'I can't tell you that.'

I became exasperated. 'But it can't just have vanished into thin air. Surely, there's some indication of what transpired.'

'Not on this file.'

'Is that usual?'

'No, it isn't. I would have expected some notation to the record sheet.'

'So, what do you think happened?'

The archivist had to think about that, and I heard her alternately sneezing and riffling paper. At last, she spoke again. 'I think,' she said heavily, 'there was other material here. Its absence may suggest it's been appropriated.'

And that was that. Was I chasing a will o' the wisp?

As far as the Mustang Bullitt was concerned, I had my answer when I found the car had been launched years before but had never been sold in South Africa.

As far as finding Anton van Zyl?-I didn't have a clue.

CHAPTER TWENTY-FOUR

I started over.

Whatever had happened to Project Hope didn't alter the fact that van Zyl had worked in the charitable sector recently. Since it was said his interest was in people seeking work, this seemed like a good place to commence.

I cast the net wide and interrogated websites that collated details of non-profit enterprises in the Eastern Cape. These were categorised into three groups: non-governmental, community-based, and faith-based organisations. Those accredited in accordance with the law benefited from enhanced funding opportunities, permissions to open bank accounts, and eligibility for tax incentives.

I had some insight into all this stuff from years earlier when I'd given away much of the fortune left me by a father with whom I'd never had a functioning relationship. But that exercise had been different. Because of the tens of millions involved, grants had been made predominantly to large national organisations having the sophisticated governance, expert management, and IT/ accounting systems in place to ensure charitable receipts were properly tallied and distributed.

By contrast, what I turned up through my efforts was a plethora of bodies, mostly small, engaged in all manner of activities from running children's crèches to organising sponsored bike rides; from advancing the merits of recycling to helping sufferers from HIV/AIDS; and from funding animal shelters to housing orphans.

None I came across met my criteria precisely, so I was forced into making compromises. At the end of it all, I was left with three possibilities where the purpose was strongly aligned with the promotion of work opportunities in all its forms.

Having done enough desk-based research, I headed out that afternoon.

Maybe I should have put in some calls from home because I'd have saved myself time.

The problem with the internet is that it can be misleading as information, not updated, ages fast. Also, that state-of-the-art website with its fancy graphics and maybe a revolving message board may lead you to make assumptions that are without merit.

I became a victim on both counts.

The first place I visited was off the Old Cape Road. Its wide concrete apron was jammed with cars but on close inspection the single storey building behind it was burnt-out. When the fire had occurred was anybody's guess but, from the maturity of the buddleia, which had seeded itself in every place it could gain a foothold, it must have been at least a couple of years before. There was no visible forwarding address I could see, only a sun-faded estate agent's board telling me the site was available for redevelopment.

The other charity, with all the bells and whistles as regards its web presence, occupied a unit on the other side of the city. It was in a line of tired retail outlets whose business offerings had mostly fallen foul of the tech revolution. Amongst others, I spotted a camera shop, an internet café and a laundrette. The place I was interested in had windows so grimy it was impossible to see inside.

As it turned out, this didn't matter as a crude sign hung in the window declared: OPEN TUESDAYS AND THURSDAYS 2-5 P.M. APPOINTMENT ESSSENTIAL. This was followed by a curt invitation to ring a mobile number. I rang and let it ring several times until it cut out. Repeating the exercise delivered the same result. From this, I concluded that after developing a website perhaps either enthusiasm or money or both had run out.

I headed west and found the last of the charities, by the name of Work It Out, in Circular Drive. It was situated on the first floor of a detached building above a veterinary practice and beneath a firm of accountants. I parked in a bay out front and strolled across to the guy who was acting as guard.

'You got a cell?' I asked. He said he had a cell. 'OK, let me give you my number.' He took it and I gave him a 20 Rand note. 'You see anybody near the car you call,' I said. 'I'll be on the first floor. Not sure for how long. You gonna be around a while?'

'Man,' he said with a grin, 'I got nowhere else to be.' I turned to leave but he was curious. 'What's with the car?'

'I'm tired of people keying it.'

But this wasn't the real reason. In truth, it was about a mood swing. One of those that creeps up like a rabid dog, then bites and infects all my senses. Where this comes from, I can't say. Its origin is as nothing in comparison with its impact. It leaves me edgy and feeling unsafe. At that moment it centred on the vulnerability of my car. Perhaps with good cause after previous experiences.

I climbed marble steps to the ground floor and passed along a corridor with floor- to-ceiling glass. It gave a view of the vet's waiting room where two middle-aged women sat huddled in animated conversation while their dogs, a Maltese poodle and a Jack Russell, each animal exhibiting disdain for the other.

If the vet's oozed sterility created by white light, white walls and white furniture, upstairs was different. By contrast, its reception area was cluttered and the rooms that led from it each had a brown door and a wired glass viewing panel.

As I arrived, one of those doors was flung open and a boisterous group of students cascaded out. They skirted me like a deluge from a breached dam and headed down the staircase in a laughing throng. Within seconds, they'd vanished like water dumped on hot sand.

I stood irresolute until a woman emerged from the room the students had vacated. She looked harassed and stared at me through horn-rimmed spectacles. Cradled in one bony arm, she carried a sheaf of papers. 'Can I help?' she asked.

'I hope so. I'm a PI and was wondering…'

'What's a PI?'

I smiled. 'Private investigator. I was wondering if I could ask you a few questions.'

Her look told me she was sceptical. 'What are you investigating?' she asked sharply.

'A disappearance.'

'Surely not one of our students?'

I shook my head. 'I think he could have been a volunteer. Does the name Anton van Zyl mean anything?'

It evidently did because a look of surprise visited her thin face. 'Just let me put these reports down.'

I watched as she approached the reception desk. For the first time, I was aware of somebody sitting there for I heard a man's voice. He remained hidden though behind a tall crystal vase of strelitzia and a stack of files.

A moment later, I joined her in the room where she'd been teaching and took a seat opposite at one of the wooden tables. Its surface was pitted with age and graffiti. 'We inherited these from a school,' she said mournfully following my gaze.

'Doesn't matter,' I said. 'It's the quality of teaching that counts.'

She beamed at that exposing a set of teeth as yellow as a bad case of jaundice. Her name, she told me, was Mrs.Martin and I told her mine was Mr. Nemo.

'Nemo?-That's a strange name,' she remarked.

'I had a strange father.'

If Mrs. Martin thought I was going to say more, she was disappointed. 'I haven't seen Anton in months,' she volunteered. 'And now you say he's disappeared?'

'He went AWOL several weeks ago. I've been making enquiries for a while.'

'On whose behalf?'

'Initially his father-in-law's.'

'Initially?'

I shrugged. 'It got complicated.'

Mrs. Martin smiled ruefully. 'That sounds like Anton. There never seemed to be an easy route to any destination.'

'What did he do for you?'

'Are you familiar with Work It Out?'

'Broadly,' I said. 'I had a look at the website earlier.'

But it was as though I hadn't spoken so keen was Mrs.Martin to evangelise. 'We're about empowering people, often young people,' she began. 'We run part-time courses to instil confidence and a strong work ethic. Most of our students come from poor backgrounds. We believe by getting them into the right place psychologically we can then graft on practical skills in areas such as customer relations, merchandising, IT, cashiering etc. Those accomplishments make them valuable and therefore much more employable.'

'And where did Anton fit into this?'

'He ran evening and weekend classes in personal finances. He also taught bookkeeping for those interested in accountancy. He was dedicated and well-liked. It was a great pity he left.'

'How long ago was that?'

Mrs.Martin thought for a moment.' Perhaps a year or so. I can check specifically if you wish.'

'Not necessary,' I said emphatically. 'Do you know *why* he left?'

'He had a falling out with one of the trustees.' Her answer brought a quizzical look to my face, so she added: 'Anton questioned the trustee's integrity over a series of transactions with a third party. The trustee and the party were related. As it turned out, I think Anton was over-sensitive after what later emerged at Project Hope when he was there.'

I pricked up my ears at that. 'I talked to the Municipality about them only this morning.'

'Was it a fruitful conversation?'

'Your guess is as good as mine. Their archivist thought much of their file had been appropriated.'

Mrs. Martin gave a snort of derision. 'Destroyed more like.'

'I wondered about that. Do you know what happened?'

'There was a rumour that about a million Rand went missing. As a result, the city closed it down.'

'I don't remember seeing a story like that.'

'You wouldn't have done. They buried it. Those of us in this line of work were told it would probably affect fund-raising if it came out. I think they were right. People don't like to think that money given in good faith ends up lining the pockets of fraudsters.'

'I can see that.' I changed the subject. 'My information is that Anton went on volunteering until quite recently. Would you happen to know where?'

'If I remember, it was somewhere off the Uitenhage Road. Algoa Park rings a bell.' Mrs. Martin got abruptly to her feet. 'There'll be a card in reception and maybe it's got his contact number.'

'An address would be more use.'

'We'll see.'

I followed her back out of the room and across to the reception desk. The vase of strelitzia was still there but the heap of files had been removed.

It took Mrs. Martin no more than a minute to find what she was looking for. Wordlessly, she passed across a small card. I recognised the cell number and knew it was dead, but I hoped the address printed in neat capitals would prove to be a breakthrough. I figured I was due a change of fortune, but in doing so conveniently forgot that sometimes those who are newly fortunate don't recognise when they're already well off.

CHAPTER TWENTY-FIVE

Surprise was my immediate reaction when I rocked up at the address the following morning.

The place proved to be a huge warehouse filling a hundred metre width adjacent to the highway and with parking at the front. An access road at the side ran so far into the distance I couldn't make out what was written on a container stored at the site's perimeter.

I pulled the Mustang into a bay marked Visitor and followed signs that directed me to what was described as the Customer Care Facility. This was a small building attached to the front elevation.

Inside, I approached a scruffy trade counter with a well-worn computer terminal, assorted leaflets advertising construction materials and a phone with a cracked receiver. Heavy footfall was apparent from the crumbling lino beneath my feet and the battered drinks machine in one corner on which was scrawled 'Out of order.'

I pressed an electric bell on the counter. It made not a sound, and nobody was to be seen when I gazed into the warehouse's cavernous interior through a glass panel. I wondered whether my arrival had coincided with the mid-morning break. Hovering for a moment or two, I rang the bell again and, when there was still no response, gave up and walked out.

With no specific idea what I was looking for, I strolled past the Mustang as far as the corner of the warehouse, before turning left down its long side. My view to the perimeter was now obscured by an articulated lorry loaded with bricks. A couple of forklifts had started unloading and transferring the heavy pallets inside. Other than a smile from one of the guys as he pirouetted in his truck, no one paid me the slightest notice.

Closer to, I identified the container against the perimeter fence as being the property of Maersk. But the lettering on it was much faded and the weeds and dust around its base told me it hadn't moved in a long time. One of its doors was ajar and a child's bicycle with a wheel missing was propped against it. Nearby, several sacks full of clothing were piled up on an expanse of concrete which stretched back to the rear of the warehouse. Along this back wall stood a Kwikspace cabin I'd not noticed. It was mounted on brick piles and a short flight of stairs led up to a door painted eggshell blue.

Curious as to what lay inside the container, I made my way over but took no more than a few steps. 'Where the hell did you spring from?' stormed a voice unexpectedly from behind my shoulder.

I turned slowly. 'Some might ask you the same question,' I said evenly to a short, lightly built man whose expression was a few clicks away from being chummy.

'*I* happen to work here,' he seethed, 'while *you* are clearly trespassing.' Eyes that were hard dots in a pale and freckled countenance signalled his anger.

'There was nobody in Customer Care,' I said carelessly, 'so I used my initiative.'

'All visitors have to be logged in.'

'Yeah, I know, but I'm not a customer. I'm making enquiries into…'

'Enquiries?' he snapped. 'What enquiries?'

'Into a disappearance.'

'What are you talking about?-Who's disappeared?'

'A guy called Anton van Zyl.'

Watching him closely after I spoke, I had to be impressed. He scarcely missed a beat at the mention of my quarry's name. If I'd been less alert, I'd have missed his reaction. But that morning I was as fresh as the breeze off Algoa Bay, so I noted the way those pinprick eyes became momentarily furtive, hunted even. 'Never heard of him,' he said dismissively.

'I was given this address by a charity he worked for,' I persisted.

The only response to that was a shrug but after that the man's body language underwent a transformation. The stiff and aggressive stance he'd adopted melted away and he visibly relaxed before putting his mind to giving me a smile. 'Which charity was that?' he asked. He really made it sound like he was interested.

'One called Work It Out located off Circular Drive.'

'And they gave you this address?'

'They gave me the site address,' I corrected him.

'How curious.'

'Isn't it?-What exactly do you do here?'

The charity worker, if that was what he was, became almost expansive. 'This place is a collection point for donations,' he said. 'The focus is children's clothing and toys, but we take anything that's usable. People bring us stuff they no longer need, and we distribute it in the locations.'

'You open every day?'

I got a shake of the head to that. 'It varies but usually a couple of times a week.'

'How do people find you?'

'Word of mouth mostly. We've been around a while. Best if charitable work is not advertised. Don't you agree?'

'Depends from whose perspective you're looking,' I said. 'If you're raising money for instance, you need…'

I was abruptly interrupted by the loud ringing of a telephone. Shifting my gaze to the Kwikspace cabin, I spotted a bell on the outside wall. It was there so anybody outside wouldn't miss calls.

'Sorry, but I'm going to have to get that.'

'Of course.' I watched him hurry away, mount the stairs to the cabin and disappear inside. As the day was hot, he left the door open and, curious as to what lay in the cabin's interior, I strolled after him.

Drawing nearer, his voice became louder. I made no effort to listen because, I soon realised, he was speaking Xhosa. There was no reason why he shouldn't, but it was an unusual accomplishment for a white man. Most of them use interchangeable English and Afrikaans. Xhosa is something else altogether.

He finished talking as I crossed the cabin's threshold. If he was surprised to see me there, I didn't mark it because my attention had already been drawn to something inside the door. It was a noticeboard with handwritten statistics added to a chart. What grabbed my attention was that the numerals were recorded in the French style, the most obvious being 7 with a bar through the upright.

But the game changer was the connection I made. The last time I'd seen anything similar was at van Zyl's house in Sunridge Park. There they were jottings on bank statements, and I'd been struck by how the numbers looked careless and slapdash, the defining feature to my mind of the French style.

'Was there something else?'

Distracted, I dragged my eyes to him. He was sitting behind a desk that was empty but for one opened lever-arch file and a large resin model of an Alsatian dog. His gaze had followed mine to the noticeboard and was now quizzical.

'Nothing really,' I said casually, 'though I'm impressed you speak Xhosa.'

'Oh that,' he said getting to his feet. 'I was brought up on a farm. It was always useful to know what the blacks were saying. The secret was never to let on you understood. Could be quite a challenge sometimes.'

I gave him an indulgent smile. 'Thank you for speaking with me. I'm sorry you couldn't help.'

'That's the way it goes. By the way, what did you say your name was?'

'I didn't.'

That brought him up short and the hostile expression came back into his eyes. Swiftly, he crossed the space between us and parked himself by the door. 'I think you'd better leave,' he said.

I shrugged and sauntered out.

CHAPTER TWENTY-SIX

I'd got made.

Or had I?

Maybe, I should've been circumspect and not come right out with the object of my visit. Perhaps, I should've have left Anton's name out of the frame and spun the guy some bullshit while taking stock of the place and what was going on.

But, in thinking I'd got made, what was I relying on?-Possibly instinct that told me he'd been warned to expect me at some time plus perhaps my too obvious interest in those French-style numbers. And, oh yeah, the fact I'd seen the guy staring after me as I exited the site. By that time, he had a cell phone glued to his ear and, through the lenses of the small pair of bins I trained on him from the car, he was mightily exercised about something. Paranoid to the last, I could only conclude yours truly was the cause.

Or was I?

I debated this but the upshot was I didn't change my plans. I drove north-west past Motherwell and away from the city. I was long overdue some shooting practice and I'd booked time that morning at a place I knew. The deal was you paid over the phone and that gave you an entry code providing access to a secure site. There were no facilities there, nothing but shallow three-sided pits where you could drive in, set up and blast away at the paper targets you arranged for yourself on fixed mounts. Sometimes the owner came by, and we'd exchange a few words. It was always about how our Rainbow Nation had gone all to hell, and he'd tell me it was about time everyone got their fingers out. Most of the time though he didn't show and that was A-OK with me as I found his company kinda depressing.

After shooting both the Tomcat and the Glock I needed feeding, so I stopped at a diner. I'd used the restaurant before when hunger outweighed my lack of enthusiasm for what it had to offer. I reckoned the people operating it were in the wrong business. They should have been running a garden centre, judging by the amount of greenery they had around the place, not paying dues to some chiselling franchisor in Jo'burg for the privilege of working all day and half the night in a fifties-themed eatery.

I parked and crossed an expanse of dusty earth interspersed with well-pruned, wild olives planted in high-sided wooden boxes painted white. The diner's entrance was set between dwarf palms in large terracotta pots and tiers of seasonal flowers in which hibiscus seemed to predominate. A waitress was spraying water on the blooms with such a look of intensity on her face I reckoned she must be communing with them in some secret language.

'I guess that beats serving customers,' I said conversationally.

She gave me a smile. 'You better believe me when I say I multi-task,' she said with a grin. 'You have yourself a seat and I'll be right over.'

I found a booth with a view over the car park. The restaurant was experiencing its mid-afternoon lull with a few people lingering from late lunches and a few others taking drinks and snacks. My table was decorated with a potted succulent in rude health displaying pink flowers and it complemented a flesh-coloured neon sign above the bar that was on the blink. At the far end stood an old-style, American juke box with a curved, tubular top playing a Johnny Cash number.

Despite saying she'd be right over, the waitress left me to my own devices. Restlessly, I looked around and after that gazed out of the window. The car park was deserted except for half a dozen scattered vehicles.

My eyes came to rest on the Mustang. What I could see of its lower flanks through intervening foliage was streaked with dust and dirt. If I went home via Russell Road, I could take it to the God's Time Car Wash. They'd see me right and restore the lustre of the blue metal. Alternatively…

A shadow fell across the car's roofline. Before, it had been glinting in the sunlight. The cause was a motorbike that had drawn up alongside. There were two helmeted guys in leathers. Idly, I watched as the pillion passenger dismounted and investigated the Mustang's interior. He turned back to his companion and each of them lifted their visors.

Their discussion lasted only seconds before the passenger moved away. Thickset, he lowered his visor and began walking towards the diner. His step was unhurried but purposeful.

The only party looking at him was me. So, the only party who saw him unzip his jacket was me. Same again when he reached inside, and his hand took out something dark and heavy. Lowering his arm, the hand holding the gun fell to his side. He kept coming.

'I'm sorry to keep you waiting,' a voice broke in suddenly. 'Have you decided what you want?'

Startled, I swivelled round to confront the waitress. 'W-What?'

The tension in my voice made her recoil.

Dealing with her upset wasn't my priority. Fact was she was blocking the aisle. 'Move!' I hissed. She didn't get the message fast enough. 'Move now!'

Shocked, she stepped back and I stepped out. Glancing out the window, I saw the biker ten metres from the entrance. I turned and moved away, heart like a jackhammer, adrenaline pump in overdrive. Holding it all together just. Every nerve screaming: Run! Run, for God's sake!

The kitchen was up ahead, and I made for it. In summer, the back doors in such places will usually be open. This one was no exception, and I crossed to it. Somebody called but I ignored them. There was a red baseball cap lying on a worktop. Grabbing it, I jammed it on my head.

Outside, the sun made me squint. I reached behind my back for the Tomcat. Taking the safety off with trembling hands, I crept along the side of the building. Getting back to the Mustang was vital. With the car, I had options. Without it, I could be dead meat.

I drew level with the building's front elevation. From there to the boundary fence was a five second sprint. I ran for it relieved those olives in their boxes hid me from view.

Crouched behind a tree and next to the perimeter fence, I peered out. My mouth was dry, my breathing ragged. The distance to my car was no more than 30 metres. The other biker was sitting astride the machine and facing the restaurant. The engine was running which masked my approach.

I came up fast. He didn't know what hit him as my shoulder cannoned into his. He toppled sideways and the heavy bike pinned him to the ground. I left him to it as I made for the Mustang. Reaching for the door, I glanced back to the restaurant. The biker with the gun was standing outside the entrance. He was scanning the car park away to my left.

He spotted me about the time I hit the Start button. In the mirror, I saw him brace and lift his arms. His second or third shot shattered the rear screen. By that time, I was in reverse and flooring the throttle. The Mustang leapt backwards spewing dust from its rear wheels. A cloud went up making me invisible but not invulnerable. I rammed the shift into Drive and turned the wheel hard. More shots slammed into the bodywork as I slalomed towards the exit.

The way out was a narrow passage between pillars. Another car was crawling towards it. I braked but the gunman was running after me and still firing. Out of options, I hit the accelerator and made for the gap.

I knew the space was too tight. There were sounds of tortured metal as I scraped the Mustang's sides. Next, I heard a crash as the smashed nearside mirror struck the side window. Fragments of shattered glass struck the side of my face and neck.

But I was through and away. Behind, a dust cloud blossomed in the hot air. For a second or two I watched it drift.

Back on the highway, I floored the accelerator. Putting distance between me and the restaurant was calming.

With the passing kms, I slowed down as did my heart rate.

Eventually, I pulled off and cut the engine. The road was quiet, and the sudden silence engulfed me like a tidal wave.

I felt a trickle of blood down the side of my face. In the rear-view mirror, I saw cuts to my cheek. Small glass crystals stuck to my T shirt and shorts and to the bare skin of my left thigh. The crystals littered the central console and covered the passenger seat and the Tomcat. In the foot well I noticed a deformed slug that had hit the bullet-proof screen after passing through the cabin.

I slung the baseball cap into the back and knuckled my eyes. My mouth was as dry as sand. I took a long drink of water. After that, I wetted a tissue and dabbed at the cuts. I went on dabbing like an automaton. Shock had brought on a numbness leaving me unable to think. I settled back in my seat and stared out.

But not for long.

A speck in the distance was coming straight for me. Next, I heard a high revving engine being driven flat out. Looking through the windscreen beyond a couple of cars, I saw a motorcycle. It was coming up so fast that in no time what had been no more than a dot became a blur as it shot past on the far side of the central reservation. So quick was it, I wasn't even sure it was two-up. I watched in the mirror as it diminished in the distance.

Diminished, but failed to disappear. Next, a brake light came on. It seemed lit for a long, long time. I realised the machine had come to a halt. As though viewing a film, I watched in a detached way. The distance between us was maybe a half kilometre on that straight road. The unexpected scream from the bike's engine brought me back from somewhere deep. My senses all kicked in at the same time. The mirror told me the bike was on the move once more. More than that, it was coming back and straight for me.

The choice was fight or flight.

Fight meant standing my ground. It meant getting out of the car and firing. Firing at a narrow target approaching at very high speed. My efforts on the range left me none too bullish. Besides, suppose I was wrong?- Suppose the bike's antics were nothing to do with me. Suppose I'd put two and two together and come up with 22. Seemed to me like I'd found myself a Catch 22.

I jabbed the Start button. The next instant I took off: a Mustang with its tail on fire. The bike was maybe a couple of hundred metres back. Lead-in-foot acceleration meant I increased that distance.

But I knew trying to outrun it was futile. Ultimately, I didn't have the same punch. Power to weight wasn't in my favour. But still I wound it up: 150, 190, 220 came and went. The bike though kept coming. Their intentions were clear when the pillion passenger began shooting.

Panicked, I shrank into my seat. If I did nothing, this was going to end one way. In the rear mirror, the bike came up close. I acted when a couple of car lengths separated us.

I slammed on the brakes. Not for a second or two or three but as a full-on, hard stop. 250 kph in-

Five…

Four…

Three…

Two…

One…

Zero seconds.

My recollections after that are hazy. I know the Mustang started to fishtail. Next, there was a huge impact at the nearside rear flank. It was like a train had hit me. Airbags went off as I was flung against the side window. My seat belt grabbed me so tight it hurt. After that, I think the car spun. I remember seeing the bike cartwheel, seemingly in slow motion, across the road in front of me. Next the Mustang careered off the highway. Under its own momentum, it slithered down a stony slope throwing up a dust cloud as it went. It came to rest parallel with the highway and ten metres below it.

CHAPTER TWENTY-SEVEN

It took me time to assimilate what had happened. Vacantly, I looked up through a star-crazed windscreen and watched the occasional car or truck pass by, oblivious to my presence below.

Shock though left me quickly enough because panic replaced it. If anyone was searching for me, they'd seek out the Mustang first. I felt unsafe and suddenly hot, very hot. In the closed cabin, I could smell fear, and it belonged to me.

Getting out proved a challenge as rock obstructed the door. The gap between door and frame was narrow. I worked the adjuster to push the seat back. Next, I released the seat belt. After that, I contorted myself and crawled head first. Once I was half out, I reached my arms down to the ground. Seconds later, I was lying dishevelled and hyperventilating in the dust.

Still panicky, I rose to my feet. Anxious to put distance between myself and the car I set off half-walking, half-running. There was a *kopje* not too far away with a view of the surrounding country. I'd not gone far though before I was aware of an ache in my shoulder. There was also a stinging pain at the side of my face.

The *kopje* was no more than tumbled rocks, so the ascent was easy. Soon, I found a niche amongst them with support for my back. From that vantage point, I had a view across to the road and my car. In my haste to be gone, I'd forgotten to retrieve either water or a gun.

More than an hour went by before they showed up. I knew they must be the two from the restaurant. They came from my right and were cruising slowly on the hard shoulder. I imagined them scanning areas below the road where bushes grew intermittently but thick enough to conceal something like a vehicle.

This effort was abandoned as soon as they observed my skid marks on the road. They slowed to walking pace for the short distance before the

Mustang was revealed. At that point, they both climbed off and put the bike on its stand. The driver stood by while the pillion made his way down the slope. I watched him walk round my car a couple of times, his closest examination being of the nearside rear panelling. After that, he climbed back up to his sidekick. In his leathers, I reckoned he must be boiling like a crayfish in hot water.

The two of them stood together for a few moments and scanned the horizon. I imagined what was going through their heads: If he got away on foot how much of a head start did he have? In what direction did he go? How fast was he moving? Was he injured? Or alternatively: Was he able to hitch a lift? If so, when? Where would he head for? How far could he have got?

Soon enough, they realised there were no answers to any of these questions. Only then did it seem to register that there was no sign either of their accomplices or their bike. So, after waiting for a lone SUV to pass, they crossed the road, and I watched as they dropped out of sight on the far side.

They were gone for a while, and I could only speculate as to what they were doing. When they did appear once more, they looked like men who had been given fresh orders for they mounted up, turned the bike and roared off.

I wasn't in any hurry to move. I thought the bikers might change their minds and come back. More important to me was the cooling breeze where I was sitting and the view over miles of open country.

This combination soothed and calmed my spirit, but not my body.

There was a dull and continuing ache in my shoulder and worse still was the sharp pain in the side of my face. Gingerly, I felt it with my fingers. It was hot and raw, and the sun's rays aggravated it. I thought maybe it was some chemical burn from when the airbags went off.

I made my way back to the Mustang slowly. Like the biker had done, I walked round it a couple of times which did no more than confirm it was a write-off. There wasn't a single panel which wasn't damaged in some way and, where the bike had struck the rear quarter, the metal looked as though it had been shaped using a sledgehammer.

The passenger door opened with difficulty because I was working against the force of gravity. Once in, I delved until I retrieved the Glock and the water bottle.

I had a drink and bathed the burn on my face with a piece of rag from the boot. After that, I climbed up to the road and crossed the tarmac.

As I surmised, there was a deep gully on the other side and, judging by how healthy the scrub looked, it had a better water supply. I scanned this greenery without enthusiasm born of my fear of snakes.

Like the rest of my fears, it's irrational but that doesn't stop it being a baleful influence. Fact is you just need to watch where you are stepping. It also helps to have the right footwear. Me, I was wearing low-sided loafers without socks. Ergo, I needed to be cautious.

I found the bike quickly enough. It was buried in a thicket with only half the rear wheel protruding. It looked like it had been flung there by an angry giant.

One of the bikers was nearby at the base of a large boulder. From his appearance, he'd shattered his spine when his helmeted head had struck the rock with all the weight of his body behind it. He was lying on his back which struck me as strange until I realised, he'd been searched. All the zip pockets on his leathers were open and they were empty.

It was the same with his companion after I located him. It took a while because he'd evidently survived the initial impact and crawled back towards the road. What had finally overtaken him I didn't know and cared less. He too had been searched, his possessions and any identification removed.

Nonetheless, I did discover one thing when I rummaged through his pockets. It was a receipt from a petrol station for fuel and a pack of Pacific Blue. It was dated weeks before and had become badly crumpled which was probably how it was missed at the bottom of his pocket. Its significance was that the garage was located a few kms outside Plettenberg Bay. More than that, it was within a couple of kms of the place along the coast where I'd met Moti.

Coincidence?-Maybe, but experience, some of it bitter, had taught me that events written off as the work of coincidence have a nasty habit of coming back to haunt you.

With that in mind, I retraced my steps across the road, picked up my stuff from the Mustang and called a taxi.

When it arrived, the sun was no more than a golden ball seemingly resting a few metres above the horizon. It was set in a sky that darkened from crimson to black almost as fast as the time it took me to climb in for my ride home.

CHAPTER TWENTY-EIGHT

'What time did you say this was?'

'Must have been around 11.30 this morning,' I said.

'You were gone a long time.'

I bridled. 'Is that a statement or a question?' Despite putting Deep Heat Rub on my shoulder and holding a cold compress to the side of my face, I was still suffering.

'I'm just trying to establish the facts,' retorted the policeman. If he was irritated by my question I couldn't detect it from my end of the line.

'Of course,' I conceded. 'Thing was I was planning to buy some clothes, but I didn't see anything I liked. Later, I caught a film at The Bridge Centre and after that I was hungry, so I went to Mugg and Bean. When I came out, my car was gone.'

The policeman was business-like. 'You'll need to come in and make a statement.'

'What tonight?' I made my voice sound suitably shocked.

'No, not tonight.'

'I should hope not. I'm very upset I can tell you. It's not the sort of thing I've experienced before.'

The policeman commiserated, took the details he needed and rang off.

I put the phone down wearily and crossed to the kitchen where I'd eaten a half hour earlier. Running the compress under the cold water tap and reapplying it to my face was soothing. After that, I poured a brandy and Coke before walking out into the roof garden. It was pleasantly cool, and, on a whim, I lit up a corona.

Getting home had been undertaken with care. The taxi dropped me in a street at the back of my apartment block and from there I used an overgrown cut-through to gain access to the gardens at the rear. Behind a line of bushes was the rear wall of the underground car park pierced with several openings for ventilation. All were covered by wire grilles except one near where the Mustang was usually parked. I got to this before jumping down onto the concrete floor inside and using my pass key to ride up to the penthouse.

Despite being ten floors up in the sky, I felt beleaguered. Unquestionably, it was safe enough where I was, short of an attack by a helicopter gunship, but the prospect of being anywhere else made me feel vulnerable. Each time the thought came to me, I began to shake. It must have been delayed shock. Draining the brandy and refilling the glass seemed like a good idea.

Thinking things through, it wasn't the police that were the problem. Reporting the Mustang stolen kept SAPS out of my face for a while and that wouldn't have occurred if I'd tried to explain everything. There would have been endless questions while they investigated, and I could have spent time locked away while they asked away. One dose of that barely a week before made me more than anxious not to repeat the experience.

No, I figured mine was the best way of playing it. Of course, there'd have been a report filed with SAPS about the incident at the restaurant, but it wasn't me that had done the shooting. Whether there was one filed after the accident on the highway I rather doubted: the place was hardly the Cape Road at rush hour. I accepted at some point my car would be found and maybe somebody would notice the skid marks on the tarmac and investigate. What would they find?–Certainly, the crashed bike, but it was probably stolen, and some human remains, probably unidentifiable. The appetites of hyenas or vultures would see to that.

My real fear stemmed from the other forces ranged against me. They were apparently directed by my erstwhile client Mahumapelo Matsunyane, aka Moti. All he'd used me for was as a stalking horse to find van Zyl. What he wanted with him was still anybody's guess but, whatever it was, it wasn't about embezzled cash. Nor did I think it was about his daughter's happiness. Moti had found Namzano an embarrassment a long time ago and sent her away.

It also came to me not to disregard the Security Services. They too had threatened me in their own special way. Their remarks about homelessness and statelessness hadn't been without impact on my sense of wellbeing. But how van Zyl was relevant as far as they were concerned was the aspect that most baffled me.

The Juliany Petit cigar was very good and brought clarity to my thinking:

thinking that, I had to admit, was too often clouded by emotional, sometimes even sentimental, factors. In this case, I'd transferred my allegiance from a client who was trying to kill me to one who was now dead. Fact was I had met Amy just once and yet had given an undertaking to find van Zyl for her. While the manner of her torture and death was traumatic, was this event going to continue dictating my actions? Besides, from what little I'd seen of van Zyl, he seemed like a guy who could look after himself. More than that, having survived two attempts to kill me, was it wise to tempt providence further? Didn't I owe it to myself to safeguard my interests?

I followed this train of thought a distance, liked it and stuck with it. Given that I felt under attack, the best thing might be to take off for a while. Out of the country, I was no threat to anybody and by the time of my return things would have moved on. Or so it seemed to me.

The night had become chilly, so I stubbed out the cigar and moved back inside. Firing up the laptop on my mahogany desk-bookcase, the search for a trip overseas began. I started with Venice if only for the reason there was a small oil of St. Mark's Square, painted by Bouvard, in the niche above the computer. Making excellent progress until a temperature chart caught my eye, I suddenly understood the consequences of flying into Europe in February. Whether staying in Venice, Rome, Paris, Berlin, or London if I was desperate, the weather was going to be against me.

After some thought, I turned my attention to California. Having done a post-grad course at UCLA some 15 years earlier, I retained pleasant memories of the place, particularly its climate. A while spent there would be a good move and took me a long way away from Africa.

There was much to choose from but eventually I settled on finding a road trip providing plenty of variety and new experiences. Working through several websites, I made notes with a gel pen on a small pad until stretching my legs became a priority.

When I returned, the pen had disappeared. It was neither on the desk nor was it on the floor. After that, it could only be in one place and that was the laptop bag propped at the side of the kneehole. This was the carrier in which I'd brought back Anton's laptop from Sunridge Park. It had been discarded after the computer had been transferred to the floor below and secured in the safe.

I rummaged in the bag. There were several compartments, and it was difficult seeing inside because the material was black. I worked by touch rather than sight and with growing impatience until my fingers encountered the smooth casing of the pen.

But those same fingers found something else which wasn't expected. It was a small object and was covered in bubble-wrap for protection. Wedged into a corner of one of the pockets, it was located where there was no risk of its falling out.

I looked at it uncomprehendingly, before setting to work with a pair of scissors to remove the tape bound around it. What I discovered beneath was a cheap USB stick which I pushed into the side of the laptop.

The stick had no password protection though the opened database was identified with the one word SECURE. Clicking on it brought up several files. I opened each in turn, but they were all empty. Empty that is except for one. What I found drove from my head the search for a vacation in California.

There were several screenshots, all overexposed because of bright sunlight. They depicted what looked like extracted record sheets. I reckoned they'd been taken in a hurry, or by someone who was nervous, because they were slightly fuzzy and difficult to read. But, after puzzling for a while, I deduced they were lists of Xhosa men, each with a unique reference number plus a recorded first name and clan name. This information was followed by a series of figures in five columns. Where the pictures had been taken wasn't difficult to establish because in one there was the partial outline of a model dog. It was the one I'd seen on the desk in the Kwikspace cabin, only 12 hours earlier.

Getting to grips with the figures that followed the names was more of a challenge. I printed them out in different sizes, examined them under different lights and even hunted around until I found a magnifying glass. What finally emerged were extracts like these:

71 8 568 120 448
65 7 455 108 347
77 9 693 141 552
56 6 336 102 234
81 7 567 117 450 ...and so on.

I went to bed with those numerals swirling around in my head and I was hardly less confused by them the following day. Sure, it wasn't difficult to see the interrelationship between them: in the first line 71 multiplied by 8 equalled 568, from which if 120 was deducted, what was left was 448.

To what they referred hit me as I was grilling bacon for a club sandwich. So surprised was I that the spatula dropped from my hand and fell to the floor. Stooping to pick it up, the enormity of my discovery overcame me.

They were payroll records, but none like I'd ever seen before. The first column was hours worked, presumably over a week, followed by the rate in Rand per hour which, when multiplied, gave gross pay. What someone actually received in their hand from this princely sum was derived after the taking of deductions.

Deductions?! -Deductions for what? The gross rate of pay per hour was significantly less than half the statutory minimum wage and was substantially below that paid even when the rates used were in respect of extended public works programmes. This was to say nothing of the excessive hours and without considering what sort of work might be involved and where it took place.

Beyond that, I speculated as to how all this was tied in with a charity ostensibly engaged in collecting and distributing goods to people living in the locations.

What I didn't need to ponder for more than about a nanosecond was the political dynamite that material like this would set off if it ever saw the light of day. More than half the population in our Rainbow Nation lives in poverty and unemployment is upwards of 30% or more depending on who you're talking to, and which axe they happen to be grinding at the time. Whatever the affinity that might exist generally between Zulu and Xhosa, the proven exploitation of one group by the other was unlikely to win anyone a government-sponsored, good citizenship award.

All that aside, I now had a reason as to why Anton made himself scarce. He'd stumbled on something and fearing for his life had disappeared with neither a backward glance nor a word to Amy. I guess he'd done that to protect her. As it turned out, it availed her and her unborn child nothing. I felt for him, an emotion enhanced by the fact that aspects of my situation seemed to mirror his.

What to do was the next question. I kicked that around in my head for the rest of the day but didn't come to any conclusions.

CHAPTER TWENTY-NINE

A few years back, I turned on its head the assumption upon which all altruistic Christianity is founded. That says you give unto God 10% of whatever you earn and retain 90% for your own use. In my case, it wasn't earnings I was disposing of but hundreds of millions of Rand in assets. They came to me as an inheritance after my father died and I believe he bequeathed them as his way of trying to atone for having rejected me during his lifetime.

I'm telling you this, so you understand something of my mindset. I could no more spend my life bigging it up in the company of a bunch of idle-rich arseholes than I could walk away from injustice. What I'm asserting is that it's the wise man or woman who listens out for the still, small voice of conscience and the wiser one still who acts upon what it says. Of course, I admit to having the luxury of independent means, the 10% I retained is still a lot of *geld*, and that gives me the latitude to tell anyone with whom I don't find common cause to get out of my road, and fast.

This was my reasoning after a lot of thought for pressing on with the case and not walking away. But the situation *had* changed and with it my focus. It was now less about finding van Zyl and more about getting to grips with something that looked like a nasty form of modern slavery.

I'd wanted to take time rehabilitating myself before making my next move. After all, there was extensive bruising to my shoulder that had turned to vivid shades of yellow/ green and the abrasion to the side of my face was even now forming a large scab. Both injuries caused me ongoing pain and discomfort.

But this was all very well only until I came up against reality. And that was if I didn't move fast, I'd likely miss the opportunity of finding out more about what was going on. I guess a sense of duty these days is regarded as rather old fashioned so you can call it something else if you wish. For me the words are not important. It's action which counts and the time for this was now.

CHAPTER THIRTY

The warehouse had powerful arc lights that illuminated the concrete apron between the Kwikspace cabin and the ancient Maersk container. Beyond the perimeter fence, the glare bled out until it disappeared in the vastness of the moonless night. Crouched on the other side of the barrier, I was invisible amongst a landscape of low scrub and uneven stony ground.

My plan was simple. It was to pick the cabin's lock and search the interior for clues, for information, for anything that would give me a way forward. Without this, I might as well give up.

With wire cutters in one hand and a small torch in my pocket, I moved towards the fence where it ran parallel with the container. The gap between the two was no more than half a metre but that was adequate for my purposes.

I set to work with a will on the wire and was about to pull out the square I'd cut when the arc lights suddenly went out. I froze in the blackness wondering what I'd done. For long seconds, fear seized me and made breathing difficult. Irrationally, I could believe someone was drawing a bead on me. I looked down half-expecting to see a red dot on my T shirt. Scrambling, I moved back from the fence and lay flat.

No more than a minute passed before I heard an engine and saw headlights. They were approaching down the side of the warehouse towards me. Their beams and the noise grew in intensity until the lights passed over me and curved away. The vehicle, whatever it was, halted on the far side of the container and its engine was cut. Silence and the darkness reigned once again.

It didn't last long because I became aware of voices.

'I can't see a fucking thing,' said one.

'Good,' said another. 'If they've CCTV it won't be able to see you.'

'You bring a torch?'

'You don't need a torch. Coupla minutes you'll be fine.'

'My eyes aren't as sharp as yours.'

'Quit moaning *domkop*. Ten minutes tops and we're outta here.'

This dialogue continued but grew fainter as they moved away. Heartened, I crawled back to the wire and removed the cut square. Crouched down, I negotiated the gap and then rose to my full height on the other side. With my face inches from the cold metal of the container, I side-stepped its length. Peering round one corner at last, there was a view of a Ford Ranger backed up close to the Kwikspace cabin. The two guys I'd heard talking weren't visible but the door to the place was open.

I watched as the minutes dragged by. There was nothing to be seen inside the cabin but the erratic movements of a pencil torch but there was a deal of noise.

An explanation for this became clear when the men emerged carrying a drawer between them. It was from one of the filing cabinets and detaching it had evidently proved problematic. It was also very heavy judging by the way the two slowly manhandled it to the back of the truck and set it down on the ground. As my observation continued, they lowered the Ranger's tailgate and lifted the drawer with muttered oaths onto the flatbed.

'Ten minutes, my fucking arse!' said the man I'd first heard speak. 'We gonna be here all night at this rate.'

'The other drawers'll be easy. First's always the most difficult.'

'You're forgetting there are two other cabinets.'

If there was a rejoinder, I missed it, but the information was valuable. Three filing cabinets meant between nine and twelve drawers altogether. That meant more time and several trips to stow everything.

The Ford was a short distance away. Its bulk would hide me from anybody looking back from the cabin or standing on the steps outside. On that basis, the risk of being spotted was small.

Yet caution was uppermost in my mind. I watched the men bring out four more drawers and gauged the time each trip took.

Then, as they strolled back to the cabin yet again, I crouched low and ran as far as the Ranger's bonnet. After that, I crept along one side until, lifting my head, the load area became visible.

Even if there'd been plenty of time, there was little light to appraise anything in the drawers spread before my eyes. All I could see was a mix of lever-arch and hanging wallet files. In that situation, my only option was lucky dip, particularly as there was a limit on how much I could carry.

I selected stuff at random from each of the drawers keeping a close eye on the cabin. But it seemed they were having further difficulties if the noise was anything to go by.

My arms laden with as much as I could transport, it only remained for me to retrace my footsteps.

And if at that moment it had come to me that this was all too easy, I wouldn't have heeded the warning. Not that I could have done anything about it.

Passing by the partially open window of the Ranger's cab, I glanced in. I was taken aback to see a small dog standing with its rear legs on the passenger seat. It was staring at me, its front paws resting on the window sill. In that split second of recognition, I knew how things would pan out.

I wasn't disappointed because the mutt began barking. It may not have been the loudest or deepest sound but, what it lacked in volume, it made up for in energy and persistence. One look at its furious countenance told me I should be much relieved it was on the other side of the glass.

Unfortunately, one thing led to another. The dog's yapping brought me unwelcome attention from inside the cabin. To the accompaniment of angry shouts, I fled but not before dropping part of my load.

With no time to retrieve it, I made it to the container in record time. After that, I stepped into the gap between it and the fence. It had been a tight squeeze before, only now my hands were full. I inched my way towards the gap. It seemed to take forever. As I crouched to get through the wire, one of the files snagged. In the act of freeing it, I looked right and saw the route I'd come blocked by a bulky figure.

'Bastard's here!' the man shouted to no one in particular, before addressing me. 'You wait till I lay hands on you!'

I decided he'd have a long wait and made haste to get through the wire. With what I was carrying, it was a slow process. But it was slower still for my pursuer. Trying to force his gut through such a narrow gap was never going to work. It left him immobile but not quiet. 'Musa, bring the gun!' he shouted. 'Bastard's getting away! Can you hear me, Musa? -Bring the gun now!'

But Musa was apparently the strong, silent type for there wasn't a sound. Unhappily though, he was also the action not words type. As I rose to my feet on the far side of the fence, something hotly fanned the side of my neck. It came from a point by the far end of the container.

I dropped to the ground as though hit and the files dropped with me. Once flat, I crawled away fast using my elbows until I found a hollow. It was screened by a line of undernourished scrub.

'You hit him Musa?'

'Not sure. I can't see a fucking thing.'

'I think you hit him. You better get the torch though.'

'*I've* got the gun. *You* get the torch, and I'll keep him covered.'

There was no response to that, so I waited with my head down. The gunman was perhaps 30 metres away from me. He had the same problem getting to me as Musa. I was safe for the present unless they could conjure up a pair of cutters and sever the wire at a point where the container didn't impede access.

Had it not been for the files, I'd have made a run for it. At present, the material was lying scattered on open ground beyond my reach. And that meant I had to take the initiative. While a torch beam wouldn't locate me if I kept my head down, it would certainly show up the files I'd filched.

I reached back and retrieved the Tomcat from its pouch at the base of my spine. Fully loaded, it was still only seven shots. That's one of the reasons it's a back-up gun. Light and easily concealed it may be, but right then I'd have preferred the Glock with its much larger magazine.

I peered above the line of the hollow, my dark complexion an advantage in what little light there was. The container was no more than a wide black shape set against a backdrop of charcoal grey. Just as they could discern nothing of me, I could distinguish nothing of them.

Nevertheless, I fired one shot at the edge of the container where I thought the gunman had stood. It ricocheted off the metal. I rolled three or four metres to my left, aimed again and loosed off another round.

The response was muzzle flashes and the sound of reports. Neither bullet was even close, but it gave me the gunman's position. I returned fire with three more shots. The result was a choked cry followed by silence.

Quit while you're ahead is great advice. I pocketed my gun, crawled out of the hollow and went to the files. Quickly gathering them up, I turned and at a stumbling run headed for my car parked on the far side of the waste ground.

Behind me, I left consternation and fury and pain.

CHAPTER THIRTY-ONE

Sometimes, the toughest things you do yield the smallest returns. Examined under the harsh illumination cast by the Fiesta's interior light, I worked through the files I'd nabbed. Unhappily, nothing of any practical use emerged and finally, in disgust, I threw the lot into the passenger foot well and headed home.

I left the Fiesta parked half a mile from the apartment block and went the rest of the way on foot. As it was around two in the morning, the streets were kinda empty.

Though my mood was as flat as the palm of my hand, the adrenaline rush I experienced earlier took time to dissipate and so sleep was difficult to come by. In the end, I gave up the struggle at sunrise and parked myself in the kitchen with a mug of coffee and a slice of French toast for company.

I ate slowly and distractedly as my mind turned over the events of the previous night. Increasingly, I was struck by one oddity and that related to the warehouse's arc lights. Whatever their effect on me when I was plunged into darkness, they proved mighty helpful to the guys in the Ford Ranger in concealing their identity. As belief in coincidence is often the playground of the naïve, I concluded they might well have been switched off deliberately. That meant somebody with access on the inside of the place.

I put in a call later that morning to Ralph Rainier. He was an accountant in Jeffreys Bay I'd known for many years through my surrogate father. From experience of navigating the government's Companies and Intellectual Properties Commission website, putting the matter of information gathering in someone else's hands was a smart move. I possessed neither the patience nor the cast of mind for the task.

As Ralph said he'd get back to me that day regarding the warehouse's ownership, I delved into the holdall brought up from the car. It contained all the snatched material, and I decided to go through all of it again.

I did so from a place of low optimism. Much of what was randomly taken from the filing cabinet drawers related to the work of the legitimate charity. Going through it once more left me believing I was doing little more than killing time.

Yet, after an hour or so, I did find something that intrigued me. It came in the shape of a collection of invoices generated by a bus company. They were for the hire of coaches over a period of more than two years. In each case, they specified the points of departure, of which there were several, and named one common destination called Triton. The name meant nothing to me, and I couldn't find it on a map. Be that as it may, somebody had helpfully added a note *Checked-483kms* on one of the invoices. The point of departure against which it was recorded was a township by the name of Blue Location lying on the west side of PE and close to the sea.

There was one further document that grabbed my attention. It was an invoice which had got itself snagged to a sheaf of other bills. It came from a wholesale distributor in Kwa-Zulu Natal and was for items including significant quantities of rice, mealie meal, sugar and samp; all staples needed to provide the raw energy to be expended by a substantial body of men. Unfortunately, the invoice didn't record a delivery address or any further detail but evidently it had been a satisfactory transaction as it was marked Paid.

I spent a long time trying to determine all the points, accessible by road, which were upwards of 450kms from Blue Location. The problem was lessened to the extent that perhaps 200 degrees of the compass were eliminated by reason of the fact they lay in the sea. But that still left a whole lot of landward possibilities tracking into the Western and Northern Capes plus the Free State and almost as far inland as the Lesotho border.

Having unearthed a large map, I cut a piece of string to scale to represent around 450kms as roads don't run in straight lines. Then I anchored it to the point on the chart where Blue Location was situated. I could then swing the string through an arc and identify all the points at the far end of it. After that, it wasn't difficult to mark the map appropriately.

At that point, I came to a halt. South Africa's a large country and vast tracts of it have few people and less infrastructure. That said, what I was looking for had to be close to a reasonably maintained highway as coaches are not SUVs. I worked on that a while and, because of the number of roads, became more and more depressed. It was at that point the phone rang.

'How are you doing, Sol?'

I ignored his invitation to chat. 'What have you got for me Ralph?'

'Not had a great day, have you?-I can hear it in your voice.'

'Had better,' I growled.

'Maybe I can cheer you up a bit.'

'Go on then.'

'We got to the bottom of your warehouse story.' There was a pregnant pause as though Ralph was working an audience before pulling a rabbit out of a hat. 'It got quite complicated I can tell you.'

'OK, amaze me.'

'The trading company that operates the warehouse is part of a large private group with diverse interests. It in turn's majority owned by a conglomerate headquartered in Jo'burg. They got themselves into financial difficulties a couple of years back and three brothers who speak for most of the shares couldn't agree what to do.'

'Right, I've followed you so far.'

'But now it gets convoluted. One of the banks providing a credit line to the conglomerate called in their loans. That precipitated a cash flow crisis that meant urgent re-financing. Part of it was resolved by a large injection of new capital from a high-net-worth businessman. He was particularly interested in the PE operation and secured a put option while he assessed its future. Apparently, there are some issues I won't bore you with. That said, there is speculation that the strike price makes the deal highly advantageous provided the underlying business is sound. This is all according to the stuff we've looked at in the press.'

Ralph fell silent. I didn't know whether he was waiting for me to catch up with him or whether he thought some plaudit was now in order. 'And?' I queried impatiently.

'Well, obviously this guy's now calling all the shots. It just goes to prove the old maxim: Cash really is king.'

'Yes, but who is he?'

'Ach, didn't I say?-It's Mahumapelo Matsunyane otherwise known as…'

'…Moti,' I interjected quietly.

CHAPTER THIRTY-TWO

Blue Location may have got its name because of its proximity to the sea or maybe it was because there were already Red and White Locations elsewhere. Frankly, it didn't matter what it was called. Its name was the least of its issues when measured against the grinding poverty and deprivation its existence spelt out in letters about ten miles high.

The following morning, I picked my way along a dirt track that was as close as the place got to a main street. It was partially flooded but rain wasn't the cause judging by the appearance of the standing water. It had the colour of excrement and under the hot sun the stench was close to overwhelming. I quickened my steps as my gorge rose and my heart hardened at the apathy and incompetence this situation underscored. Such is too often the character of our Provincial Assemblies where words are as plentiful as swarming mosquitoes and actions about as rare as black rhinos dancing.

A line of shacks ran on either side of the track each with a few metres of open space and partitioned one from another with whatever had come to hand: chicken wire, lumps of plasterboard, splintered wooden pallets. The earth they enclosed was beaten flat and devoid of vegetation except for a few blades of grass. Lines strung with washing provided the only splashes of colour against a uniform backdrop that was faded, flaking, and dirty.

No architect had designed the hovels thrown up behind them though some were as different from each other as any of the fancy homes you might see in Framesby or Charlo or Springfield. What they did have in common was the meanness of their vision and the make do approach of their construction. Make do with anything that came to hand whether it be corrugated iron, old boards, plastic sheeting, even cardboard and lengths of rope. Overlooking all this, above the rusting tin roofs, were sagging electric cables strung from poles that leaned every which way.

I'd come up with a cover story for my visit and now I looked for someone to tell it to. But the faces I saw blanked me or else were so caught up in their own dramas they had no room for an interloper like me.

Making no progress in starting a dialogue, I made a turn onto a narrow path no more than two metres wide. Here the dwellings crowded each other with little space between and everything looked as though it was held together by something other than physical forces. I spotted a couple of small children ahead of me in the open doorway of a shack. They were sitting on the bare earth and playing with a battered plastic fire engine. I noticed one of its wheels was missing and the turntable ladder had become detached.

At my approach, they looked up curiously before shyness took over. With one accord, they scampered through the doorway leaving me with the toy. I bent down and, lifting the ladder, tried to re-attach it.

I fiddled with it for no more than a few seconds before two black legs, the feet bare, intruded into my peripheral vision. Above, I heard a voice address me in Xhosa. Abruptly, I straightened up and came face to face with a tall woman. Standing with arms akimbo, she wore a tired blue skirt, her thin wrists adorned with cheap bangles.

'You speak English?' I asked.

She stared at me and shrugged; her eyes watchful.

I pressed on,' I'm looking for a young man. Thabo Butshingi. Tall like you. 20 years old.'

'Why you want?'

'He disappeared. His brother's very worried.' I didn't think she understood so I reached into my pocket. I took out my ID and passed it to her. 'I'm a detective.'

'SAPS?' she asked, my silver security industry card evidently meaning nothing to her.

I shook my head and gave her a broad smile. 'Not SAPS.' The apprehension which had flooded her face vanished in an instant.

'No knows Thabo,' she said.

That his name signified nothing wasn't surprising as I'd made it up purely as an icebreaker. But having to break through the language barrier wasn't something to which I'd paid sufficient attention. I said OK and smiled a goodbye but, turning to go, was confronted by a man of indeterminate age. Much of his weight rested heavily on a pair of crutches because he only had one leg.

'What do you want?' he asked sharply in English.

I repeated my story before adding, 'My client said Thabo had friends living here. That was why I came.'

'Do these friends have names?'

I shook my head. 'Unfortunately, he didn't know.'

'I don't suppose you know his clan name either.'

'The clan name's Nala,' I said, thinking fast. 'Perhaps I should have mentioned that first off.'

'Perhaps you should. The clan name's more important than the surname in our culture.' He stared at me defiantly. 'It doesn't change anything though. There's nobody using that name here.'

'Is it possible he might be working away?'

The disabled man shook his head. 'I know all the people here. Not many from clan Nala.'

I changed tack. 'Come to think of it,' I ventured. 'You're the only adult male I've seen.'

'I'm the only cripple is what you mean.'

'It wasn't,' I said evenly. 'It's just there aren't any other men. Lots of women and small children. In a place like this, that's kinda unusual.'

He said nothing but the shiftiness that came into his eyes told me plenty.

'Are they all working away?' I persisted. 'Maybe a long way from here? So far in fact they must be bussed.'

I didn't think he was going to tell me anything and I was right. His mouth stayed as clamped as a closed vice.

Thus, it is that the exploited are complicit in their own oppression. But rebellion's frequently a luxury to be indulged only by those who have means and the necessary wherewithal. Fact is you don't have too many options when the government steals the bread from the people's mouths and sees mass unemployment as just a part of life's rich tapestry.

CHAPTER THIRTY-THREE

When first I learned of the size of the inheritance from my father, I was overwhelmed. The sums of money were so large that for a time I lost my head. I spent money like there were no consequences and even had I continued to do so for years there still wouldn't have been much of a price to pay for my extravagance.

One of the things I did for a while was to take flying lessons. I joined a school up in Jo'burg and was introduced to the challenge of learning to handle a Piper Warrior, a single-engine monoplane with dual controls. It was all very sociable too spending time in the company of a pilot who was back in SA temporarily for family reasons. But however much the personal relationship between us blossomed, that regarding my latent skill as a flier never took off.

And in all the time spent there, I was never tempted to take the controls of a helicopter, though the opportunity was offered more than once. There was something unnerving about the way in which choppers manoeuvred, the level of noise they generated and what precisely might happen if the engine cut out say at 500 feet. Irrational it might be but all the reassurance in the world about the ability of a helicopter to auto- rotate didn't change my view. Hence, I've always stood well clear even as a potential passenger.

Now it seemed I was going to have to cross the Rubicon. There was no other way of conducting such a large-scale search within a measured distance of PE without resorting to the air. Using a helicopter was the obvious answer because of its flexibility.

That was my take on it but Markus, the guy to whom I was introduced at the airport later that day, wanted to complicate everything. The fact he towered over me gave him a sense of natural superiority before he opened his mouth to put me right on several issues.

'Let me get this straight,' he began after I'd given him my opening pitch. 'You want to fly out from here and then describe an arc ultimately taking in all landward points which are about 450 kms from PE.'

'I guess.'

Markus scratched his blond beard and gave me a disapproving look. 'Guessing's not going to be much help with this. You familiar with Pi, Mr Nemo?'

'Pi?'

'As in the mathematical constant equating to about 3.14.'

'I remember something of the sort,' I said, giving a hostage of fortune to truth.

'2 x Pi x R,' he went on, warming to his subject, 'gives you the circumference of a circle. In this case, a radius of 450kms equates to a total distance of almost 3000kms.'

His faded blue eyes searched mine closely, but I wasn't going to give him the satisfaction of batting the proverbial. 'Half's seaward so not relevant,' I pointed out.

'Something over half,' Markus corrected me. 'But it's still 450kms out and the same back before you've explored anything along the arc.'

'Which means what exactly?'

'We won't be using one of the whirlybirds,' he replied flatly. 'Not enough range to do the job. Even with a much larger helo you could be looking at upwards of a week or more. That's unless you get lucky of course.'

'Well, it's gotta be done.'

'And it's gonna cost plenty, I can tell you. You sure it's worth it?'

'My principals are adamant,' I said. 'They take a dim view of their building materials being diverted. Apparently, this has been going on a long time and the losses run into millions. Trying to get a lead on it at ground level hasn't worked. Don't ask me why because that was before I got involved. Now apparently, they've some intel saying they're being used on a particular project well away from PE.'

Markus shrugged and brought his mind to bear on practicalities. 'Have you given any thought to where you want to start?' he asked.

I'd given much thought to this but that didn't mean there were any valuable insights to be had. 'Maybe fly due north towards Bloemfontein,' I said gazing over his shoulder at the large-scale map of Southern Africa pinned to the wall.

'And at the point of intersection, what then?'

'I guess we toss a coin.'

CHAPTER THIRTY-FOUR

To my eyes, the chopper looked as though it should have been retired years ago to the SAAF Museum located at the far end of the runway. But I tried to discount first impressions and reassured myself as to the machine's size and payload capability rather than dwelling on its dull, silver fuselage and worn decals.

In the act of climbing aboard, Markus registered the expression on my face. 'Don't worry,' he said. 'This old girl's given solid service ever since the Angola bush war. With drop tanks and only the two of us aboard we've got plenty of range.'

This wasn't necessarily my main concern as I followed him in but, playing along, I stared at the array of instruments before me and asked pointedly, 'Which one is the fuel gauge?'

Markus grinned and tapped one of the dials. 'Chill,' he said, lifting his headset.

I sat back and stared out of the glass to the runway where a passenger jet was coming into land. The air around me was hot and laced with the aroma of aviation fuel. I turned to say something to Markus but by then he was talking to the control tower.

After that, the main rotor began to turn, accompanied by a whooshing sound from behind me. Very soon, this became a high-pitched whine as the blades overhead reduced to a blur against the cloudless vault of the sky. Markus tapped my arm and pointed to the headset in front of me. 'There's a delay,' he said after I put them on. 'Flight from Cape Town's overdue.'

I shrugged and waited. A few more minutes wouldn't make any difference. It had been three days since Markus and I had first spoken. In the intervening period, he'd had to clear time in his diary and sort out, as he put it, all the logistical issues. Darkly, I wondered whether this included effecting some repairs and renewals to the contraption in which I was now sitting.

We took off a quarter of an hour later, Markus nudging the cyclic lever to move us forward. Initially, we headed east over Algoa Bay before turning back inland and climbing towards our cruising altitude.

Uitenhage and its VW factory were bypassed in minutes after which we headed north towards Bloemfontein.

At an altitude of 4000 feet, and two hours out, the ground beneath us was a patchwork of ash grey and olive-coloured scrub set within endless plains broken by rocky outcrops and buttes. It was a parched landscape with occasional steep-roofed, sandstone homesteads each with its own steel windmill to draw up water. Little of any note moved in this wasteland, the most common sight being Merino sheep and sometimes the odd buck. The small towns we flew over were isolated one from another and lay beaten into submission under the glare of the sun.

At a distance of 450kms from PE, I'd agreed with Markus we'd bear left and begin exploring the line of the arc we'd agreed.

'Around 200 kms is the limit,' Markus warned me, 'before we head back. Keeping adequate reserves is a must.'

I couldn't disagree but was disappointed when, the distance flown, we had to turn and set a heading back to PE.

It was the same after the second day which brought home to me the physical size of the area I was trying to reconnoitre. Even activity on the ground of scale and substance could so easily be missed in a landscape that was seemingly limitless under those huge skies.

On the third day, we were still exploring a westerly arc at a height of 7000 feet. 'We lose nothing by flying higher if the sky's clear,' said Markus.

I was philosophical about the whole thing because there was no choice. It was either run with this or pursue a ground search. Doing that though would take weeks and I knew could well prove fruitless.

But I couldn't deny I was sick of it all: sick of the incessant racket from the helicopter's engine; sick of a seat that seemed to have lost much of its lumbar support over too many years of use; and sick of the unrelenting strain of looking through binoculars into near featureless landscapes. On more than one occasion, I'd directed Markus' attention to some anomaly I spotted, and we'd alter course for a closer view. Invariably, the effort was wasted, and I'd have from him such looks of disdain that those alone made me want to be out of it.

As it turned out, the breakthrough, when it came, was signalled by him, not me. 'Two o'clock,' I heard him exclaim as he nudged the cyclic to change direction. I swivelled the bins to where he was pointing but discerned nothing. Payback time, I thought; my turn to cast a condescending eye in his direction.

But I was wrong. As we approached, I saw the broad blue ribbon of a body of water running between raised banks. Rivers in this part of SA are notable by their absence so its mere presence was a sight for sore eyes. More compelling than this though were the construction works being executed in the water and on the far bank.

Those in the river divided it and comprised a line of steel caissons, some empty and some filled, that ran as straight as an arrow for perhaps 100 metres before turning in a shallow curve towards the bank. A temporary bridge provided access to the caissons so that cement, delivered by lorry, could be pumped sequentially into the empty structures. I knew that because I saw a mixer parked on one of the filled caissons and several workers standing around it.

Behind the bank, extensive earthworks were under construction with the purpose of creating a waterway or canal. A part of it had already been dug and the work was being continued using a small army of navvies. I watched excavated soil being shovelled into wheelbarrows before its transfer into a couple of battered trucks parked beneath a ramp. It was a labour-intensive solution to a problem that would otherwise have required the use of prohibitively expensive, imported earth movers.

'Take us down,' I ordered Marcus. 'I want a closer look.'

I watched as the altimeter needle fell back and the chopper went with it. At the new height, and with the aid of the bins, I saw how the future line of the waterway had been marked out using a series of stakes with wooden cross-members. Without my telling him, Markus throttled back and followed the stakes for perhaps half a kilometre. At that point, the ground fell away into a shallow valley that was roughly circular in shape.

'What do you reckon?' I asked.

'Looks like they're diverting part of the river.'

'I can see that but for what purpose?'

Marcus shrugged. 'Maybe a reservoir?' He caught my incredulous look and grinned. 'You're asking me to speculate on a project whose rationale was probably the last thing anyone thought about.'

'Government you think?'

'Could be. The nearest town's De Aar about 100kms away so I'm guessing it's nothing to do with them.'

We lapsed into silence as the chopper crossed the width of the valley and then made a slow turn to the west. With this new perspective and after crossing over a butte, the view changed.

Spread out before me was a large materials handling site including a mixing plant and conveyor that towered over large piles of loose sand and bagged cement. Several vehicles were parked up close by including three old coaches and several trucks. Beyond lay a work camp comprising a dozen or more large wooden cabins in two lines with some adjacent structures that must have been kitchens and stores and washing facilities. As it was the middle of the day, the place seemed deserted but for two men in cement-stained clothing who looked up as we passed overhead. A dusty and well-used track wound its way out of the site and disappeared in the direction of the river.

'Seen enough?'

'I guess.'

Marcus gave me a nod and operated the pedals, so we made a right turn. Simultaneously, he used the collective to open the throttle. As we rapidly picked up speed, I brought the bins up for a final look and caught something in the periphery of my vision. It was bright red in colour and in that landscape as incongruous as an ostrich strolling around the BayWest shopping mall.

'Turn back,' I shouted. But Marcus, focusing on gaining height and setting a new course, didn't respond. 'Turn back,' I urged him.

At last, he glanced in my direction. 'Turn back where?'

'Back the way we've just come,' I said impatiently.

'Are you sure?'

It was a dumb question, and I gave it short shrift. 'At over 200 kph? -Of course, I'm not sure.' Marcus withered me with a look. 'I think I saw something, that's all.'

Without a further word, he did what I asked and brought the chopper round. After that, he throttled back and descended a couple of thousand feet. When it became obvious it was a struggle to locate what I'd seen, he hovered and slowly boxed the compass while I raked the ground.

The bright red showed up at last in the lenses and I motioned Marcus to move in closer. We descended further and continued to hover.

'We need to land,' I said firmly when it was plain what I was looking at.

'Where do you suggest?' asked Marcus sarcastically spreading a contemptuous arm in front of him.

So engrossed had I been that the state of the terrain hadn't registered. It was an area of uneven broken rocks interspersed with patches of tough wild thorn. Some of those were a couple of metres high and looked as though they'd survive most acts of God. 'As close as you can,' I said.

Marcus lost more height and began seeking out a landing ground. 'You reckon it's a body?'

'What might have been one,' I said soberly.

The helicopter finally touched down about 400 metres away. It came to rest on a narrow promontory of sandstone but at least the ground was clear of obstructions.

'Coming?' I asked Marcus as I opened the cabin door and admitted a blast of heat from outside.

He shook his head. 'Somebody has to stay here,' he said scratching his beard. 'Besides, I doubt anything over there is going to raise my spirits.'

I couldn't disagree so stepped down alone and closed the door, the handle hot to the touch.

Staying crouched beneath the turning blades, I negotiated a steep slope and descended into a wide gully. Whatever breeze there might have been elsewhere had no chance here. Before achieving any distance, I felt sweat break out in my armpits and my T shirt stick to my torso. I also struggled to breathe as the hot air seemed to minimise the oxygen entering my lungs. Whatever the temperature actually was, I knew the mercury must be well on the wrong side of 40 degrees.

Making my way proved a challenge. The rocks underfoot were loose and the patches of thorn so dense that in places I had to skirt them. As a result, it took almost 15 minutes to cover the ground. By that time the sweat was running in streams off my face and my bare arms were wet and slippery.

The red top I'd seen covered the ribcage of a body lying atop a large boulder. The shirt was ripped in several places exposing broken bones and a fractured spine, all picked clean. As the bile rose bitter to my throat, I saw the cadaver was missing both its head and one leg. The arms, strangely splayed, were little more than smashed, bare bones and the remaining leg was in a similar state, the femur white as snow from bleaching by the sun.

Whether the man, and that was an assumption, had been alive or dead when he'd fallen was a moot point. What a moment's thought made clear was that he'd plummeted from a great height; I had to wonder whether that had been accidental. From there, the connection with the construction site was kinda easy.

I used my cell to take pictures from different angles, paying particular attention to all those bone fractures. No doubt someone qualified would be able to verify my conclusion as to their cause.

Next, I thoroughly searched the area in the vicinity of the body but found nothing more than a skeletal hand. Meagre traces of dried and blackened skin were still attached to it.

After that, I felt unwell. Whether from shock, the heat, or dehydration, or a combination of all three, I voided my guts. Uncontrollably, the retching went on well beyond the point where I had anything to bring up.

When at last it stopped, I looked weakly across to the chopper. Getting back to it was a priority for my throat was on fire and I had no water to soothe it.

I started out retracing my steps in the white blaze of the midday sun. The way back seemed longer and was certainly hotter. Twice, I caught an arm on thorns. On the second occasion, the encounter drew blood, and I stopped to dab at it with tissue. I was feeling sorry for myself only until the sound of a shot rang out.

In my line of work, quick reactions count. Don't bother trying to work out what's happening: Just get your head down and fast. Mine was down faster than it takes to count honest bankers.

From my prone position, I heard another report. Gunshots can be distinguished from each other, and these came from a rifle. Nor was it me being shot at. That was a safe assumption as soon as I heard bullets striking the chopper.

Then the gunfire ceased and time from the last shot began to stretch. I lay there, the sun flailing my back, my sweat-covered face centimetres from a patch of sand.

I waited a while before adopting a crouched position. Thinking the bullets had come from behind me, I turned my head. As I did so, there was a further crash of gunfire.

Silence wasn't the consequence this time round. Quite the contrary for the helicopter's rotor blades began to turn and the familiar whoosh of the engine starting up came to my ears. Within seconds, this was transformed into a maelstrom of noise as Marcus opened the throttle.

Powerless, I could only watch as the machine took off and charged away into the wide blue yonder.

CHAPTER THIRTY-FIVE

Distressed didn't begin to describe how I felt as incandescent rage gave way to disbelief. I watched helplessly as the chopper soon became the size of a mosquito. Then it disappeared and even the echoes of its existence were silenced.

Despite everything, I waited impatiently for the *whop whop* of those rotor blades to herald its return. Or at least to signal it was standing off near by and hadn't abandoned me.

Nothing though reached my ears in the sultry stillness.

What a jackass I'd been not to have taken water with me when I left Marcus. Worse, the cell in my pocket was useless. Large swathes of South Africa have no coverage, Wi-Fi being restricted to population centres.

And with that revelation, suddenly, I couldn't breathe. My airway closed up. I gasped for air. It was like I was about to have a seizure.

All classic symptoms of my nemesis, the panic attack.

I fought it by driving every thought from my mind. Every thought, that is, except the one to do with the act of breathing. With my eyes closed, I focused on inhaling and exhaling, one hand pressed against my diaphragm. Pressed against it to measure its rise and fall. In and out, in and out, in and out: as reassuring as the ebb and flow of waves on a beach.

Calmer, my priority switched to getting out of the sun. It was frying me alive, particularly as I had no hat, and exacerbating my dehydration. I found a camel thorn near a tall rock and slipped into its shade.

Light-headed, I wasn't sure what to do which meant doing nothing became the obvious choice. It occurred to me the shooter might instigate a search, and I had no intention of being found. As a precaution, I checked over the Tomcat and placed it on the ground next to me.

I waited a long hour. Nothing though stirred in that desolate spot except the sun shifted a few degrees west.

The forced inactivity gave me time to think. I was in the shit and no mistake. I couldn't contact anyone, and no one knew where I was, except Marcus. He might report in and say he'd been shot at, and he'd left a passenger on the ground. On the other hand, he might not. And even if he did file a report, how long would it be before anyone took the matter up?-I was in the back of beyond and the nearest help was probably hours away.

No, I was going to have to extricate myself from this mess and the first thing to decide was in which direction I should head.

I had two options. One was to strike out for the river. This had a couple of major advantages: access to drinking water and, because rivers attract settlements, the prospect of some human habitation within walking distance.

The alternative was to head for the work camp. This had significant disadvantages that I didn't really have to spell out.

Nevertheless, for the present, I kept an open mind. Getting my bearings was a priority and finding higher ground the first part of that.

I got to my feet reluctantly and put the Tomcat in my shorts. I felt weak and my throat was as sore and dry as a piece of sandpaper. Pacing myself was essential so I took my time in leaving the gully and ascending to where the chopper had landed.

But the view from there revealed neither the location of the river nor the work camp. That meant climbing a butte visible away to my left. It was maybe three or four kms away, but perceived distances can be deceptive.

As I found out, the distance walked was never determined. All I can say is that it took me two hours and the climb up the steep side of the flat-topped hill another hour. By that time, I'd fallen more than once on loose stones and grazed my arms. But that was as nothing against the raging thirst that the pitiless sun mocked during my exertions.

The top of the butte was as barren as every place else, but it did offer a panorama. I studied those views from every point of the compass with great care. Then I studied them again, but this time with a growing sense of desperation.

There was no fucking river.

There was no fucking work camp or construction site.

There was nothing but mottled vistas of green and brown stretching away on every side to the limitless horizon. It brought home the reality of the Northern Cape wasteland which occupies a third of South Africa's mass yet accommodates just two percent of its population.

But statistics weren't exactly uppermost in my mind at that moment. What was beginning to dawn on my exhausted and overheated brain was the possibility I might not find a way out of this. That I might wander for a day or two, it could hardly be longer, before suffering a complete collapse.

It tired me standing so I sat down on a rock. Its surface was blistering to the touch but the sun on my back was no longer so intense. Idly, I observed my shadow lengthen as the afternoon wore on.

Deciding to move again when it was dark, I waited impatiently. It would be less exhausting and, if I was favoured with a moonlit night, negotiating the broken ground and obstructions along the way wouldn't be so difficult. My aim would be to find a track and then to follow it wherever it took me. Tracks connected places and people, and the presence of people meant I could get help and get away. For how long, I'd have to walk was an unknown, but it wasn't as though there were a whole lot of other options.

Night encroached faster than I expected. In truth, it was my belief I closed my eyes at some point because I was surprised at how fast the light had weakened. The panorama spread out before me had turned from those mottled greens and browns to soft-edged and indistinct shades of grey.

I got up and stretched and put my intertwined hands behind my head to flex my spine. The action felt good, so I repeated it and rotated my body at the same time. It brought my gaze to bear elsewhere and what I saw grabbed my attention in an instant.

There was a faint glow in the distance. It was too diffuse to be an aircraft's navigation light and besides it was unmoving. But what it did do was to increase in brightness as any remaining daylight was leached out of the sky.

I watched it for many minutes until it formed a sharply defined cone of light in the sky. It was as constant as that star that had once shown above Bethlehem, and I had to hope it would prove to be as auspicious.

CHAPTER THIRTY-SIX

The reason that the South African Large Telescope, known as SALT, is situated at Sutherland in the Northern Cape is because light pollution is minimal.

I had little idea where I was in relation to Sutherland but could give compelling testimony as to the darkness of that night out on the veld. I only made it down from the flat top of the butte without injury by taking my time over each step of the descent.

But, once I was on what passed for the flat, I looked up and saw the cone of light had vanished. Dumbfounded and panicky, I turned and hurriedly retraced some steps, tripped, and fell heavily into a bush. The relief when I looked up and saw my guiding star once more far outweighed the pain in my arms and legs from the thorns puncturing my skin.

I walked for almost three hours. By that time, the soles of my feet, encased only in a pair of light deck shoes, were on fire and my head seemed as though detached from my body. More than that, my mouth was as dry as Kalahari sand and my breathing came in rasping gasps.

Nor could I be sure I was any nearer my objective. In a sky devoid of competing light sources, I believe a solitary point of illumination may prove to be many, many kilometres farther away than one might think.

This far from comforting thought had the effect of driving me on relentlessly. Ignoring painful feet and an aching body, I stumbled on as fast as my weakened legs would carry me. I became increasingly careless of my personal safety as I weaved my way across an undulating plain strewn with low scrub, sharp stones and small boulders. I fell several times but wasn't sure why. Maybe I fell over something in my path or perhaps I passed out.

On the last occasion this happened, I woke up lying on my back my gaze fixed heavenwards. My guiding light had vanished, yet I was bathed in something that emanated from a point behind my left shoulder. I turned my head and saw a window from which a yellow glow spilled into the dark night. This occurrence struck me as very strange unless I was in fact hallucinating.

Thinking about this took a little while after which I turned my head the other way. On that side, my peripheral vision spied another light source high in the sky and white in colour.

Bemused, I focussed exhausted eyes and saw it was fixed to the top of a silo, specifically a cement silo. I guessed the powerful halogen light should have been pointing towards the ground but instead its beam was at 60 degrees pointing into the night sky. It was that which had undoubtedly saved my life.

I'd arrived at the work camp-cum-construction site.

CHAPTER THIRTY-SEVEN

I had sufficient presence of mind to crawl away from the block of light cast by the uncurtained window. After that, I passed out and, when I woke up, found it was almost two in the morning.

There was no sound except the hum of a generator and that was so subdued it must have been on the far side of the camp. Turning on my side, I looked across to the base of the silo.

A sluggish realisation that water is required in the production of cement caused me to move closer. I accomplished this on hands and knees, certainly to maintain a low profile, but also because I found my feet very painful.

There was a large water tank at the base of the silo, and it was mounted on steel supports. The area beneath was wet and I crawled my way round until I found a spigot.

What trickled out when I turned the tap a fraction was as welcome as an 18-year-old brandy. I lapped at it, let it linger on my tongue and then let it slowly massage my sore throat as I swallowed it down.

Yes, I sipped that water with the same reverence I'd have given the brandy but for different reasons. Rehydration of a parched body takes place quickly, but I didn't want stomach cramps or other side effects from imbibing too quickly. So, I took my time until the point was reached where my thirst was sated. Then I used the water to splash on my sticky face.

Later, I sat for a few minutes with my back to the tank, my legs and feet stuck out in front of me. The silo was positioned on an incline which meant I had a view over the camp's buildings and beyond saw the vague outline of a small helicopter. Apart though from occasional exterior lights, the complex was in darkness and the only sound came from cicadas lodged in a stunted tree.

But, for all that, I could sense the press of slumbering humanity nearby. This was a population that had chosen to live and work in this place: there were no constraints upon anyone leaving as the lack of guards and fences proved. Yet those who laboured were as surely fettered as any slave chained to an oar in a Roman galley or forced to toil at the behest of overseers on an 18th century sugar plantation.

Security may have been non-existent but that didn't mean the site's managers were careless about safeguarding their transport. Fondly imagining I might nab one of their cars or perhaps a coach was a doomed ambition from the outset. There was nothing doing as everything was locked up tight and I had to turn my eyes elsewhere.

For a long moment, I cast covetous eyes over a small motorcycle. Had I the skills to hot-wire it, I might have made a noisy but quick escape. Gaining that sort of practical experience though wasn't something I'd acquired and once again I had to look to alternatives.

By that time, I'd explored the limits of the transport area except for one small hut at the rear. The door to it was locked but there was a quantity of junk outside. I went closer and spied a solitary wheel poking out from a collection of boxes and filled plastic bags. Closer inspection in the darkness revealed it was attached to a frame at the end of which was another wheel.

Freeing the bicycle from the stuff piled around and on top of it took a while. I was paranoid about making a noise and that further slowed the process but eventually I was able to wheel my find away.

But the machine surely dated from when a youthful Mandela attended Methodist college. Certainly, any association with the description *lightweight* was misplaced. The bike was of robust construction with a heavy frame and similarly weighty chain and mud guards. It had no gears, but it sported a luggage rack I didn't need and a pump which I did because the tyres were flat.

When I was finally ready to leave after strenuous efforts with a leaky pump, I was about all in. Watered I might have been, but I'd eaten nothing in the best part of 24 hours and during that time my exertions had been more than taxing. With no food available, I had to content myself with filling a small plastic bottle from the tap on the water tank.

At that juncture, it might have occurred to me that things had gone too well in the past couple of hours. But that realisation only intruded when, walking away along a track parallel with the camp and wheeling the bike, a dog started barking. The sound came from my left and prompted my throwing caution to the winds, leaping astride my new mount and pedalling furiously. As I tore away into the night, I fancied the sound of angry voices reached my ears.

CHAPTER THIRTY-EIGHT

Every year in Cape Town, there's a cycle race covering over 100 kms in which 35,000 people compete.

35,000!

Frankly, I wouldn't have thought there were that many bikes in the whole country.

You may gather from this that cycling isn't a sport in which I have any interest. Nor is this defect in character likely to be rectified after my experience of riding the machine I pinched.

My furious pedalling died a death not more than 200 metres from the camp. Fact was nobody was chasing me. It was also the point at which I became aware of how difficult it was turning the pedals. No doubt there was more than one reason for this but predominant, I suspect, was my shattered strength.

Nevertheless, I struggled on till I reached a metalled road and a while after that spotted a road sign in the approaching dawn telling me there was a town 18 kms ahead.

It might as well have been 180 or 1800 the way I felt but I had little choice in the matter. Sure, I could wait for daylight and hope somebody would pass by and pick me up. But I had to wonder, if I saw me thumbing a lift, whether stopping would seem a sensible idea.

I ditched the bike in a deep gully short of the town as questions about it might have been awkward. Besides, I had by that time concocted a story to explain my distressing appearance.

It was only later I worked out the name of the place I fetched up at. I think that was a measure of my exhaustion. Certainly, the town's sole landmark was the single storey guesthouse I discovered in one of its side streets. Coming upon it by chance, I was attracted by the deep shade offered by its brick arcade. Even under the rays of the early morning sun,

I was already uncomfortable as my skin had burned the previous day.

I limped a few steps along the arcade and descended two steps into a spacious vestibule. It was lined with photographs displayed around a cluttered cubby hole with a brass bell. Distracted by the seductive aroma of cooked meat, I pressed for service and then let my eyes to roam vacantly over the black and white pictures of 20th century film stars. Uncaptioned, I tried idly to recall who some of them were.

'*Kan ek jou help, meneer?*' queried a voice.

At that moment, I considered my appearance probably didn't justify calling me 'sir.' But then my questioner couldn't have been more than 15 years old.

'I need a place to rest up,' I said. As this produced only a questioning look, some further explanation seemed to be necessary. 'I was off-roading yesterday afternoon. Broke an axle and couldn't find my way back. I've been walking all night. Didn't realise there's no phone reception.'

'It's restricted to built-up areas.' The youth looked at me curiously. 'Where have you come from?'

'Cape Town.'

This reply evidently provided a satisfactory explanation for my naiveté, so I played on it. 'It was a new Q8. I drove friends up yesterday morning and then headed off on my own. Big mistake!-Shan't be doing that again.'

There was an awkward pause. 'If I give you a room,' the boy began doubtfully, 'and you clean up a bit, perhaps we could fix you some breakfast.'

I beamed. 'Sounds like a plan.'

In the event, whatever shock he thought my appearance would have inflicted on his guests didn't come to pass. As soon as I saw the bed in the room and he'd closed the door behind him, I kicked off my shoes and lay down.

Hours passed in an instant. None of the usual fitful tossing and turning or pacing up and down in the early hours, just a spell of long unbroken sleep like I'd not experienced in…I couldn't remember how long.

When I did awake, there were two sensations. My feet felt as though somebody was applying lighted matches to them and I was as hungry as a forest fire.

Three bananas taken from a wooden bowl, embellished with San decorative art, put a dent in my appetite. After that it was the outer man who caught my attention. Actually, caught wasn't the right word. More like stuck my eyes to the glass of the wall mirror when I placed myself in front of it.

First there were my clothes. I'd left PE the day before wearing a bright blue Billabong polo shirt, a pair of light brown shorts, and sneakers with soles as thin as ice-cream wafers. After all, I'd been anticipating nothing more strenuous than a day in the air.

Given that my stuff was all new, my rig had taken a hammering. Everything was coated in a layer of dust and beneath my arm pits there were thick white bands of dried sweat. The shirt itself was ripped and there were multiple scratches to my arms and legs. When I took off the shirt, the waistband of my shorts had also turned a dirty white and one of the pockets was torn.

I didn't spend too long looking at my face. Like everything else, it was caked in dust and my hair was matted and filthy. The dark eyes that contemplated me out of the glass were sunken and red-rimmed, their gaze devoid of life.

I stripped off all my clothes and washed them as best I could. After wringing them out by hand, I laid them on the tiles of the small balcony outside my room. Fortunately, it faced west and despite the lateness of the afternoon the sun remained fierce.

After that, I got in the shower and let cold water sluice down my body for a decade or two. Washing bare skin was painful until it struck me that, for the first time ever, I was unquestionably sunburnt.

Worse though were my feet. My heels had broken blisters, all my toes were red and raw, and the balls of my feet had bullae which would have to be drained. In the absence of the right equipment, I contented myself by bathing them in a small bowl of water until my clothes were dry and I could head out.

The shopping area was 200 metres from the hotel and described itself as a mall. In fact, it was no more than a few shops huddled together under a single roof of corrugated iron sheets painted apple green. Limping very slowly and painfully from one place to another, I made several purchases including new clothes and took my first proper meal in two days.

Later, dealing with the bullae on the balls of my feet required the use of a sterilised safety pin. Applying it to the edge of each large blister,

I pricked the skin and slowly drained the fluid beneath. Once that was done, I applied antibiotic ointment and covered up with gauze and sticking plaster.

I got away from the town late the following morning. It had taken time to organise a hire car as the rental company's nearest hub was 80kms away.

Once I was on the move, I was anxious to get back to PE as quickly as possible. That anxiety though turned to panic when, at a halt for coffee and cake, I phoned home and punched in my remote access code for messages.

I'd expected the usual sepulchral voice, but I was surprised instead to hear Effie. She sounded strange, her tone an octave higher than normal; as though someone had her by the throat.

'Effie?-Is there …?'

'T-Thank God it's you Sol,' she interrupted. 'How soon can you get here?'

'Why?-What's happening?'

I didn't recognise the voice that answered me. It was male, elderly, well-educated. 'I believe the *kaffir* asked you a question.'

'About two hours,' was my shocked response.

'We'll wait but understand you're to contact no one and you're to come alone. It would be most unfortunate if there was any misunderstanding about this.'

The phone went dead.

CHAPTER THIRTY-NINE

I made it back a fast as I could. The whole journey was a blur, my only focus being the steady march of time as I neared my destination. It was one of those occasions where I could have wished to have made the trip by means of some out-of-body experience. That would have delivered me home in the blink of an eye. As it was, the journey took me almost three hours by which time I was wound tighter than an overwound watch.

When I finally I stepped through my doorway, an old man sat facing me in my favourite recliner, an electrically operated, cream-leather affair. He'd made himself comfortable by operating the independent foot and backrests such that he regarded me from a semi-horizontal position. His faded eyes were as blank and unyielding as a brick wall.

'Please put the gun down,' he said in a matter-of-fact tone. 'You might get a bullet off, but it'd be your last.' He looked at me quizzically. 'And why would you do that when you don't know who I am? Or for that matter the purpose of my visit? Such impetuosity would betray the ability to reason given you by an expensive education.'

Nonplussed, I dropped my right arm to my side. As I did so, there was a rushing sound from behind and my arms were simultaneously seized by two men in a powerful grip. The Tomcat was wrested from my fingers and the ammunition clip removed before the gun was tossed on a sofa. At the same time, my other arm was released by a muscled guy who gave me a mocking smile.

'How the hell did you get in here?' I spat, recovering my wits. 'And where's Effie?'

'As to your first question, the answer should be obvious,' said the old man. 'Corruption, in what's laughingly known as our Rainbow Nation, is endemic. Ergo everything has its price. Honesty, integrity, loyalty are all commodities to be bought.' His gaze shifted to my left. 'What was the janitor's price, Gustav?'

'250 bucks.'

The man smiled but the gesture did no more than crimp the corners of a small mouth set beneath sunken cheeks. 'It's pathetic, isn't it?' he said. 'For the price of not much more than a passable steak in a half-decent restaurant one dumb *kaffir* was prepared to give you up. He wasn't to know I might wish to kill you, was he?'

This bullshit was getting on my nerves. 'Where's Effie?' I shouted.

A lazy flap of the arm from the recliner sent one of the men who'd grabbed me across to a party door which he pushed open. On the far side was the dining room and sitting in one of the carvers turned to face me was Effie. Her arms and legs were bound with duct tape and a piece of the same material had been stuck across her mouth. It was her eyes though that caught my horrified attention for they were liquid pools of fear. When she saw me, she struggled hopelessly to free herself and those eyes, huge in her terrified face, pleaded despairingly with me.

'You do anything to harm her,' I yelled, 'and so help me you'll pay for it.' I started forward and would have lunged at him but one of the guys, still standing at my back, grabbed me in a bear hug.

In response, the old man did no more than give me another of his excuses for a smile. 'Observe,' he declaimed to no one in particular, 'how miscegenation dilutes the blood, thus permitting the cancer of sentiment to take hold. In this case, you see a lineage dating to the Dutch founding fathers polluted via some casual coupling with a servant girl. Doubtless, *her* ancestors were no more than slum-dwellers from Madras, or Calcutta, or some similar shithole.'

At that point, I'd had enough. Enraged, I pushed back violently.

Unfortunately, the outcome was no more than a tightening of the grip around my body. I was being immobilised by a guy whose forearms were the size of lions' haunches. But I still had my voice. 'For one hell of a geriatric motherfucker,' I stormed, 'you've got plenty to say for yourself! What I want to know is who are you and how you found me?'

'My name's Aaldenberg,' he replied quietly. 'For your information, I was well-acquainted with your late father.'

Given what he'd already said, this shouldn't have come as a surprise, but I must confess it was. There hadn't been another occasion when someone had told me my father had been a close friend of theirs. 'If you knew my father, you have the advantage of me,' was all I was able to say, struggling to keep any traces of bitterness from my voice.

Aaldenberg shrugged. 'It's of no importance one way or the other. I mention it only to underscore your duty to collaborate.'

'Duty!-Duty regarding what?'

'Someone who's of mutual interest.'

'And who might that be?'

'His name's Anton van Zyl. You've been looking for him and made enquiries at the Merryhills Golf Club. There are only a handful of private investigators in Port Elizabeth. Finding you wasn't difficult.'

I did a double take but there was nothing wrong with my hearing. 'How exactly is he of interest to you?' I asked. 'More to the point, how does this interest justify your breaking in and terrorising my associate?'

Aaldenberg sighed. 'There was no break-in as the door was opened to us. After that your helpmate became overwrought and had to be restrained. It was as much for her protection as that of my men.'

I seethed inwardly as I looked across at Effie. She'd been following the conversation and was calmer now, but her eyes were watchful and very scared.

I badly needed to grab the initiative. 'Release her and I'll talk to you,' I said. 'Otherwise, you can go screw yourself.'

The old man abruptly swung his legs onto the floor and stood up. He was taller than me and without a gram of surplus fat on him his height was emphasised. Leisurely, he walked across to me until his expressionless eyes were only inches from my face. When he opened his mouth, I caught a whiff of violets. It was odd that the menace in his balled fists had such a precursor.

'It doesn't work like that,' he said sharply. 'Accordingly, let me explain your position.' His eyes bored into mine and, as he opened his mouth again, the smell of violets suddenly became overwhelming. 'I believe you possess certain information that may be helpful to me. I know something of van Zyl's recent history, but I must confess there are gaps. Like you, I'm looking for him.'

'Why would that be?'

Aaldenberg hesitated before replying. 'Van Zyl's a longstanding compatriot. He was somebody who rendered valuable service at a time when it was most needed. I believe he's now in trouble and would benefit from my help. You should understand I always take care of my own.'

Taking care may be viewed in more than one way, but I put that aside. For the moment, it was curiosity that got the better of me. 'Service?-What service?' I asked.

'The highest form,' retorted Aaldenberg proudly 'The sort that shapes events and affirms a people's identity.'

As he spoke, I saw something ignite in his eyes. I would describe it as the flame of fanaticism and at its heart I could well imagine a ruthless single-mindedness. It was then I came to understand just how dangerous this man might be.

But there was no time to ponder this because he began speaking again. 'What I require,' he said, 'is an account of your investigation to date and what lines of inquiry you're currently pursuing. You'll tell me everything you know because, if you don't, there will be consequences.' Aaldenberg turned away from me. 'Gustav,' he ordered, 'a small demonstration if you please.'

Sensing something unpleasant was about to happen, I seized the initiative and once more tried to free myself. This time, the back of my head collided with the guy's jaw and made him stagger. His response was to clasp me tighter than the steel bands they put round barrels.

And it was in that state, that Aaldenberg seized his opportunity and kneed me in the groin.

'Aaargh!' I cried out. Expletives were torn out of me as excruciating pain ripped me apart. Nauseous, I slumped forward and gagged several times before Aaldenberg grabbed me by my hair and jerked me upwards.

My vision blurred, I found myself looking into the old man's eyes which were now as remote as those beaches along the Skeleton Coast. 'You're beginning to try my patience,' he said. 'And your little outburst interrupted the demonstration I ordered.' He turned towards Gustav who was now standing by Effie's chair. 'Please proceed.'

What I witnessed then would replay over and over in my mind's eye in the days that followed. At the time, it seemed to unfold in slow motion as the flat of Gustav's hand stretched sideways from his body before describing an arc across it. Then, with a sound like a whip cracking, his hand struck Effie's cheek and threw her head to one side. I saw blood start from a gash made by a ring and heard the strangled cries that came out from behind the tape over her mouth.

'I'm going to fucking kill you!' I screamed, despite the pain emanating from my groin.

Aaldenberg was unmoved. 'I think not,' he said matter-of-factly. 'What you are going to do is cooperate fully. If I have any suspicion that you're being less than candid, you know what'll happen. Not to you, but to her.'

Of course, falling into line was my only option. I had no choice in the matter. The bastard had the measure of me, and he was relaxed about exploiting his advantage as bullies always are.

So, mindful of Effie's welfare, I began to take him through everything, starting with my initial meeting with Moti and my agreement to search for his missing son-in-law.

Telling my tale, in a level of detail that left no room for Aaldenberg to punish Effie further, brought home to me how much had happened in a few weeks. From discovering the smashed-up flat in Central; to discovering Amy's body in her sister's swimming pool; to my arrest and incarceration; to my separate meetings with van Zyl and his disturbed wife; to the attempts on my life by the motorcyclists; to my theft of documents from the charity office; to my visit to Blue Location; and to my abandonment by Marcus when he'd flown off, I'd ridden a roller-coaster and then some. Hindsight told me it would have been better if I'd never got involved. But hindsight's the guest who arrives too late at the party and makes you beat yourself up.

Aaldenberg mostly heard my monologue in silence, but he did question me about one thing and that was my meeting with our mutual quarry.

'What did you discuss?' he asked.

'It wasn't like that,' I said. 'I'd barely introduced myself before a grenade came through a window.'

'Yet here you still are.'

'It was a stun grenade. There was a bright light and a lot of noise. For a while, I was deafened.'

'And who do you believe threw the grenade?'

'Men sent by Moti. They'd been tracking me for days.'

'What happened after the grenade exploded?'

'In the confusion, van Zyl took off and I wasn't far behind.'

The old man looked hard at me and directed his gaze towards Gustav. I saw the thug's hand flex, anticipating a command to administer a further blow. 'Look, that's how it was,' I said desperately. 'The grenade caused the place to catch fire. There was even a news piece afterwards saying the house had burnt down.'

Aaldenberg's gaze resumed its search of my face. 'What did van Zyl look like?'

If I'd been able to shrug, I might have done so. Unfortunately, I was still tightly pinned. Despite this, my thoughts were with Effie who sat slumped in the carver. I couldn't see much of her face because her hair was dishevelled but her body language told me she might have slipped into something like a catatonic state. 'Tall, slim guy with fair hair,' I said. 'Heavy glasses with black frames. He looked like a school teacher or a college lecturer.'

'What was he wearing?'

I made an effort to recall. 'Jogging bottoms and a printed T shirt.'

'And what did he tell you?'

'As I said: he told me nothing. The explosion occurred almost as soon as I clapped eyes on him.'

'I assume he had a car. Tell me about it.'

'It was a small Fiat. I think it was blue.'

'I believe he's given that up.'

This was the first time Aaldenberg revealed he had any information of his own, but I made no comment. 'I tracked him down about three weeks ago,' I said. 'Anything could have happened since.'

'But what do *you* think has happened?'

'How should I know?' I retorted, but I saw from the expression on the old bastard's face that this wasn't cutting it. 'In his shoes,' I added quickly, 'leaving the country would make a lot of sense.'

Evidently Aaldenberg hadn't considered this. 'Why?'

I summarised: 'He'd have the means, following his thefts of company money. Also, Moti believes he has information about his labour scam. If it comes out, it will seriously damage Moti. In fact, I believe it'll destroy him altogether. It's evidently vital which is why he's tried to kill me. He thinks I know something about what he's up to. In short, all the time Moti's around, van Zyl has no future.'

But Aaldenberg decided to be dismissive. 'I'm not interested in how one group of *kaffirs* exploits another. What I must know is what enquiries you're pursuing as of now.'

With an effort, I looked straight into his eyes. 'I'm out of options,' I said baldly. 'And frankly I'm sick of the whole business. I'm no closer to van Zyl than was the case when I started. I've really no idea where he is now.'

Aaldenberg pondered this for a moment. 'Nevertheless, your enquiries will continue,' he said slowly. 'They'll continue until you achieve a result, or I inform you that you're to stop. Is that understood?'

'How does that work?'

'You're a resourceful man, so that will be for you to determine. Besides, I'm going to incentivise your efforts in a way you'll find meaningful.'

I didn't think I was going to like what he said next, and I was right.

'The *kaffir* will stay with me until this matter's resolved,' Aaldenberg went on. 'She'll be my guarantee you don't do anything contrary to my interests. I shall require you to provide me with daily updates. Have you any questions?'

No words came out of my mouth because I was overcome with rage. My silence though caused Aaldenberg to assume I was acquiescent, so his eyes slid away from me. In the same instant, the guy holding me relaxed his grip.

This time, with all the pent-up fury at my disposal, I flung myself backwards. After colliding heavily with my captor's chest, I managed to free my arms and drive myself forward. Aaldenberg recognised his peril too late for my hands were already around his scrawny neck. Remorselessly, I began to crush his windpipe. Another minute and I'd have succeeded in throttling the life out of him. But time wasn't on my side. Even as my grip further tightened, I felt a crashing blow to the side my head. As that happened, my vision exploded into a thousand brightly lit fragments.

CHAPTER FORTY

'I want… to speak to… Lydia Estleman.'
'Who's calling?'
'Sol…Sol Nemo.'
'Please hold.'

I held, but the phone placed against the left side of my face wasn't comfortable. That was because my usual habit was to wedge the instrument between my right ear and shoulder, so my hands were free. I couldn't do that as there was a painful gash and a large bruise. It was where a gun butt had caught me behind my ear in the act of throttling Aaldenberg.

I'd regained consciousness an hour earlier but for how long I'd been out, I wasn't sure. What I did know was it had become dark, and I could hear a fluttering sound that came from the dining room. I was puzzled about it for all the time it took me to lift myself from the floor and stagger with an aching crotch and a bursting head to a light switch. It was then I saw the streamers of duct tape hanging from the empty chair Effie had occupied. A stiff breeze from the direction of an external door standing ajar was agitating the cut lengths and making them dance. After that, the shock of Effie not being there hit me, and I fell back against the wall. A wave of nausea overtook me, and I slumped to the floor.

Eventually, I did manage to pick myself up and shamble towards the bathroom. Locating some codeine tablets, I took a couple and splashed water on my face. What I saw of the wound behind my ear dissuaded me from giving it any immediate attention. There was some congealing blood soaking the hair and the area was very painful to the touch.

Booze and pills are considered to be a bad combination, but I have to say they've often served me well in situations like the one I now found myself in. Moderation though in the quantities of each taken is essential and it was on that basis I poured myself a brandy overlaid with a large measure of Coke.

After that, me and the brandy did some hard thinking in the recliner that Aaldenberg had so recently occupied. My first thought was to call SAPS to report the break-in and Effie's kidnap, but it didn't take me long to appreciate that this was purposeless. I mean what was I to tell them?- That three men had ambushed me at home, assaulted Effie, and me, asked a lot of questions about somebody who was missing, and after that had disappeared into the night taking Effie with them? Sure, I hoped they'd be sympathetic and promise to come back in the morning with scenes of crime personnel. But when they were done, I'd be no further forward than I was right now.

On the other hand, Aaldenberg and Anton van Zyl were connected and possessed some sort of history that sounded like it dated back a while. The only other party, except Moti, who was actively interested in my quarry, was the lady in the two-piece suit and pearl accoutrements I'd met on the N7. It was wise to have omitted any mention of her to Aaldenberg though I was apprehensive he might know something leading to consequences for Effie. The other reason I left Lydia out of my account was because it wasn't difficult to believe he might just be the sort of individual State Security could be interested in. His explicit racism and casual resort to violence was confirmation of that.

'Are you still there?' It was the guy who'd asked me to hold on.

'Y-Yes,' I said, startled by the intrusion into my thoughts.

Next, I heard a female voice. 'Mr.Nemo, this is Lydia Estleman. I'm sorry to have kept you. What can I do for you?'

'You said to call if I had anything regarding Anton van Zyl.'

'I did. What have you got?'

'A party called Aaldenberg,' I went on, 'broke in here today with a couple of heavies. He told me he was looking for van Zyl. He wanted an account of my attempts to trace him.' I paused for a few seconds. 'Rather like you did when we met.'

'Aaldenberg?-I'm afraid the name means nothing. Can you describe him?'

'Tall, spare figure. Dead eyes and a spirit to match. In his mid to late seventies, I reckon. He told me he knew my father.'

'And who was your father?'

I said the name and waited for some reaction. There's usually a comeback as the old bastard was a prominent Afrikaner plus a successful entrepreneur and businessman. But, on this occasion, there was nothing. 'Is there anything else you can tell me?' asked Lydia.

I reflected. 'There *was* one thing: his breath smelt of violets.'

That got her attention. '*Parma* violets?' she queried.

'I haven't a clue. What'll stick in my mind is the association between the smell of them and getting kneed in the balls.'

But Lydia wasn't listening, her thoughts having taken wing. 'His name isn't Aaldenberg,' she said at last. 'It's Steganga. Johannes Steganga.'

I took a large slug of the brandy. Between the alcohol and the codeine tablets, I was beginning to anaesthetise the pain. 'I've never heard of him. Should I have done?'

'Not unless you're a student of apartheid-era politics. Johannes Steganga led a group of right-wing terrorists. That was back in mid-to-late eighties. They were in the same mould as the *Afrikaner Volksfront* headed by Terre'Blanche. You remember Terre'Blanche, surely?'

She was talking about stuff from my teens. 'Vaguely,' I said, 'but wasn't all that baggage dealt with by the Truth and Reconciliation Commission? It was where the idea of a Rainbow Nation came from, wasn't it?'

'It was, but you overemphasise the TRC's significance. Certainly, as part of its brief, it had the power to grant amnesties as regards criminal acts. But that was only in specified circumstances. In fact, thousands of applications were turned down by the TRC because they didn't meet the criteria.'

'So, there was stuff that wasn't resolved?'

'Yes.'

'And what of Steganga?'

'He's been below the radar for a long time now. As I recall, he retired to Constantine. It's a settlement near Cape Town.'

'You've a good memory.'

'Not really. I had an aunt who lived in a place called Constantine in England. I stayed with her sometimes, so the name has always stuck in my mind.'

'But where does van Zyl fit into all this?' I interrupted impatiently, sensing the conversation was in danger of degenerating into reminiscing.

She gave me no answer.

'Look,' I went on, 'Aaldenberg stroke Steganga told me van Zyl had rendered him some sort of service. He told me what he did influenced events and gave me some bull about it confirming a people's identity. What the hell was he talking about?'

'Steganga's group was called Strike Now! As I've already said, it was a terrorist organisation. It committed itself to violent opposition to any dismantling of apartheid. To that end, it orchestrated assassinations and bombings. I'd need to refresh my memory as regards the details.'

'OK, but why do you want to find van Zyl?'

'He's a person of interest.'

'That's what you told me before. I seem to recall we had a discussion as to what the term meant.'

'Did we?-I don't remember.' Lydia paused. 'We want to locate him because of that unresolved business we spoke about. There may be a need to protect him. You've had an encounter with Steganga so you've an idea of what he might be facing.'

'So why don't you deal with Steganga?'

'Deal with him how?-I don't believe there are any criminal charges pending if that's what you mean. If there were, they'd have been processed long ago.'

'So, you can't help me?'

'I didn't say that. Rest assured, I'll institute a case review at this end and update our records in the light of what you've told me. And if all that sounds terribly bureaucratic, I'm sorry but that's the way it is. The Republic's priorities have rather changed over the years as I'm sure you can imagine.'

'Accepted, but your response gives me nothing.'

'Not quite. I think you should alert SAPS to the break-in and the assault. They are after all the appropriate authority and will institute their own enquiries. No doubt, that will require an internal referral between the Eastern and Western Capes because of the jurisdictional issues. I'll ensure that SAPS in both provinces are informed of our residual interest and that we're to be kept fully informed.'

This sounded to me like a kiss-off. Self-evidently, it was van Zyl they were interested in, not some misogynistic relic of the apartheid era whose crimes had presumably never been provable in a court of law.

Anyway, that's where we left it.

Why didn't I say anything to her about Effie?-I suppose it was because of my lack of faith in the system and what Lydia had just told me confirmed my cynicism. If I wanted anything done, I was going to have to do it myself as sitting tight isn't my natural inclination. In the particular situation of Effie's abduction, the best place for me was to be up and doing. In short, I had to make for Constantine, and fast, however bad I felt in myself.

CHAPTER FORTY-ONE

Referring to a place as a ghetto has its genesis in the Jewish quarter of 16th century Venice. Despite its being a Venetian language term, there's no concurrence as to the word's origins. That said, there's general agreement that describing a place as a ghetto has kinda pejorative connotations. Constantine was no different, but its defining characteristics weren't poverty and squalor but rather wealth and privilege.

Not that there was much of that to see when I pitched up after an eight-hour drive west from PE along the N2. Exiting the highway, I missed my turn into the settlement and had to back-track. The residential street I joined ran parallel with the main road before bending left. A couple of hundred metres farther along, I pulled up adjacent to a high granite wall and beneath the dense canopy of some tree with wide-spread branches. It was only after switching off that it became apparent there was no ambient light for the darkness was as impenetrable as that within a vault.

But, with the luminous hands of my Omega telling me it was after three, I moved into the passenger seat and closed my eyes. There was nothing to be achieved before the new day dawned and besides, I was shattered.

The spot in which I was parked remained in deep shadow long after the sun had risen. Consequently, my melatonin levels stayed elevated, and I slumbered on until the sun was visible above a distant mountain top.

I surfaced with a raging thirst and ached all over. The first I dealt with by taking a long pull from a bottle of water. The second I acknowledged sequentially: there were pain centres in my head, in my shoulders, and in my feet. There wasn't much I could about them, other than pop another pill or two.

As I considered my next move, I contemplated my surroundings. The road was built on a hillside ledge with detached houses above and below.

Along the way from me, a young guy in faded blue, cut-down jeans was taking equipment out of a *bakkie* advertising pool maintenance services. I watched him idly for several minutes as I worked my way through a couple of cereal bars and a banana.

Constantine wasn't a big place. It comprised perhaps 300 properties situated along a network of roads at different levels, all overlooking a sandy beach strewn with smooth, granite boulders. Thinking it over, it seemed I could walk around the estate to see whether there was anything to be learned regarding Steganga's whereabouts or I could visit the local Electoral Commission office and find somebody to bribe. Neither option appealed much, particularly the first, because, if Steganga was there, I could be spotted. It was this dilemma which engaged me as I sat chewing.

Up ahead, the pool guy had quit unloading and was starting to shift stuff from the kerb into the garden. Or he was until a small van, painted bright yellow, passed me at speed before pulling up close behind the *bakkie* obscuring my view. Squinting at the black lettering on the rear doors I read the words *Speedy Gonzalez*. A few more seconds allowed me to work out I was looking at a courier either picking up or dropping off.

Quickly, I jammed on a baseball cap covering most of the wound at the side of my head and opened the car door. Stepping out too quickly, my left leg gave out and I staggered, a consequence of having been off my feet for 12 hours.

I wasn't the only one though with mobility problems. The courier, evidently employed for reasons not connected with his bulk, was awkwardly levering himself out of the driver's seat. After that, he shambled to the back of the van, eyes down.

I limped slowly and painfully towards him and caught up as he busied himself removing a small parcel from a collection on display in the loading area.

'Hi,' I said displaying my winning smile, though I wasn't feeling much like a winner.

Startled, the courier looked round and focused tired eyes. 'Hi,' he replied in a neutral tone.

'I think you may be able to help me.'

The man's expression told me he disagreed. 'I'm on a tight schedule,' he said. 'No time for helping.'

'This won't take long. And I can make it worth your while.'

About to turn his back, he decided not to. 'How?'

'With information.'

'What sort of information?'

'You been working this area long?' I countered.

He ignored me. 'Who are you?'

'I'm a PI out of Cape Town.' The courier looked baffled. 'Private investigator. My name's Shah. I'm looking for a missing teenager. Her parents are frantic.'

This appeal to his better nature didn't seem to work. 'You said you'd make it worth my while.'

I shrugged. 'If you've got what I want…'

'And what do you want?'

'I'm trying to trace a party by the name of Steganga. Apparently, he has some connection with this place. One of the girl's friends mentioned it. It's a long shot but that's where I am right now. If I give you money, can you help?'

'How much?'

At that point, the courier started to get on my nerves. I balled my fists but kept them in my pockets. 'There's no budget,' I said tightly. 'What have you got?'

'Cost you 500 bucks.'

'OK, 500 bucks it is.' I looked straight into his sore eyes. 'Now spill, before I forget my manners.'

'I've delivered to Steganga once or twice. Last time was a few months ago. He lives out on the west side in Bay Road.'

'What number?'

'I don't remember.' The courier saw my look of impatience and added quickly. 'Bay Road's a cul-de-sac. His house is the second, maybe third, from the end.'

'Describe it.'

'What can I tell you?'

'How the hell should I know?' I hissed.

The courier looked vacant, before his face cleared. 'It's got more security than the other places.'

'What exactly?'

'High walls. Razor wire. CCTV. That sort of thing.'

'Anything else?'

The man shook his head. 'What about my money?' he asked pointedly. Without a word, I gave him five bills and painfully turned my back.

CHAPTER FORTY-TWO

I passed by Steganga's place in the car, made a U-turn at the end of the street and passed back the way I'd come. If further reconnaissance would have been risky, it was also pointless. There was no easy access from the road as steel gates protected the driveway and these were set into a high brick wall. Nor could I see anything of the house from the car, apart from what looked like glass-panelled decking on the top floor.

I made no better progress when I gained some height. The street above, which ran almost parallel to Bay Road, offered no views of Steganga's place because of the intervening roofs and other obstructions. Deeply frustrated, I left knowing I was going to have to find another angle.

I headed for Camp's Bay up the coast, the towering crag of the Lion's Head becoming increasingly prominent the closer I got. I finally pulled up in the main drag a few minutes later, found a café offering a cooked breakfast and settled myself at a corner table with a view of the beach.

Genteel and refined though Camp's Bay is, the town brought back uncomfortable memories. It was there I'd been led when making enquiries about the kidnap of Frank's wife; Frank was the man who'd been like a father to me. Her subsequent murder had killed him as surely as a bullet in the brain. And, in turn, his loss had left me rudderless as he'd been my only family.

I was staring unseeing into the middle distance when my gaze alighted upon an estate agent's board planted at the side of the pavement. It was in the usual format with the company's name and logo, a telephone number and a mugshot of the selling agent. This last attempted to convey, all in one smile, the attributes of expertise, honesty and approachability. Personally, I often struggled to get beyond the impression left by teeth that might have been better deployed marketing dental services.

But whatever ghost of a grin might have appeared on my face at this thought disappeared abruptly as something else struck me. In the next moment, I got up, crossed over to the car and retrieved my laptop.

Returning to my half-drunk cafetiere, I opened the computer and began searching for a street map of Constantine. When I found one, it was the work of only a moment to note down the street names close to Bay Road before scanning websites advertising houses for sale.

In all there were a couple of dozen scattered around Constantine with nothing available for less than eight figures. Helpfully, some listed addresses which made plotting their locations regarding Bay Road easy, while others required a telephone call to the agent of record to get further details.

When my research was complete, I had one strongly preferred option because of its apparent proximity to Steganga's place. In fact, it seemed it wasn't much more than a stone's throw from my objective.

'Hi,' I said a moment or two later when the agency's phone was picked up. 'You're advertising a place called Four Winds in…Yes, you're quite right I did call. About half an hour ago. Look, I'd like to arrange a viewing…No, I'm flying out later this evening… Could we say later this afternoon? Thank you so much. I'll look forward to it…Yeah, you have a great day too.'

CHAPTER FORTY-THREE

Ginny Rebolo was raven-haired and older than I expected with myriad crow's feet at the corners of her startlingly blue eyes. While this corvine likeness continued to find an echo in the hand she offered me, for it was as delicate as a bird's claw, her painted nails only found correspondence with her bright red lipstick.

Standing on the driveway of Four Winds, I hoped I'd passed muster as she approached me. Time and trouble had been taken with my appearance; courtesy of the facilities offered by a hotel room in Clifton. For me it was money well spent as, having arrived dirty and dishevelled, I'd emerged a couple of hours later spruced-up as befits a man calling on 40 million bucks of prime South African real estate.

'Delighted to meet you, I'm sure,' said Ginny though her voice didn't sound that sure. I guessed that was down to the baseball cap I was wearing, concealing where I'd been slugged, or it could have been down to the patina of my skin, or maybe I was being paranoid. 'Did you have any difficulty getting here?'

'None at all,' I answered truthfully. 'I've done a lot of research, so I've got this spot pretty well taped.'

'Relocating out of the city centre?' she asked.

'Not Cape Town. I'm from PE.'

'Port Elizabeth?-I can't remember the last time I was there.'

I smiled. 'That's the problem. PE's not really where it's at in my line of business.' Seeing a further question spring to those ruby red lips of hers, I stepped in quickly. 'Film industry pre-production,' I said. 'These days that means Cape Town. I'm spending more than half my time here as it is.'

'That would explain a lot,' she replied.

What exactly was explained, I didn't bother to ask but I thought it time to move her along. 'Shall we get to it?-My schedule's a bit tight.'

'Of course.' Without another word, she operated a remote for the garage doors and I heard a high-pitched screech as they started to rise on their rollers. Beyond was empty space with enough parking for three cars.

'Is the house unoccupied?' I asked.

'Has been for the last six months.'

'What happened?'

'This is an executor sale. The old lady who used to live here was admitted to a nursing home.'

'So, completion could be quick?'

'Weeks if you have the asking price.' I detected a needle in her voice.

'Maybe we'll get to that presently,' I said.

She shrugged and led me to a door at the back of the garage. On the far side was a short staircase leading to a cloak room and the kitchen. Passing expanses of marble tops and stainless steel, we walked out to the adjacent living spaces. How each of these rooms could have been arranged wasn't apparent because they were devoid of furniture.

I turned to Ginny with a questioning look on my face. 'Shame there's nothing here,' I said. 'You really have to use your imagination, don't you?'

For the first time, the estate agent tried to look sympathetic. 'There were antiques and some furniture the family sold to pay nursing home fees. The rest of the stuff was old and outdated. We advised getting rid of it as it did nothing to promote the potential.'

I found the potential best observed from standing close to the floor-to-ceiling glass. It provided a 180-degree panorama over the beach and out to sea where, beyond the breakers, I saw a group of surfers lining up.

'I'll show you upstairs,' said Ginny.

I turned my back on the view to face her. 'Not necessary,' I said, the pain in my feet giving urgency to my words. 'Four doubles with en suites, including a master bedroom and dressing room. You've given me the floor plan so what's to see? Right now, I'm more interested in the outside.'

Without a word, she unlocked one of the sliding glass doors and we stepped out onto an empty stone-flagged patio with a staircase at one side. At the bottom was an area of close-clipped grass with borders and a small rim flow pool. A heron, fashioned out of bronze, stood in the water, its gaze permanently focused seawards.

It wasn't that though that held my attention but rather the low retaining wall at the boundary. I made for it across the lawn without so much as a by your leave and didn't halt until I stood in the shade of the sweet thorn that grew in one corner. The tree's flowers, in the shape of yellow balls, were nearly done for the year but the air was still heavy with their scent.

On another occasion, I might have revelled in this feast for the senses but there was no time now: getting my bearings was the overriding priority. To do so, I inclined my head and looked down

Steganga's house lay perhaps 20 metres below and away to my left. It was a four-storey pile which I was viewing sideways on, its reception rooms and outside decks facing north. Painted a brilliant white, the place seemed empty for it was as silent as a cicada in winter.

But this wasn't my major preoccupation. I was more taken with working out how to gain access to the grounds from where I was standing. From what I could see, the only route was along the tops of connecting walls. These, like the one behind which I was standing, were made of brown granite and were almost a half-metre wide. Fine, but the problem was that the route to Steganga's house turned twice through right angles; at one point stood four metres proud of the ground; and at another descended in several steep steps before passing close to a first storey picture window.

'What do you think?' asked Ginny, breaking in on my thoughts.

Turning back to her, I raised my eyes above her head to Four Winds' soaring elevations. 'I'm not sure. It's a pity there isn't something more by way of a garden. I'm afraid this is all rather cramped.'

'You have children?'

I'd never been asked that question before. 'Children?' I queried stupidly.

For the first time, she smiled. 'Children like to run around. Kick a ball. Let off steam.'

'Ach, I see what you mean.' After that, my forked tongue came to my rescue. 'My partner's a keen gardener,' I said. 'I doubt this would be enough of a challenge for her.'

'That'll be a problem with most property here. Few houses have much of a garden and some have none at all.'

'I understand. But there's a house across the way which is different. It has plenty of open space, particularly at the back.' Ginny followed my arm as I pointed out Steganga's place. 'Do you have anything like that on your books?' I asked.

Ginny shook her head. 'That's one of the original houses built here. And before you ask, it's not been on the market in at least 30 years.'

'Who owns it?'

'I don't know, because I've never inquired. But apparently the owner's a recluse and rarely leaves the place.'

I felt like pressing Ginny further but resisted the temptation. I thought it unlikely she knew anything more than she'd already told me. The information though that Steganga was seemingly a recluse piqued my interest as it further confirmed that his trip to PE must have been vital to the way he perceived his interests.

CHAPTER FORTY-FOUR

I had no wish to call Steganga, but what I wanted didn't count for much. My duty was in respect of Effie's welfare and fostering that had to be my key objective.

By then, I was back in the hotel room in Clifton and preparing for the night ahead, my feet planted in a bowl of hot water laced with bath salts. As I worked my way through a plate of sandwiches, I turned over the best way to play the call. But that went on only as long as I came to realise that second-guessing wasn't going to work. The only way this could be played was by ear. Once that was settled, I punched the digits into my cell from the card Steganga had left on my dining table in PE.

'I was wondering, Nemo, how long it'd be before I heard from you,' Steganga said, before I could say a word. Either he recognised my number, unlikely, or he was using a unique phone.

'I want to talk to Effie,' I said.

'I'm sure you do, but first what have you got for me?'

'Zip,' I snapped. 'I've spent the day recovering from being beaten about the head. Not to mention kneed in the balls. I'll get started again tomorrow.'

'And after that will be the time for you to call again. Assuming of course you have something for me. At that point, you'll be able to trade.'

I breathed hard and regrouped. I needed a different approach: something that would get inside the old mother's guard. 'Please,' I said in a whining tone of voice. 'I must know Effie's OK. I couldn't forgive myself if anything were to happen to her.'

Steganga chuckled. 'I suppose,' he said unpleasantly, 'you're not to blame for the deficient genes that make you a weak-minded fool. Of course, it's that which lets me bend you so easily to my will. We'll leave it that when you've something concrete to report, you'll call again. In the meantime, rest assured the *kaffir* still lives.'

For a moment, after he rang off, I felt like throwing the phone at the wall. But that was only until recalling that he was under the impression I was 800 kms away and had no idea where he was living. That gave me the element of surprise and for that I had to be grateful as there was nothing else on offer.

CHAPTER FORTY-FIVE

Long black pants.
Black T shirt.
Black windbreaker.
Black gloves
Black Gucci loafers.
Glock plus spare clip.
Lock pick.
Pencil flashlight.

What I couldn't wear, I stored in my pants and in the pockets of the windbreaker before gathering the rest of my stuff together. A few minutes later, I checked out of the hotel.

I headed away from Clifton along the exposed coast road, a rising wind occasionally buffeting the car as I made the journey south again for the third time that day. But, unlike before, the picturesque highway was now dark and deserted and all that could be seen of the sea on my right hand were angry whitecaps.

Once I reached Constantine, the weather had deteriorated further making it difficult for me to open the car door. After that, I fought my way in the dark along the street, step by footsore step, the wind trying to tear the windbreaker from my body. If I'd harboured any fear of being observed, it was soon dispelled on that moonless night as the gale tore across land and sky.

But there was no rain and for that I was thankful as I fetched up outside Four Winds. A spear-topped gate stood at the side of the garage, and it gave access down a flight of stairs to the garden. Unfortunately, it was locked but a fence panel set between a grass bank and the gate soon gave way under my determined shoving. Once through the gap, I replaced the panel as best I could and descended the stairs. A moment later I was at the spot beneath the sweet thorn where I'd been that afternoon.

Under my feet lay hundreds of the yellow blossoms that had been ripped off the tree. Above my head, the gale harassed the branches and set them swaying crazily as I looked out towards the sea. To be sure, lights were visible in some of the houses, but it was to the foreshore that my attention was drawn. There, huge white-capped breakers crashed onto the beach and boiled and frothed in a maelstrom of angry water that looked like it might overwhelm and drown the land.

My first thought of walking along the top of the wall was stillborn. The gusting wind saw to that as it mauled me and then forced me onto all fours. In that fashion, I navigated about ten metres, turned through a right angle and kept moving. As it turned out, it proved easier than I thought and even the section that descended in a series of steps caused me little difficulty.

I had bad moments though where the wall ran close by a house. As I crawled past, a light abruptly came on in a room which was level with me. I froze in a prone position and watched as an elderly woman peered out into the darkness. For what seemed like a long time, she stood immobile. I stopped breathing and waited. At any moment, I expected some sign she had spotted me.

But, in the event, nothing happened. Whatever she was contemplating beyond the glass didn't include me. Next, the light was gradually extinguished as she slowly drew the curtains. Having unconsciously held my breath too long, I gasped for air like a half-drowned man.

After that, I pressed on again until I reached the rear wall of Steganga's house. But it was with dismay I viewed the drop into his garden. It wasn't less than two metres and meant, if I jumped down, it would be very difficult for me to climb back up. Nor would it help much to pass along the side of the house to the front. My reconnaissance from the car earlier had made me aware of the high wall and steel gates facing the road. Getting out of there could be as difficult as it would have been getting in.

Then the rain came. It arrived without warning and in no time became torrential. One minute I was being buffeted by the wind and the next a deluge overwhelmed me. Soon it penetrated every inch of my clothing leaving me cold and miserable, my pants stuck to my skin. Plainly, I needed shelter.

I turned my attention to the house from my vantage point. I'd already noticed there were only two sources of light. One was high up from a living room looking out over the sea and the other was at ground level and a short distance from me.

This last was no more than a glow and it came from a small window. Using the torch, I shone its beam into the wet blackness and made out an adjacent door protected by a steel grille.

Could this be where Effie was being held?-The ground floor location at the back of the house suggested staff quarters. Most wealthy South Africans don't want the help living cheek by jowl with them, nor do they want them within general sight. Tucking them out of the way has long been the norm and this looked like an efficient piece of tucking.

But speculation wasn't getting me out of the rain. Either I could return to Four Winds and give up or go for it and jump down. Becoming colder by the minute, I decided to bet the farm. To hell with it it, if the need arose, I'd shoot my way out of the place.

I dropped down from the wall, fell awkwardly and sprawled on the grass. Picking myself up, and clearing rain from my eyes, I crossed to the lighted window. It was little more than a slit set high up in the wall and it was shut tight.

I turned to the steel grille. It was of the sort incorporating a bolt secured with a padlock. Judging by what I saw in the beam from the flashlight, it hadn't been disturbed in a long time.

Using a lock pick competently is a job for a pro. At best, I'd never been more than an amateur and my skills were as rusty as the padlock I was working on. I gave it my best shot but after several minutes with rain coursing down my back, I gave up.

That meant using the Glock and that was risky. No matter that the wind was howling, and I could hear the crash of the sea, a gunshot might trump all that. And anybody who did hear it would know instantly what it was and would likely investigate. Or more likely, make a call and ask their private security or SAPS or both to come out, as I had no idea what the local set up was.

In the event, it took three shots to break the shackle. The first missed when the pencil light in my left hand slipped because it was wet. The second only did half the work so a third was needed to finish the job. After that, I raced into the lee of a shed by the wall and waited.

I was patient and gave it a quarter of an hour; a quarter of an hour when I strained my ears for the sound of revved engines or the wail of sirens and kept a lookout for the glare from approaching lights.

But nothing interfered with the storm's unabated fury as it continued to lash the coast.

The door behind the grille yielded easily to the pick; perhaps I was more determined this time round or previous practice had stood me in good stead.

On the other side, lay a corridor dimly illuminated by a light in the ceiling. At the end, there was a cement staircase leading upwards and on the opposite side a closed door.

Curiosity though first took me to the top of the staircase where there was a landing and a lift. There was no need to explore farther.

I descended and cautiously tried the door handle. I was surprised when it swung open. Beyond, all was darkness except for a thin strip of light at ground level on the far side. I moved towards it, but not before bumping against the corner of a heavy, stinkwood table. With a silent oath, and a sharp pain in my thigh, I waited for some reaction. As a precaution, I drew the Glock.

With the gun held tight and my finger inside the trigger guard, I pushed against another door. On squeaky hinges, it opened a fraction emitting enough light for me to see I'd just crossed a small kitchen diner. To one side, was a basin and worktop where I saw a microwave oven, a small fridge and a kettle.

I pressed against the door harder, but it needed a shove to open it fully. What I saw was a small, barred window with a bed beneath it. An adjacent door led to an en-suite bathroom.

I was more interested though in the figure curled up on a tartan counterpane on the bed. It had its back to me facing the wall. The light from a solitary lamp wasn't bright, but it was bright enough.

I'd found Effie.

CHAPTER FORTY-SIX

I called softly to avoid startling her but there was no movement. Swiftly, I crossed over and gently shook her shoulder. This too was in vain, and I began to think she might be drugged.

That thought instilled a sense of urgency. This time I shook her hard. 'Effie, wake up!' I hissed.

That brought her round for she turned her head and slowly looked over her shoulder. She did a double take before her lips shaped the one shocked word, 'Sol?'

Distracted, I didn't respond. When Effie had moved, I heard a rattle of chains. Inclining my gaze, I found myself looking at a heap of steel links fastened to a hook set in the wall. At the other end, they terminated in a bracelet locked around Effie's wrist.

'Got to get this off,' I said shortly.

But Effie's mind hadn't processed my miraculous appearance. 'H-How did you find me?'

'Tell you later, Effie. If you sit up, I'll try to release you.'

I stood back so she could swing herself onto the floor. It was difficult for her because of her disabled leg. I wondered where her walking stick was. It hadn't been left behind when she'd been kidnapped.

Crouched in front of her, I set to with the lock pick, her wrist held out rigidly. That was so I could get a purchase with the wrench as I manipulated the pick. She remained still and made no sound. Periodically, I lifted my eyes and gave her a reassuring smile, my gaze taking in the scab on her face where she'd been struck. It was only visible against her black skin because the surface of it was rough.

How she was feeling, I couldn't tell for her eyes were as impenetrable as tar pools. But, as the minutes ticked by, whatever reassurance she had must have started to ebb. Try as I might, my attempts to get the bracelet off proved fruitless.

At that moment, I heard a loud whirring noise. Effie heard it too and her demeanour changed. 'Please hurry, Sol,' she urged. 'It's the lift. Somebody's coming down.'

I'd have liked to oblige, but knew it was impossible. Time and luck were against me. I put down the tools and rose to my feet. In a few quick strides, I crossed the kitchen diner and closed the door to the passage. As it shut, I heard the lift doors on the floor above open. I went back to Effie who was now on her feet. A length of chain from her wrist trailed down and across the floor. The expression on her face was panic-struck.

'Lie down and face the wall. Pretend to be asleep,' I ordered. 'I'll hide next door.'

She nodded dumbly and lay down again. I drew the Glock and retreated into the bathroom, shutting the door behind but leaving a small gap. Effie wasn't visible but I had a large portion of the room covered. Everything was under control.

Momentarily, I relaxed and became conscious of just how my pants were coldly stuck to my skin; how despite the windbreaker, my body was soaked through; and how my feet were both soaked and very tender.

It was only then it hit me, as unexpected as a stone striking a moving car. Closing the door to the passage had availed me nothing. Evidence of my entry would be evident in every wet footprint left on the cement floor outside.

I'd lost the element of surprise.

More than that, I was trapped.

With that revelation, my breathing came faster, my windpipe suddenly constricting. Beads of sweat sprang unannounced from my pores. I fell back faint against the bathroom wall.

I fought it the usual way; the only way I knew: Closing my eyes, I focused on my breathing; forced myself to slow the rate of intake; forced myself to slow the rate of output. Slow it right down, until I moved back towards a place of equilibrium.

And once that was close, I put a finger inside the Glock's trigger guard and pointed the gun into the room. Breathing now nice and easy, I waited.

It seemed like a long time before anything happened. After the event, there's no means of calculating these things. Experience told me though it would have been a much shorter period than I thought.

Of course, I heard him move before seeing him. Heard him descend the stairs, one steady step at a time. Heard the silence as something, no doubt my footprints, brought him up short. Heard nothing more until the light went on in the kitchen diner.

Next, he was in my line of sight: a tensed figure I knew by the name Gustav and holding a gun in his hand. It was the same hand that had crashed into the side of Effie's face. Now the arm it was attached to swivelled towards the bathroom door.

I was taught you don't open fire unless you feel threatened. Was Gustav a threat if he didn't know I was there?-Even though his gun was pointing at me.

It was a moot point. And so it stayed because Gustav's sixth sense must have kicked in. Without warning he fired, the bullets splintering the door panel. Whizzing past my left shoulder, they smashed into the tiles behind me and ricocheted.

Gustav hadn't been sure of his target; wasn't sure he even had a target. My position was different. I had a bead on him throughout and now I had malice aforethought.

I squeezed the trigger twice. Before the crash of the shots had finished echoing, he crumpled and fell to the floor.

I didn't linger. Storm or no storm outside, the fusillade was likely to bring trouble in spades.

I exited the bathroom and crossed to the gunman. A glance was enough to see the state Gustav was in. It didn't need a medical degree from Stellenbosch to confirm the holes in him were kinda fatal.

I kicked his gun into a corner and turned back to Effie. She was transfixed by what had happened. Uncomprehendingly, she gazed at me.

'We gotta go,' I said bluntly. She didn't answer but her eyes shifted to the corpse. 'There's no time Effie. We must leave.'

'I-Is he d-dead?' she queried.

'As a door nail.'

'You k-killed him?'

'Sometimes it's like that.' I looked over to her, but my words hadn't registered. 'He fired first. It was him or me.' Still nothing, so I assumed the initiative. I took a length of Effie's chain where it lay across the bedding and straightened it. 'Keep still,' I ordered her, lifting the Glock and aiming.

The explosion made Effie scream. Panicked, she began to retreat along the length of the bed. Next, she raised her legs and turned her body away from me. A few seconds more and she'd have rolled into a ball.

There was no time for this. I put the gun down, stood in front of her and grasped her shoulders. 'Effie, you're free,' I said, lifting the length of cut chain. 'We can't stay. We must go.'

Momentarily, her eyes blanked me. 'Go?' she asked.

I smiled. 'Yes, go. Where's your stick?'

The mention of something so necessary to her everyday existence resonated. 'They took it,' she said simply.

I made light of her reply, though I'd never seen Effie move unaided. Wordlessly, I helped her to her feet and to skirt Gustav's corpse before following her across the kitchen diner. A length of chain about half a metre long swung from her wrist as she moved.

She turned into the corridor and slowly clumped along its length, her body rocking from side to side. The action was as regular a rhythm as that of a metronome but at a fraction of the speed. I curbed my impatience with difficulty, my ears straining for any sound from the lift.

It came as Effie was about to open the external door. It was the same loud whirring noise as before. 'Keep moving,' I hissed. 'The lift has to go back up.'

She nodded, pushed open the door and headed out with me behind her. I thought to turn out the passage light but decided against. The pool it cast into the garden was small and was confined to a narrow cone that soon bled away in the darkness.

Though the rain and the gale had died down, it was still a wild night. The wind buffeted the two of us and I felt the cold chill my wet legs.

'If you make your way to the back wall,' I said, raising my voice, 'I'll join you.' I indicated the direction she was to take.

'What are you going to do?'

'Wait a while.' She was about to say something further, but I got in first. 'There's a storage hut back there. If it's open, see if there's anything we can use to climb on.'

'Climb?-Why climb?'

'To get over the garden wall.'

'But...'

'No buts. Just go and wait for me. It won't be for long.'

I watched her walk lamely away until she was swallowed up. I looked back to the open doorway assuming it was from that direction trouble would come. The problem was there was no cover where I was standing. The garden was grassed without even an intervening flower bed, let alone a tree.

With no choice in the matter, I stepped back a few metres and reluctantly lay flat on the ground. It was wet, very wet so I got soaked afresh, my face level with the sodden grass. Carefully, I stretched out my hands in front of me and brought them together holding the gun. In that position, enfilading the lighted corridor would be easy.

I waited, growing colder by the minute. I wondered what Effie was doing. There was no sign of life from the direction she'd gone.

Then, in an instant, things happened fast. The light in the corridor abruptly went out. Next, I heard charging feet. That was followed by a burst of gunfire. The bullets came straight at me but went over my head. The flashes though gave me a target. I got off four rounds and heard a weapon clatter to the cement floor. Despite this, I rolled away fast, turning over and over, both hands keeping the Glock firmly grasped.

It proved the right thing to do; shots stitched the ground near where I'd been lying. They came from my right, but I was too late to see the gun flashes. Tempted to respond, I resisted. Instead, I waited, wishing the ground would swallow me up.

I didn't count passing seconds but there were a lot of them. At last, a powerful torch lit a patch of ground ten feet in front of me. It then slowly described an arc moving away.

I had my chance and went to take it. Yet, as I aimed the beam swung back fast. For an instant, it held me in its glare. I wasn't much of a target, but I felt the crack of bullets whipping past my head.

Panicked, I fired repeatedly, the Glock bucking in my hands. I stopped when the torch light arced heavenwards. Once again, I rolled clear and stayed flat.

A long silence ensued. There was no way of knowing if anyone else was out there. Eventually, concern for Effie got me to my knees. Cautiously, I stood up.

There was neither sound nor movement from the downed gunmen. Directing the flashlight parallel to the Glock's barrel, I confirmed one guy as having been in my apartment. It was he who'd held me in a vice-like grip and later belted me round the head. The other guy was unknown.

After that, I made for the shed. It soon loomed out of the darkness though there was no sign of Effie. I opened the door, but the interior was empty, except for a lawnmower and gardening tools. I stood irresolute until it occurred to me to search behind it.

The area was overgrown but there was a heap of broken bricks and other building materials, including split bags of cement. I ran the torch over all this until I heard a small voice.

I responded and saw Effie slowly rise from behind a stack of tiles. 'Thank God, Sol!' she cried. 'Thank God!-I was beginning to think you must be dead. I heard so many shots.'

'You need a hand?' I pointed the torch at her feet where she was stepping out over a quantity of broken stone.

'I-I'm OK.'

But she wasn't because she fell, and I had to help her. From the way she sagged against me, I reckoned she was about all in. After guiding her back to the lawn, I stopped and took her two hands in mine. 'Look Effie,' I said. 'I know you're tired, but we've got to keep moving. There's no way the police and everybody else won't have been called out to this. But the good news is I reckon they'll have to come from Camp's Bay. That's ten kms so we've got a little time.'

'But how do we get over the wall?' There was a tremor in Effie's voice that I knew could quickly degenerate into panic. 'I looked in the shed, Sol, and there's nothing there.'

'Change of plan.' I grinned at her in the darkness. 'We'll go out the front. You OK with that?'

She could have nodded her agreement, but I wouldn't have seen it. Besides, there wasn't time to debate the issue. 'I'll go first,' I said, 'and you stick close behind. If you want anything just grab me.'

Without a further word, I turned away and headed snail-like for the main gate, my gun levelled. On one side, the house soared four storeys, an oppressive pile on that darkest of nights and, on the other, trees and bushes encroached upon a narrowing strip of lawn.

The grass terminated in a wrought-iron gate set into a side wall. It wasn't locked and after checking the lie of the land we started down a steep cobbled drive that became wider as we descended.

We'd covered most of the distance to the steel entrance gates when we were lit up by halogen lights. They were located somewhere high up and to our rear, picking us out like targets in a shooting gallery.

I spun round making Effie to lurch into me. I braced myself for the bullets that must surely kill the two of us.

But nothing came. Screwing up my eyes, I focused on the space below and between the lights. That directed my gaze towards the house where the front door stood open. A man was standing there looking down the length of the drive towards us. He was motionless and at that distance I couldn't make out his features.

It was only when he opened his mouth, I confirmed who it was. 'Nemo!' It was Steganga. And then once more: 'Nemo!'

But it wasn't a shout I heard, it was a scream, and its high pitch riveted my attention. It seemed half-human, half-animal in its intensity and it was of someone in existential pain; in a pain so deep, there was nothing in life that could come near to extinguishing it. Effie heard it too and froze. She opened her mouth to say something when Steganga's voice rang out again.

'Do you know what you've done!' he screamed. 'You've killed my only son! My son's dead! Dead!!! Do you under…understand…what…?' His voice, unable to take the strain any longer, abruptly broke off.

I looked up to where he was standing. His eyes seemed to rest on me and then his head lifted as though he was searching for something far out to sea.

For a long moment, he was motionless before he raised one arm to cover his chest. Puzzled, I watched until his voice rang out once more. '*Lang lewe wit Suid-Afrika!*'

Maybe he tried to shout the words *Long Live White South Africa!* again. I don't know because the words were obliterated by the crash of the bullet that rocketed up through the roof of his mouth before blowing the top of his head off.

CHAPTER FORTY-SEVEN

My guess many people assume, like Macbeth, I've supped full with horrors. Years working for SAPS had exposed me to all manner of evil in which one party had sought to destroy another by bludgeoning, gouging, stabbing, torturing or burning. And that was to say nothing of the fearsome damage inflicted where the protagonists had resorted to firearms to settle their hatreds. But, in all that time, and never since, had I ever witnessed anyone commit suicide.

Actions have consequences and those unintended can often be the most challenging. What had happened was down to my having set in motion a chain of events. Four people dead by my hand said it all.

That revelation brought me up short and with it came an overwhelming weariness. The adrenaline drained from my body like water out of a holed cistern. Listlessly, I lifted my eyes to where Steganga had fallen but saw only a leg poking out over a step.

'Sol!'

I didn't answer so Effie repeated herself.

'Sol!-We can't stay here!'

I turned round surprised. For a moment, her presence had been forgotten. 'I was thinking...' I began to say.

'About that bastard?' Effie cut in with unexpected vehemence. 'Don't waste your breath! You heard what that scumbag shouted.'

That broke the spell. With a start, I looked round. The driveway was lit as bright as day. In adjacent properties, I saw lights coming on.

Rapidly, I sorted my head out. 'We're OK, Effie, once we're on the far side of the gates. There's plenty of cover and no street lights.'

We made it out through a latched side gate and crossed to the other side of the road. In the shelter of a granite wall, I took stock. The wind had almost died away though the crashing of waves on the beach below remained loud and persistent.

'My car's half a km from here,' I said. 'Do you think you can manage?'

'If I take my time.'

'That's fine. We'll get plenty of warning when the cavalry shows up.'

We set off in single file as before, but I let Effie lead. Progress was slow but she told me she could get along faster without my trying to help her.

I put the Glock in my pocket but kept my hand over it. I wasn't anticipating trouble: with the sound of all that gunfire, intervention from the neighbours was unlikely. I mean why risk your health and happiness when there were others to take the heat for a rate of pay per day no more than the locals stumped up for aperitifs at their fancy *braais*.

It panned out much as I anticipated. Various vehicles tore along past us at regular intervals, headlights on full beam and often with sirens wailing. Most numerous of course were private security and the police but there were also a couple of ambulances and a fire engine. With plenty of warning of their coming, we melted into the shadows cast by trees or hid behind walls and wood fences.

I didn't clock the time it took to reach the car but, had I been on my own, I could have covered four times the distance. Perhaps the very slowness of our progress added to my fatigue. All I can say is that by the time I was sitting behind the wheel and turning the key in the ignition, I felt about as lively as a dead sloth.

My intention had been to head for home at once but that wasn't practical. Instead, I took the road back to Camp's Bay, found an all-night café bar and bought sandwiches and coffee. Back in the car, I thought to interest Effie in what I'd got but she was out of it, her head pillowed on my jumper held against the door frame. I watched her for a moment and, for the first time in many weeks, felt a real sense of achievement. Sometimes, you must step up and take a stand.

In that frame of mind, I ate a little and drank most of the coffee before falling asleep. But the realisation the temperature had dropped and I was still in wet pants, forced my eyes open soon enough. When it did, we set out for home.

CHAPTER FORTY-EIGHT

'I want a guy from Zap-It to be here 24/7. Each working an eight-hour shift.'

'That's expensive, Sol.'

'Screw the cost. I also want a *bakkie* out front round the clock. Use a liveried vehicle so it's obvious the place is covered by armed response. And make sure I get your best people. I don't want any unpleasant surprises.'

'You mind if I ask what's going on.'

In response, I winged it to avoid having to explain what had happened to Effie. 'We had a break-in,' I said. 'There was some rough stuff. An associate of mine's very badly shaken up.'

'I'm sorry to hear that, but whoever it was isn't likely to come back.'

'Maybe not,' I agreed, 'but Zap-It provides plenty of reassurance and that's all I'm concerned about. If there was a need, how fast could you get extra people here?'

'To Marine Drive?'

'The Summerstrand end.'

'Three to four minutes. Five tops.'

'Frank'd be proud of you,' I said.

'I hope so, Sol. You must still miss him.'

'More than words can say.' Frank had been like a father to me and for years had been my sheet anchor. Zap-It had been his business and life's work until his death three years earlier. With an effort, I focused again. 'How soon?' I asked.

'How soon do you want them?'

'Now would be good.'

I rang off and lifted my eyes to gaze out over Humewood. From where I was standing on the roof terrace, I had an eagle's eye view of the links where the sundowners were winding up before heading for the clubhouse.

The sight of them made me think of van Zyl, the man who'd almost been the death of me more than once already; and the man who, even now, I was unable to ignore and put behind me. Impotently, I breathed hard and turned away.

CHAPTER FORTY-NINE

My anger wasn't only directed at van Zyl. There was also the matter of my abandonment by Marcus after the helicopter was shot at. As having it out with him entailed no more than getting off my butt and visiting the airport, I drove myself there the following day. But I remained cautious about my coming and going and so left the apartment on foot via the basement garage and walked to where I'd parked. By the time I departed, the security measures I ordered were well established. Consequently, my living space was the responsibility of a monosyllabic hombre whose array of weaponry was more than equal to the task of doing any hard talking that might be required.

This reassured me, particularly as far as Effie was concerned. I'd seen very little of her since the previous day when we returned from Camp's Bay. Inevitably, there'd been the time I spent with wrench and pick releasing the steel bracelet from her wrist. While the pinched, raw flesh revealed beneath was an outward sign of what she'd been through, I was more concerned about any psychological damage she might have suffered. But, for the present, I did no more than respect her wish that she wanted time out. That meant the door to her rooms remained closed. Each of us has a different way of coping with trauma and I reckoned if she wanted anything, she knew me well enough to ask.

I thought about what line I should take with Marcus on the way to the airport. On the one hand, I was inclined to go in with fists balled with the object of doing him some harm. On the other, his was likely to be valuable testimony corroborating the existence of the labour camp; I didn't discount the value of that moving forward. These contradictory thoughts left me in a quandary, confirming that making serious decisions about stuff is often a bit of a bitch.

Marcus shared offices with a few small, aviation-related businesses. As I stepped through the door, I recognised the woman who looked after reception. But whereas before, she'd given me a happy smile, now she looked at me woodenly.

'Where's Marcus?' I asked her pointedly.

Her reaction wasn't what I expected for her face splintered and became wet with tears. Without a word, she abruptly got to her feet and fled.

Mystified, I looked about me. The place appeared deserted until I spotted a full head of grey hair belonging to a man sitting in one of the inner offices. Making my way to a connecting door, I opened it and stuck my head through. 'Hi,' I said.

Startled, the figure swivelled away from the conference table at which he'd been working. 'Hi,' he retorted cautiously.

'I'm looking for Marcus.'

'Uh-huh. And you are?'

'The name's Nemo.'

The man's dour features registered more than a spark of interest. 'Nemo,' he said almost to himself. 'Your name came up yesterday when I was collecting this material together.' With a deeply sunburned arm, he waved vaguely at a collection of lever-arch files arranged in front of him. One of them, more voluminous than the rest, was open and a few sheets of paper had been removed. He'd been studying these when I'd interrupted him.

'Who are you?' I asked.

'The name's Tredaway, AIID.'

'Air and...,' I stumbled.

'Accident Incident Investigation Division,' he corrected me, as he reached for a small notebook. Rapidly, he thumbed the pages until he found the one he wanted. 'According to this,' he said lifting his eyes, 'you're the party who last hired a helicopter from here.'

'What of it?'

'Perhaps if you sit down,' said Tredaway quietly, 'I can explain.' He indicated a seat on the far side and watched while I settled myself. 'My presence here tells you there's been an accident. It occurred five days ago in the Northern Cape.'

'What happened?'

'That's what I'm here to try and find out.'

'You misunderstand me,' I said. 'I meant what sort of accident. Was Marcus injured?'

Tredaway shook his head. 'I'm sorry, but he's dead.'

That rocked me. 'Dead!-How the hell?'

'I think there was a mid-air explosion. Followed by a fire. Some of the wreckage supports that theory. I'd have contacted you in due course. After I've finished my paperwork review.'

'That's all this stuff in front of you?'

Tredaway gave me a wintry smile. 'I'm afraid so. There's always a lot to be looked at. In this case, it's compounded by the aircraft's age and the modifications carried out after it was converted for civil use.'

'You have any preliminary thoughts?'

Tredaway shook his head. 'It's too early to say. I might have a better idea once I've reviewed the maintenance/component records and the overhaul schedules.' He looked at me curiously. 'One thing I was puzzled about. According to the flight plans, the aircraft came down in the same area you'd been overflying on previous days. Do you know why the pilot was on his own?'

'That's easy,' I said. 'It was because Marcus left me behind.' The look of incredulity that came over Tredaway's face gave me time to head off his questions. 'The chopper was fired on.'

'Fired on!-By whom?'

I shrugged. 'Not sure to be honest. Marcus landed so I could look at something on the ground. I was a distance away when it happened. Do you think rifle bullets could have brought it down?'

Tredaway looked sceptical. 'I doubt it,' he said dismissively. 'I mean it would have to be a one in a million shot. Still, leaking fuel from a punctured tank is always dangerous so I'll bear it in mind.'

After that, the man from the AAID asked several questions based on the false premise that, because I'd had flying lessons, I might have some technical insight into the world of helicopters. Disabusing him on that front didn't take long and, a few moments later, I got up to leave. As I crossed to the door, he asked a final question. 'Of course, it's none of my business, but what were you doing up in the Northern Cape?'

'Searching for an illegal labour camp.'

If Tredaway was startled by my reply, he didn't show it. 'Did you find it?'

'Yes, I did.'

'Have you told the authorities?'

'No, I haven't.'
'Don't you think you should?'
I shook my head. 'Right now,' I said, 'I've a better idea.'

CHAPTER FIFTY

Without corroborative support from Marcus, I thought my chances of interesting anyone in authority about what I'd found in the Northern Cape were small. At best, a lot of time might be spent navigating the labyrinthine workings of any one of several government departments that might conceivably have some involvement in what was happening. Without taxing my brain overly, Public Works, Water Affairs, Transport, Human Settlements, and Trade and Industry all popped into my head and formed an orderly queue. Only it wasn't likely to be very orderly if any of these entities were doing anything they shouldn't. Once found out, there would instead be frantic activity directed towards getting out from under and covering up any tracks as fast as possible. After all, while the term State Capture might have originated with the World Bank, its greatest resonance has been in none other than our Rainbow Nation where the ruling elite have suborned numerous organs of government for their own nefarious purposes.

But never fear, railed against this racketeering and gangster culture is the fourth estate. Over 40 mastheads figure in print or its digital equivalent and, even if they don't all have national coverage, they have strong regional focus. Most are not afraid to call out incompetence or criminal behaviour wherever it may be found, even at the highest levels, and to use a vernacular by way of describing it which leaves its recipients no room to doubt the vitriol being poured down upon their heads.

But I wanted something more than this and it was then my thoughts turned to Moses. Despite the name, *he* was in fact *she*, though this wasn't something that was publicly known. I'd met her years before when I'd been disposing of the bulk of my father's estate to charity. In that task, I'd spent a fascinating hour being briefed by her on why it was a very bad idea to give R50m to one particular not-for-profit.

Her subsequent revelations, syndicated on a national basis, rocked the foundations of the charity world and cast a spotlight into some dark corners. Its release though to the media hadn't occurred before the forces of law and order in the shape of the Hawks, SA's very own super-cops, had swept in and made several arrests as well as seizing a mass of incriminating material.

This, and other investigations before and after, had established Moses as the freelance, investigative journalist *par excellence.* But her work had upset powerful people and, after she'd narrowly survived an assassination attempt, she disappeared. Nevertheless, her efforts continued unabated, though it was rumoured she'd withdrawn from the frontline and worked through associates. Despite this change of *modus operandi,* Moses' by-line remained the same and always grabbed attention because it heralded something special.

Tracking Moses down proved problematic. It was a while since there'd been any contact and it wasn't as though I'd had a cell number and an email address even then. But her spiritual home was the offices of one of the dailies based in Jo'burg and it was there I started. I asked for Editorial and was put through a long minute afterwards.

'Moses been gone a long time, bro,' quipped a voice.

'I meant Moses the investigative journalist.'

'Sure, you did. And who might you be?'

'My name's Nemo. I'm calling from PE.'

'PE?-Might that be Port Elizabeth?'

'It might,' I snapped. 'Look, I haven't got all day. Is she there and, if not, could you take a message?'

Identifying Moses as female got me off first base. 'What did you say your name was?'

'Sol Nemo.'

'What's your action with Moses?'

'Charity fraud a while back. She gave me some good advice.'

'You want Moses' advice again, bro?'

'No, I've got a story for her.'

'Might be an idea if you gave me your best pitch.'

'On the other hand, it might not,' I said firmly. 'Thank you, but I'll talk to her direct.'

'She might not remember you.'

'How often does she persuade somebody not to piss away 50 million bucks?' I retorted.

'No idea, bro. I'd have to ask. You got a number where you can be reached?' I gave it to him before I heard him say, 'Might be an idea not to get your hopes up. Might be a fair while before she hooks up.'

In fact, I heard from Moses that night while I was fretting about what to do about Effie. Since returning from the airport, it occurred to me I ought to take the initiative in respect of her welfare. I was half of a mind to reach out to her, but the ringing phone forestalled that plan.

'Always wondered what you did with that 50 million,' said a female voice without preamble.

'It was allocated to other projects.'

'Not tempted to keep it for a rainy day?'

'There was enough of that money already.'

'In your shoes, I'd have been tempted. I'd have seen it as a message from the great beyond.' Moses suddenly laughed. It was an exhalation full of phlegm that soon deteriorated into a cough. Without enthusiasm, I recalled her incessant cigarette smoking. 'I was told you got something for me,' she pressed.

Swiftly, I summarised what I had. It didn't seem like it took a whole lot of time to tell and, of course, there wasn't much in the way of corroboration. Evidently, she thought the same because there was a silence after I finished speaking.

'You said you had some payroll records,' Moses said at last. 'I'd be happy to look at them. But it'll have to be tonight.'

I glanced at my watch and saw how late it was. 'OK,' I said cautiously, 'but where are you?' Half my mind was already imagining a journey cross-country to one of those remote locations favoured by kick-ass journalists who possess a penchant for the melodramatic.

'I'm staying at the Phoenix,' she said. 'Will an hour give you sufficient time?'

CHAPTER FIFTY-ONE

The Phoenix Hotel is an institution in PE and, like all institutions, has characteristics you don't find elsewhere. It's located round the corner from the Opera House which I guess explains why its restaurant is called The Stage Door. What isn't explained is why it says it's The Place Where Real People Meet. I pondered this as I crossed the street and hobbled in beneath a line of limp flags displayed above the arched balconies.

The Stage Door was a few metres across the vestibule, its furnishings of dark wood and its floor strewn with sawdust. Whereas this combination might have created a sombre mood, here it was unabashedly relieved by brightly coloured signs, posters, advertisements and old number plates that occupied every inch of its walls and most of which evoked the fulfilment of the American Dream in the nineteen-fifties.

Looking over, I saw Moses positioned at a table in one corner with her back to a wall. She must have finished eating a short time before as the remains of a meal had been pushed to one side so she could put her elbows on the table. Slim hands cradled a coffee cup, her eyes focused somewhere into the middle distance. The place though was quiet, so when I slipped into her field of vision, she had no difficulty recognising me. About to get up, I waved her back down and offered her a wide smile.

'You're a long way from Jo'burg,' I said, after we'd exchanged greetings.

'I've been here for personal reasons, and I also had a meet earlier.'

'Productive?'

Moses shrugged thin shoulders beneath a saffron cheesecloth top. 'Could be, but I don't think it justified the face time. Not at this stage anyway.'

'Perhaps I can offer you something more compelling.'

For the first time, she smiled, the skin at the corners of her eyes squeezing itself into closely packed ridges. 'Tell me again what you said earlier.'

I told her, only this time I slowed it down and added some detail. I find conversations over the phone a pain because there's no means of gauging the other person's reaction. Face to face, there's an opportunity to tailor a message or, put another way, to try and make an effective pitch. And it seemed that was all that was left to me. Unless Moses took up the cause of exposing the corruption I'd unearthed, however imperfectly, there was nothing more to be done. As far as I was concerned, the search for van Zyl was now at an end, though with hindsight it had taken far too long for me to come to that conclusion.

It was ironic then that it was the subject of van Zyl that came foremost to her mind when my story ended 'He's the key to this,' she opined firmly.

'Without which…?' I let the unfinished question hang in the air.

Moses must have noticed my hangdog expression because she flashed me a consolatory smile, before abruptly getting to her feet. 'I need a cigarette,' she said. 'Do my best thinking when I smoke.'

I watched her thread her way across the sawdust floor to the exit leaving me alone in the empty restaurant. From an adjacent room, I heard a vacuum cleaner signalling that the place was on the point of closing. Morosely, I gathered the paperwork I'd brought to show her and let my eyes drift over the wall display in front of me. A black and white pin-up of Elvis Presley was mounted adjacent to a poster promoting Chevy Trucks and another extolled the pleasure to be had from getting matey with Jack Daniels. It was all no more than advertising puffery but what I wanted to bring into the light of day was hard news. And news, as a wise man once said, is always something that somebody's eager to suppress.

Moses was absent all the time it takes to puff two long cigarettes. When she sat down again, the smell of smoke was all over her, as pervasive as the stench from garlic.

'Van Zyl's gone,' I said without preamble.

'Gone?-Gone where?'

'Out of the country. Mozambique, Namibia, Botswana-you name it.'

'What makes you think that?'

I shrugged. 'I've been reflecting on all the heat I've taken in recent weeks. And me, I was never the main target. Only the means to an end.'

Moses looked at me out of eyes that had the light of battle in them. 'You and I then,' she said, 'are going to have to work with what we've got. We'll have to make the best of it, won't we?'

I looked at her disbelievingly. 'OK,' I said slowly. Until that moment, I'd been of the view my discussion with her was over. 'Where do you think we should start?'

'First off, I'll arrange to put someone into Blue Location. He can infiltrate the township and hopefully get himself hired into one of the work gangs. Once he's bussed up country to the site, he can find out how things fit together and report back.'

'And then?'

'Got to find those remains you spotted from the chopper. And then check round about to see if there are others.'

'How are you going to do that?'

'By a system of mapping, using drones.'

'Will this need funding?'

'By you?'

'If necessary.'

Moses shook her head. 'It won't be. I aim to get this signed off without a hitch.'

'You sure?'

'Sure, I'm sure. What we seem to have here is a large-scale labour scam. And if that's not monstrous enough, it looks like there's murder in the mix as well.'

'Though that could be difficult to prove.'

'I don't think so. If we find other remains, like in those pictures you showed me, that's a game changer. There'd be unpleasant resonances with other places at other times. Think of Argentina's Dirty War or Mobutu's Zaire where shoving people out of aircraft was an instrument of State terror. In the present case, of course, the justification would simply have been profit by avoiding expensive med-evac.'

All this chimed with my view, but my features must have worn a different expression because Moses went on quickly: 'Remember, from what you've told me, this is a large-scale project. And it may not be the only one. Construction has a poor record regarding health and safety. I did a piece ten years back and nothing's changed. Injuries are frequent and fatalities not uncommon. For those who need it, rapid medical transfer is essential. That costs a lot of money. So much easier, don't you think, to organise a death flight when required?'

I made no reply and Moses let the question hang before turning her face towards me, her eyes hard as those of a sphinx. 'Once we've evidence proving a case, Sol, we've a story that'll run and run. It's the stuff editors wet themselves for.'

CHAPTER FIFTY-TWO

I'd been around long enough to know that at least an element of what Moses told me was wishful thinking. She wasn't going to underplay a story that had as yet not been investigated, let alone written. After all, she needed to be confident about what she was advocating and the first person to reassure in that regard was herself.

Nonetheless, after I'd finished speaking with her, a sense of relief overcame me. I hate leaving things undone and, without the backing of the media, I feared an outcome where monstrous crimes might never be exposed. Not that any of this, Moses cautioned me, was going to happen fast. A thorough investigation would take time, and I should understand patience was a virtue.

And all this was fine for a while, but the sense of relief I felt initially palled as the days wore on. Increasingly, I found myself disconnected and restless. It wasn't that I had nothing to do. It was the fact that what came to me didn't exactly bring with it an adrenaline rush.

There was the distressed father who sought me out about his missing daughter, only it turned out said daughter was his mistress and the briefest of encounters with her, after a couple of days of running around, confirmed she wanted neither communication with him nor any contact from me.

Then there was a young buck who'd got on the wrong side of gang members to whom he owed money and thought I could straighten it out. But the only straightening I achieved, having faced down a couple of these dudes with the Glock visible in a shoulder holster beneath my jacket, was his taking up a longstanding invitation to visit a favourite aunt. She lived on the far side of Durban and would, I told him, probably do a jig, particularly if he said he planned on staying for a year or three.

Later, Effie brought me up to date with her situation. I'd been concerned about her since our return from the Western Cape a week earlier. Unusually, she'd kept herself to herself and when our paths had crossed, I found her distant and uncommunicative.

It all came to a head one afternoon when I was sitting out on the roof garden. I was trying to catch up on some reading but, in fact, was making a better job of catching up on lost sleep. That was on account of my accumulated injuries, particularly to the soles of my feet which were still disturbing my night's rest. I'd been reading, but the paperback slipped off my lap and woke me up.

I reached down to retrieve it at the same moment as a voice arrested my arm. Half turning in my chair, I said, 'Hey Effie, how you doing?'

She didn't answer immediately but instead limped across until she was standing in front of me. But rather than look in my direction, her gaze was directed down towards the astro turf. Leaning heavily on her stick, she looked awkward and uncomfortable.

'Why don't you sit down?' I encouraged her, inclining my head to an upright chair.

'I-I can't stay,' she said in a small voice.

'Right,' I said. 'What's on your mind, Effie?'

For the first time, she lifted her head and met my eyes. 'Sol, I came to tell you I'm leaving. I'm going home.'

I can be slow on the uptake sometimes. 'When will you be back?' I asked.

'You don't understand, Sol. I'm not coming back. I'm leaving PE for good.'

This really was news. 'But what about your course? You told me this was the best uni in the country.'

'It is, but there are other ways for me to access what I need.'

'But that's going to limit your options, isn't it? -What I mean is...'

'You're right,' she interrupted. 'It'll limit my options, but at least I'll be safe.'

'Safe?' I queried. 'Surely, you don't feel *unsafe*? There's cover up here round the clock. And the support outside is high vis because that's what I ordered.'

She shot me a look of angry exasperation. 'You don't get it, do you Sol? You don't understand that having someone around the place who looks like he's up for World War Three doesn't exactly send the right psychological message. Quite the reverse.'

I pondered this. 'I'm sorry you feel that way,' I said slowly 'And I'm really sorry for what happened to you. Had I thought there was any risk that...'

'Risk!' she suddenly flared, lifting her stick momentarily and pointing it at me. 'What the hell do you know about risk? Your whole life is high-risk. One thing after another. So often, in fact, I don't think you even recognise the danger anymore.'

'Look...' I began.

'No, you look!' stormed Effie, cutting me off. She was shouting now. 'I could have fucking died, Sol, at the hands of those bastards. Before you came and got me, I thought I'd had it. That they'd torture me or cut me up or maybe rape and then kill me. I never felt fear like that before. Do you understand what I'm saying, Sol? I don't ever w-want to f-feel like that...?' All at once, her tirade came to a halt and her voice shattered. To my dismay, she began to sob uncontrollably.

Nonplussed, I slowly crossed over and gathered her into an awkward embrace, my arms barely reaching each other round her back. For as long as a couple of minutes, I held her like that as the racking cries slowly left her body and she became calm. After that, she let me lead her to a chair and persuade her to sit down.

While she fetched out a tissue and dabbed her eyes before noisily blowing her nose, I went inside and poured some brandy. Returning to her with the glass in one hand and a bottle of Coke in the other, I gave her the liquor and watched as she sniffed it suspiciously.

'I don't like spirits,' she said.

I tried to grin. 'You don't have to, Effie. If I dump enough Coke on top of this, you won't taste it. And I know you like Coke.' She wasn't convinced so I filled the glass and passed it to her. 'Take a mouthful or two. It'll take the edge off, believe me.'

She did as I suggested, before settling back in the chair. I fetched the one I'd been sitting in and dragged it over to face her. For a long moment, I watched her, but she avoided my eyes. 'What happened shouldn't have happened,' I said. 'It's my fault. I got complacent. This block's supposed to have state-of-the art security. It was the principal reason for my buying it in the first place.'

I broke off as Effie gave me a weak smile and took another sip from the glass. 'I really don't want to lose you,' I went on. 'And I happen to believe the arrangement we have works pretty well. Up until the time Steganga turned up with his thugs, I like to think you felt the same way.'

Effie nodded her agreement. 'You've always been more than generous, Sol,' she conceded. 'With what I have, there's no way I could afford to live in this part of the city. Being so close to the uni is a real bonus. And that's without saying anything about the apartment and all this.' She gestured to indicate the spacious dimensions of the roof garden.

'So, you might stay?' I ventured softly.

'I didn't say that,' she countered sharply. 'I need to take some time out and get a fresh perspective. Will you let me do that?'

'Of course. I'm in your hands completely. You know that, don't you?'

She said nothing but did incline her head in my direction. After that, a silence grew between us and, thinking I needed to give her some space, I made to move away. But, as I flexed my leg muscles, she said: 'You mind if I ask a question?'

I settled back and smiled. 'You go right ahead.'

'What I want to know is why?'

'Why what?'

'Why do what you do?' Why put yourself out there day after day? In your place, it's the last thing I'd be up for.'

I shrugged. 'What can I tell you, Effie?'

'You can tell the truth.'

I looked at her and saw that ducking this wasn't a good idea, but I tried anyway. 'It's not something I've thought about,' I said.

'Think about it now.'

'OK,' I said slowly. 'I guess life tends to mark us out for things. In my case, I made a switch away from SAPS. If you think about it, what I do now was an obvious step.'

'But it's not obvious now, is it?'

'I don't follow.'

'Your circumstances changed radically, Sol. Your money gives you options. Different paths you could explore.'

I took a moment before answering. 'But money also gives you obligations,' I said. 'Or it should. Ignoring them would leave me with a sense of guilt. Personally, I couldn't turn away and live a life consisting of no more than endless vacations and shopping sprees. I tried that when I first came into money, but the experience soon palled.'

'All right, but I think there's something else.'

'Like what?'

'The action's the juice, don't you think?'

I shrugged. 'There has to be a reason to get out of bed each day,' I admitted. I let that settle, before changing the subject. 'I'm not going to make it easy for you, Effie. You're way too valuable for that. Without you, remember, I might still be sitting in a police cell in Despatch.'

A few more minutes, I reckoned, would have been enough to have persuaded her to stick with it, at least for a while.

But, at that moment, one of those occurrences you later realise is kinda critical came out of the left field. It came in the form of a reverberant telephone and, instead of ignoring it, I made an excuse and hastened inside. I reckoned that giving Effie a little space could only work in my favour.

The ringing came from the landline that stands on the office desk. It's the number advertised on my website but, in these days of mobile comms, is used less and less. It was that which had piqued my curiosity.

'Nemo Investigations,' I said, picking up.

'Is that Sol Nemo?'

'Speaking.'

'My name's Anton van Zyl. Look, Mr. Nemo, I badly need your help.'

CHAPTER FIFTY-THREE

For a few seconds, I think my mouth opened and closed soundlessly like a fish out of water. When I did locate my voice, all I managed was: 'W-What did you say?'

'My name's Anton van Zyl. We met briefly a few weeks back.'

I remembered the encounter right enough, but was it with the guy on the other end of the phone? 'Where was this?' I asked, my brain catching up.

'Near the Sundays River. I was staying at a house there for a while.'

'And what happened?'

'You know what happened.'

'Maybe, but tell me anyway.'

'OK, I understand. You came knocking early one evening and I let you in. That was only because you mentioned the name of my girlfriend Amy. We started a conversation, but something was thrown through the window. There was an explosion and then a fire.'

This checked out. 'You said you needed help,' I prompted.

'I have to get out of the country.'

'What's stopping you?'

'Lack of transport.'

'I don't understand.'

'I'm under the radar. Do you know what I mean?'

'Yeah,' I said. 'Keep moving. Cash only all the way. No credit or debit card use. No bank transfers. No paper trail for someone to pick up and start sniffing around. What happened?-You run out of money.'

'Smashed shocks what's happened. Car's essentially a write-off. Even if I had enough cash to fix it, who would I call?-Right now, I'm not exactly living on Main Street.'

I heard him out in thoughtful silence. The trouble was I could find myself being sucked back into the situation from which I'd so recently extricated myself. Ergo, any renewed association with van Zyl's life and circumstances, if it became known, was likely to place me back in harm's way. And one way or another, I'd had enough of that. It was true the action might be the juice, but there was a limit.

But the other side of the coin were the factors that lay outside the circle of my personal interests: like whether van Zyl had anything to offer for my help.

'Your father-in-law hired me to find you,' I said. 'But far from being concerned about how your absence affected his daughter, he only wanted to find you to get whatever you had that could incriminate him. After that, I think he planned to take you out. And he followed me, hoping it would lead to you. When he realised, I'd got compromising material in my own right, he tried to kill me. I guess your call means you accept what I'm saying.'

'Don't worry. I took you out of the equation a while back.'

'Good to know, but why?'

'Key was your reputation. That led me to believe you'd probably been fed *kak* from the off. I've also had some handle on what's happened to you since.'

'Like what?'

'The stuff that went down close to Motherwell. References to dead bikers and a written-off Ford Mustang in the media allowed me to put two and two together. Moti's used biker gangs as enforcers before and when I left that time we met I saw a Mustang. I picked it up in my lights when driving past. My guess was it was yours.'

I let that percolate before reaching a decision. 'If I help, you got anything to trade?'

'You have something in mind?'

'Stuff that'll take Moti down. Of most interest is a construction project of his in the Northern Cape.'

'OK, but it's not the only one.'

I was incredulous. 'There are others?'

'Several.'

'And you've got hard info?'

'Hard enough to keep you reading long into the night,' said van Zyl confidently. 'Plans and technical drawings; cost estimates and quantity surveys; machinery and equipment inventories; government permissions and regulatory sign-offs; labour schedules and payroll data; inspection reports and...'

'What about accident records?' I cut in.

'As I recall, there weren't many of those. Projects seemed free of accidents, come to think of it. Certainly, in the time covered by what I have.'

'In what form's the material?'

'USB flash drives. There are two of them and, before you ask, I've got them safe.'

I thought for a long moment. 'What do you want me to do?' I asked.

'Drive me to Botswana.'

CHAPTER FIFTY-FOUR

I left well before dawn the following day passing suitcases belonging to Effie in the hallway. They'd not been there the previous night and when I'd finished talking to van Zyl I found Effie gone. The lack of opportunity to continue the discussion was more than disappointing and I now wondered whether there'd be another chance.

In the meantime, though, I had other things on which to focus as I beat a fast path towards Cape Town. Fortunately, traffic was light which did something to alleviate driving conditions made hazardous by high winds and torrential rain. But, with the breaking of a new day, I saw the piled rain clouds begin to thin, and their colour bleed out to an insipid grey. A half hour after that and the first rays of sun poked through and vaporised the overcast.

My destination lay on the west bank of a slow flowing river that debouched into the sea. I crossed via a road bridge that passed over its delta providing me with a view of the ocean on one side and thick forest on the other. On the landward side, the waterway ran between closely spaced stands of trees until a half kilometre upstream it made a leisurely right turn and was lost to view.

The road I wanted off the main highway was no more than a track with a gently rising gradient. It snaked its way through the forest and, according to the map, ran for seven or eight kms before ending at a small dwelling above the upper reaches of the river. Van Zyl hadn't exaggerated when he said he was living elsewhere than Main Street.

I drove on for several minutes, but my sense of unease grew as the distance from the highway increased. Justifying my disquiet was the narrowness of the track, its poor repair and the precipitous drops from it on the valley side. But, more than that, I questioned the wisdom of this approach as the prospect of trouble ahead couldn't be discounted.

I went not much farther before bringing the car to a halt. I thought about calling van Zyl but that went nowhere because there was no signal. Besides, thinking about it, I hardly wanted to advertise my arrival. It wasn't as though we'd arranged any specific time and it was he who'd remarked sarcastically that he was wasn't going anywhere.

Turning the car round proved difficult but the manoeuvre did much to dispel any anxiety I was feeling. Within minutes, I was heading back the way I'd come, now determined to exploit my observations of 20 minutes earlier when I first turned off the N2.

CHAPTER FIFTY-FIVE

The lodges for rent lay along the margin of the riverbank on flat ground that narrowed the farther one ventured into the site. But it was close to Reception that I parked and crossed the few metres to the entrance.

'You canoed before?' I was asked by a young black man who looked like he had a lot of time to heft weights.

'It's been a while,' I confessed.

'Can give you a lesson if you like.'

'Is that necessary?'

The guy grinned revealing gapped teeth. 'Depends on your direction of travel.'

'Strictly upstream,' I said. 'I'm hoping to spot some of the birds everybody keeps raving about.' I pointed out the binoculars round my neck.

'That's fine then. Most the time there isn't more than a metre or so under you and the current's real slow. All the same, you'll have to wear a life jacket.'

I paid for a day's hire and took a paddle across to where the water licked the sandy bank like a cat cleaning its fur. My two-seater craft, which was all they had, lay at the end of a short pontoon that jutted into the river. It had a red hull and varnished woodwork that gleamed in the strengthening sun. Before stepping aboard, I crossed to the car and retrieved a small holdall containing the Glock with a spare clip, a large bottle of water and some oddments.

It was a long while since I'd been in a canoe. Though the detail of the specific occasion was lost in the mists, I vaguely recalled an outing as part of a team, my role confined to following what the party up front had been doing.

Now, I was on my own, a fact of which I became acutely aware as soon as I stepped aboard. Unexpectedly, the canoe lurched to the left and, as a result, I staggered, almost dropping the holdall into the river.

It was then that memory flooded back and sound advice about assuming a low centre of gravity came to mind. At once, I dropped to my knees and settled myself down, the holdall placed where I could see it. After that, I released the painter and gently pushed off with the paddle.

Real slow, as far as the river current was concerned, didn't mean it wasn't running at all. I found this out when the canoe bumped back against the pontoon within seconds. Next time, I pushed off *and* tried to paddle away.

I got out into the stream quickly enough and then established a slow rhythm with the paddle. At that point, I'd recalled other advice about staying perpendicular and not slouching; about using my upper torso and muscles in a combined effort; and about keeping the paddle close to the side of the canoe each time it bit into the water.

But, for all that, the effort was taxing. I was using muscles unaccustomed to exercise which made my shoulders ache, and my kneeling position caused numbness in my legs. For a while, I ignored the discomfort and pressed on until, unable to stand it any longer, there was no option but to paddle ashore.

The spot I chose was a sandbank at the side of the river where the canoe grounded easily, and I could step ashore without getting my feet wet. After tying the painter to a tree root and taking a long pull from the bottle of water, I took off the life jacket and rubbed sore shoulders and legs before looking around me.

At this point, the river was 50 metres wide, the trees on the far bank hugging the water and creating dark shadows, in contrast to the sunlight roasting me. Other than the silent flow of the water over the flat rocks of the riverbed, the day seemed frozen in time. Behind me, as I stretched my legs by walking back and forth along that narrow strip of sand, the ground rose steeply between stands of sweet thorn interspersed with lofty Cape ash. Beneath them, well-worn trail tracks snaked up the hillside towards an illegible sign nailed to a tree.

Any doubt as to what was responsible for making the paths was soon dispelled when I heard a marine engine. Looking up, I observed a small pleasure boat with a sun-bleached canopy hove into view and make a beeline for the sandbank. As it approached, a dozen pale faces stared at me as though I was some exotic specimen of wildlife. Closer to, I recognised mostly British accents. It's hardly surprising they visit in such numbers, given all the crappy weather they have to put up with at home. Me, with no wish to do a PR job for the Tourist Board, smiled politely, pushed off and resumed my paddling upstream.

I kept at it for another half hour, the river becoming increasingly narrow. In parts, trees overhanging each bank formed a cover overhead and almost blocked out the sun. I stayed in the light though to make navigation easy but paid the price because the heat made me sweat, even though by then I'd discarded the life jacket.

Not long after, paddling round a long bend, I looked up and saw what looked like a gable. Quickly, I brought the bins up to my eyes as the canoe drifted backwards. Sure enough, on a high ridge and framed by foliage, I saw a triangular shape made up of logs beneath a pitched roof. Its dimensions indicated a sizeable dwelling.

Pulling the canoe up and out of the water was the work of a minute or two, before I stepped ashore again. A steep bank detained me until I tracked a little way along and found a gap where I could clamber up. Beyond lay a dense screen of undergrowth that had to be fought through, before I emerged in a small clearing.

From there, the only way was up so I climbed from the open space onto a hillside dotted with trees. That no one had been this way before was apparent for I was often diverted by fallen timber and startled by local fauna that fled at the sound of my noisy passage.

But the higher I ascended, the more caution became my watchword. I wasn't expecting trouble, but the Glock was readily to hand in the waistband of my shorts.

Soon, I was able to take stock from a rocky outcrop. Getting to the top of it had winded me so I was breathing hard when I raised the bins to my eyes.

The sight that met them surprised me.

For a start, I'd tracked too far over and as a result my objective lay behind and, in fact, slightly below me. Sure, it was the lodge right enough with a straw roof and a verandah, but it was its dilapidated state that took me aback. A profusion of shrubs grew out of its thatch; the preservative on its timbered walls had mostly flaked away; and one section of the *stoep* had collapsed. All that could be said in its defence was that it looked no worse than a beat-up Fiat parked near by whose offside front wing sagged alarmingly. This at least was one confirmation of what van Zyl had told me about broken shock absorbers and it looked identical to the vehicle I'd seen at the Sundays River.

I climbed down from my perch and struck out for the lodge. I kept my distance though and moved cautiously through the trees sometimes with the lodge in view but often with its elevations obscured. In this way, I made a slow circuit of the place but saw no sign of life.

Why so cautious?-Well, it was all to do with that truism: Once bitten, twice shy. I mean, I had every reason to give van Zyl the widest possible berth. He'd almost been my nemesis on more than one occasion and the only justification now for having anything to do with him was to transact a single piece of business.

At last, I approached the lodge's front door, the rail on the steps flaky under my hand. In the other was the Glock held by my side, the barrel pointing to the ground.

The door had no bell, only a knocker fashioned in the shape of an impala's head. I thumped it twice against its metal plate and waited. For a moment, nothing stirred until the silence was shattered by a frantic beating of wings. Startled, I inclined my head towards the sound and out of the corner of my eye saw a large bird wheel into the sky. But that had barely registered with me before a voice cut in sharply: 'Don't move a muscle.'

Of course I did, but it was only to turn my head a fraction. The voice belonged to a man I didn't recognise. He was about my height, had unruly hair, a sweaty, pale complexion and an untended beard. In his hand, he held a snub-nosed pistol pointed unwaveringly at my stomach.

CHAPTER FIFTY-SIX

'I.D. yourself,' the man ordered.

I opened my mouth to say something, but not fast enough.

'You've a gun!' he suddenly screamed. I saw the tension in his arm and a finger transfer to inside a trigger guard.

My racing heart constricted my throat. 'Y-You and me both,' I stammered. 'Only m-mine's not pointing at anyone.'

He ignored me. 'Put the gun down!' he shouted. 'Put it down! Very slowly!'

I bent my knees until the barrel of the Glock touched the ground and I could lay it flat. 'M-My name's Nemo. I came...'

'Nemo!' he bellowed, cutting me off. 'Nemo!-Where the fuck did you spring from? And where the fuck's your car? I thought you were bringing a car.'

It was my turn to be incredulous. 'Van Zyl!' I exclaimed. 'What happened to you, man?'

'Happened?-What do you mean what happened?'

'I saw you that once and you looked like your pictures. Now...' My voice trailed away. 'I mean where's your glasses?'

'Glasses broke two days ago.' Van Zyl looked at me in a way I thought invited sympathy. 'I had a really bad night,' he went on. 'I dozed off earlier and then heard knocking. I looked out but wasn't sure who it was. I expected to hear a car. Did you leave it down the track?'

I shook my head. 'It's near the road bridge on the N2.'

'Why leave it there?'

'I came part way to you,' I explained, 'but turned round. The track was very bad, and I felt kinda exposed.'

'So how did you get here?'

'By canoe.'

'Canoe!'

I smiled. 'There are lodges for rent near the river mouth. They also hire boats.'

Van Zyl shot me a look of incomprehension. 'You'd better come inside,' he said at last. With that he turned on his heel and retreated the way he'd come.

I shrugged, bent down and retrieved the Glock before following in his footsteps. This led me through French doors and across a bedroom where a single, stained mattress was propped against the wall.

My feelings at the sight of this weren't contradicted by anything else I observed in the place. If the exterior of van Zyl's bolthole made a poor impression, the interior did nothing to dispel it. While the rooms were spacious, they were poorly appointed and the sticks of furniture I clapped eyes on looked as though they'd been in vogue around the time of Verwoerd's assassination.

Van Zyl led me through into the kitchen where an ancient range cooker was flanked by empty, eye-level shelving and a line of large hooks. From one of these hung a single copper-bottomed pan adjacent to a wall clock with Roman numerals but only one hand. Against the opposite wall stood a chipped sink full of crockery and next to that a worktop and an array of groceries. From what I saw, van Zyl was living on a diet of cereals and nuts supplemented by bananas and citrus fruits. Packs of shrink-wrapped water were stacked close by plus a tray of soft-drink cans and several bottles of Richelieu, most of which were empty. All this, and the absence of a fridge, suggested the lodge had no electricity and probably no running water.

Was it these drawbacks alone that caused van Zyl's discomfiture?-I couldn't be sure, but there was no denying he was jumpy. I noticed how one of his legs trembled and saw the film of sweat that coated his pale forehead as though he had a fever.

'You OK?' I asked.

Embarrassed, van Zyl scratched his unkempt beard. 'Not really,' he confessed. 'This place gives me the creeps. At night, it's pitch black and the woods all around come alive. There's a lot of noise and unexplained sounds. I've never slept too well, but here's the worst yet. The other night I could have sworn there was somebody outside looking for a way in.'

'Probably some animal following its nose,' I said. 'How long you been here?'

'A week or more give or take. I've rather lost count of the days.'

'I thought you'd be long gone from SA by now.'

'Need a passport to cross the border.'

This explained a lot. 'And there've been complications?'

Van Zyl laughed but the sound came out high-pitched and strained. 'I should say so,' he said. 'The guy I was using screwed me around. Getting it has taken way too long and cost far too much.'

'So not legit?'

Van Zyl shot me a contemptuous look. 'What do you think?'

'Me, I don't know what to think,' I said evenly. 'But as sure as hell, I'm going to find out. That's if you want my help.'

With that, I crossed past him and grabbed a bottle from an open pack, unscrewed the top and took a long pull. The last of my water had been used up an hour earlier and I was parched. Choosing something to eat wasn't difficult either as there was so little choice. Slow-release energy seemed like the best idea, so I unpeeled a large overripe banana. Van Zyl watched me irritably.

'Who owns this place?' I asked with my mouth full.

'Belongs to an old friend of mine. I've not seen him in years, but I knew the lodge from way back. I also knew it was remote and seldom used.' Again, I heard that high pitched laugh as van Zyl spread his arms in a dismissive gesture. 'I mean why would you stay here,' he asked, 'if you had some other option? Some other place you could go.'

I shrugged. 'You tell me. All I know is that I was taking heat from Moti. I'm sure that happened after we met up that one time. I reckon those guys of his thought you'd given me something they needed to take back.'

'But that's only a part of it,' said van Zyl angrily. 'There was a whole other dimension and that created a perfect storm. I'm still trying to get out from under and that's why I need your help.'

'OK,' I said, 'we can talk about that later. All I'm saying now is I came up against a bunch of racist thugs who were looking for you. They got my help by kidnapping an associate of mine. They messed her up pretty badly which is why I'm very angry.'

Van Zyl's face registered surprise. 'When was all this?' he asked.

I was firm. 'First things first, so we'll get to that later. Right now, I want to know what you've got for me.'

CHAPTER FIFTY-SEVEN

At my prompting, van Zyl led the way out of the kitchen and into a room at the rear of the house. That was because I wanted to look at the flash drives. To calm his nerves, van Zyl brought a bottle of Richelieu and a tumbler for company.

'Go steady with that,' I cautioned, as he took a large gulp of brandy. 'If the stuff you've got checks out, I'll take you to Botswana but don't expect me to do all the driving. By my reckoning it's over a thousand kms.'

'There's plenty of time for that,' retorted van Zyl. 'I don't think we should move until after dark anyway.' Without a further word, he led me to a scruffy desk which was bare but for a closed laptop. Putting down the bottle and glass, he pulled it open and switched on. I heard the fan whirr into life and watched the display light up.

It took a few seconds for me to recognise the picture on the screensaver. Taken before she'd become pregnant, it was Amy, van Zyl's girlfriend. Unless I was mistaken, the backdrop was PE's Kragga Kamma Game Park. Wherever it was, she'd been caught smiling widely, her tiny hands folded in her lap. She looked as happy as a child with a new toy.

I glanced across to van Zyl and saw the pain that had leapt into his face. It was as intense as if he'd been punched on the nose. Self-consciously, a trembling hand flew to his mouth, but it wasn't enough to stifle a small cry. I suspected his reaction was exaggerated by alcohol.

'You found her, didn't you?' he asked dully.

'I did,' I admitted. It was a legacy of the apartheid era that violent deaths of whites often garnered more media coverage than similar deaths of blacks, or coloureds for that matter. Amy's untimely death was a case in point.

'What happened exactly?' he queried.

I looked van Zyl straight in the eye to make more credible the half-truth I was about to tell him. 'It was as reported,' I said. 'She fell into the empty swimming pool at the back of her sister's house. The drop was four or five metres. Death would have been instantaneous.' I didn't mention she'd been tortured; the reason she'd been running from the house. All the reports I'd seen had said only that her death was unexplained. It was a line sometimes taken by SAPS to take the pressure off having to announce yet another inadequately resourced, murder investigation.

'And the baby?' he asked.

The question was pointless, but I refrained from saying so. 'I found Amy several hours after she fell,' I said quietly. 'There'd have been no hope in that direction, I'm afraid. No hope at all.'

Van Zyl reached for the tumbler and swallowed what was left. I didn't try to stop him and consoled myself with the thought that he could drive when he'd sobered up. That was on the assumption I agreed to help him.

To break the spell cast by Amy's picture, I used the touch pad to open one of the icons. 'Where are the drives?' I asked.

Fumbling in his shorts, van Zyl produced a small plastic packet and extracted one of the sticks. With some difficulty, I inserted it into the side of the laptop. 'Now what?' I asked.

'Click on Documents and then Folders. After that, you'll need the password.' He began giving it to me, but I heard a catch in his voice. Turning my head, I watched him recover his composure. 'Capitals A-M-Y,' he spelt out. '060398-It was her birthday you know.'

I said nothing and, focusing on the task in hand, keyed in the password. At once, a new icon appeared in the shape of a zipped-mouth emoji and when I clicked on that a list of files appeared. They were numbered but were otherwise unidentified.

'So where do I start?' I asked.

For the first time, van Zyl smiled. 'Anywhere you like.' He said it casually but with such assurance that I randomly clicked on File 4.

The next couple of hours passed in a flash of bright, revelatory light. That first file was a record of email exchanges, with attachments, between one government department and a host of third parties. The correspondence had been generated by a small group of senior civil servants and their political masters. It concerned several high value infrastructure projects around the country. None had a value of less than R500m and the largest was five times that size. The reservoir and river works I'd visited in the Northern Cape was one of the bigger projects.

I had to concentrate to recognise the terminology that spelt out the scale of the fraud that had taken place. Ergo, it took me a little while to tune in to what was meant by references to sums of money variously described as *safeguarded*, or *protected*, or *conserved*. My personal favourite though was *ring-fenced* to describe one transfer of two million bucks to some undisclosed destination overseas. Of course, the reality was that the cash involved was about as safe as an open hen coop in fox country.

While I was occupied, van Zyl sat across from me in one of two tatty armchairs. Once a soothing salmon pink, exposure to the sun had bled the colour. Not that this troubled van Zyl because he dozed in a shaft of sunlight streaming through a picture window streaked with grime. The brandy stood close by him on a stool made from an elephant's foot, the nails chipped and discoloured with age. Just the sight of this relic from the colonial era depressed me.

Equally depressing was the material I viewed. All the files I looked at contained similar subject matter to that found in the first. Viewed collectively, it became plain that a small network of well-placed and influential fraudsters had succeeded in suborning the State's procurement protocols to serve their own greedy and corrupt ends.

But this wasn't the end to the revelations. When I removed the one drive from the laptop and substituted the other, I found all the stuff van Zyl had described to me over the phone. Diverting though this material was, it was the detailed labour records for the various projects I examined that held my attention. As with those few I found on the flash drive in van Zyl's laptop bag, retrieved from his house in Sunridge Park, these painted a compelling picture of abuse. In short, it catalogued long hours and poor pay offered to and accepted by those whose lack of education and skills condemned them to a life of servitude. What made this data particularly toxic was that, unlike back in the bad old days, this was exploitation perpetrated with the connivance of at least some members of a black majority government. So much for the fine words of the Bill of Rights and its bullshit about freedom from slavery.

When I'd seen enough, I shut the laptop angrily. Then, having slipped the two drives into my shorts, I walked across to van Zyl and woke him unceremoniously. He came to with a start and the panic in his eyes told me he momentarily failed to recognise me.

'Where did you get all this stuff?' I asked abruptly.

Van Zyl stifled a yawn with difficulty and straightened himself up. I settled myself into the chair opposite and watched as he stretched his arms. In the bright light cast by the sun, the bags beneath his eyes were pronounced and very black.

'Where did I get the stuff?' he asked rhetorically. '-It all came off the IT system at the company where I worked.'

'Newton Building Engineers?'

'You know it?'

'One of the places I went when I started to look for you.'

'I suppose you met Galway?'

'The name rings a bell.'

'Man's an arsehole.'

For the first time, I grinned. 'As I recall, he wasn't much enamoured of you. He said you'd ripped the company off.'

'No more than was my due.'

I parked that. 'How did you get the data on the sticks?' I asked.

'Newton belongs to Moti. I was employed there 20 years. I only got the job in the first place because I married Namzano, his idiot daughter.' Van Zyl clocked my startled look. 'I use the term advisedly,' he added. 'If you were to meet…'

'But I have,' I interrupted. 'I travelled to Port Nolloth about a month back.'

'Don't leave any stones unturned, do you?-What did you make of her?'

I cast my mind back to the tortured soul with whom I'd spent a few minutes and remembered with a shudder the canvas on which she'd been working. The painting of that oversized eye with its dilated pupil picked out in a fiery red had been as disturbing as the behaviour of its creator. Her ranting was the sort of stuff you'd find analysed and explained, or not, in a textbook of psychiatry.

'I didn't know what to make of her,' I said, 'but idiotic isn't the word I'd use. Of course, our meeting was only brief.'

'Lucky you,' said Van Zyl bitterly. 'I've had a couple of decades to regret what I did. The seeds of her personality disorder were always there. Almost from the start, she was unpredictable and headstrong. Initially, that was part of the attraction.'

'Why didn't you divorce?'

Van Zyl looked contemptuous. 'You're the detective. Work it out.'

'OK,' I said slowly. 'I guess it was about economics. Or it was until you decided to grab yourself some options.'

'Got it in one, Mr. Detective.' Van Zyl brought his hands together and clapped them mockingly. 'I'm a white guy living in a country run by blacks. I had no fancy upbringing or education, no big inheritance to bail me out and now I'm rising 50 years of age. What options has a guy like me got in a country like this?'

It was a valid question, but it wasn't only about discrimination against the whites. Like all else in our Rainbow Nation, the issue of race often sticks its ugly mug in where it's not wanted. The result is blacks distrust whites and vice versa, and both groups distrust coloureds /Indians who, in turn, distrust them. And if I chose to get hung up about it, where did this leave me as a half-breed, other than stranded somewhere between elite Afrikanerdom and the Natal descendants of migrant labourers?

I resisted the urge to get sidetracked. 'Looks like your options expanded some,' I suggested. 'How did that come about?'

Van Zyl yawned again, leaned back and crossed his legs at the ankles. 'By accident,' he said. 'I'd been around Newtons so long I knew how we did things from way back. Like every other business, we'd upgraded systems over the years. One day I was doing some IT housekeeping when I came across a server that should have been decommissioned. I must have had a brain-freeze because I typed in a superseded password. You can imagine my reaction when I found what was there.'

'And Moti knew about this?'

'Knew about this?-Do me a favour! Moti's the one with the connections and the clout to make it all happen. Of course, that fat bastard knew about it, but he never lifts a finger if he can find somebody else to do the grunt work. All that was handled by a guy called Dubazana, the Managing Partner. He and Moti were as close as fleas on a baboon's fur.'

'What did you do with this piece of good fortune?' I asked.

'I regarded it as an insurance policy.'

'How did that work?'

'Moti was on to me about the missing money. My downloading the information brought me some time. Or that's what I thought.'

'Best laid plans went awry?'

'Totally. Moti tried to take me out. Sent a couple of his guys but I got the drop on them and managed to get away. Didn't achieve nothing though. After that, I had to disappear and real fast.'

What I was hearing now made it difficult to reconcile my impressions of the man in the photo given me by Moti. I remember thinking van Zyl looked like a schoolteacher or a college lecturer. And that was on account of his regular features and those heavy glasses with black frames. What I mean is he had the sort of appearance that was reassuring, not one that might lead you to believe he could be dangerous, or it might be risky being around him.

'But Moti wasn't your only problem, was he?' I ventured. 'Had he been, maybe things now would be simpler.'

Van Zyl nodded his head, tried to sit upright and then leaned forward. 'Would you like me to tell you a story?'

'Floor's yours,' I said expansively.

'You familiar with a group called Strike Now!?'

It was the name Lydia Estleman had given me when we'd spoken after Effie's abduction. Nonetheless, I chose to play dumb. 'Can't say I have.'

'It started up when things began to fall apart. Politically, I mean. This was at the back end of the eighties.'

'Before my time.'

'Ach, man you're not that young. You must recall something from that period.'

I shook my head. The truth was that events at that time in the wide world beyond the limits of my eyesight hadn't registered. I was far too self-absorbed, far too engaged with all the issues that had almost overwhelmed me through my teens.

'Strike Now! was about direct action,' van Zyl resumed. 'The country was in crisis and heading into chaos. Law and order were at risk of being destroyed. There could have been civil war.'

'By which you mean the apparatus of apartheid,' I said. 'Racial classification, the pass laws, the forced removals, the internal security set-up and so on.' I clocked the surprise in van Zyl's face. 'Yeah,' I went on, 'I got educated. Eventually. What form did this so-called direct action take?'

'Strike Now! found targets for assassinations and bombings. To make that happen it needed arms and ammunition. All in the name of the struggle. The aim was to fight a race war, if it came to it. After that, *baasskap* would be restored. You know what I mean by *baasskap*?'

I nodded. 'White supremacy. How did you become involved?'

'During my time in the Army. Mine was one of the last groups called up before National Service finished.'

I waited for van Zyl to say something more, but he simply looked at me expectantly. 'What was the connection between Strike Now! and National Service?' I prompted.

'The Army was fertile ground. And not only for us. There were other groups as well. The most prominent being the AWB.'

'The neo-Nazis?'

Van Zyl looked irritated. 'Name-calling's childish.'

I shrugged. 'But you were sympathetic?'

'Let's say I found myself persuaded. There was a lot going on and the atmosphere was feverish. Restoring stability was paramount. Otherwise, everything was likely to go up in smoke. To prevent that sort of thing is one reason for having an army in the first place.'

'But this wasn't to do with the army, 'I snapped. 'This was about aligning with forces opposed to the transition. I don't know what sort of mental gymnastics would make you believe that was a good place to be. By then, South Africa had become a global pariah and was in economic free fall because of sanctions.'

I'd become animated. When that happens, my voice rises an octave and words run away with me. I paused to draw breath and, when I lifted my eyes, discovered van Zyl eyeing me quizzically. 'Whatever enthusiasm I had didn't last,' he said quietly. 'Thing was I was young and got carried away. All that cloak-and-dagger stuff was a terrific adrenaline rush. I was made to feel like I was important and...'

'What happened?' I cut in.

'Infiltration's what happened. Not at once, but soon after the transition in '94. It came out of nowhere, though I guess it's often like that. I was working in Cape Town. I'd been there only weeks when I was picked up and taken somewhere along the coast. I never did find out exactly where.'

'You were arrested?'

Van Zyl gave me an enigmatic smile. 'It doesn't work like that,' he said. 'The Security Service plays by its own rules. It started with what they knew of me and my activities. And what they knew was one hell of a lot. It was then explained that everything I'd done was treasonable. I was warned I could find myself on the wrong end of a 20-year sentence, maybe more.

They left me to think about that for a few days while letting me enjoy all the creature comforts of a spacious home.'

'So, you agreed to be turned?'

'What makes you say that?'

'A low opinion of human nature.'

Van Zyl guffawed. It was an unpleasant sound and inwardly I recoiled. 'I can see why you're a detective,' he said, still laughing. 'You're right of course. I quickly saw the error of my ways and where my real interests lay.'

'How long did this arrangement go on?'

'More than ten years.'

'What form did it take?'

'I was assigned a handler, and we'd meet up as and when.'

'And the stuff you were passing over?'

'Anything and everything I was asked about. You see I often acted as a courier. That meant driving high value loads round the country, but also passing on messages. Those were ones thought too sensitive to be sent by other means.'

'Would I be right in thinking the loads were arms?'

'Guns and ammunition mostly,' said van Zyl casually, 'but sometimes grenades and explosives. And anything else that might fall into our hands.'

'From Army depots?'

'And from SAPS. Both from supporters and people prepared to sell us stuff.'

'Yeah, I know the sort you mean,' I said bitterly. 'People ready to sell their souls for the right price. Tell me about the messages.'

'Strike Now! had a network of affiliates around the country. The leadership needed to keep in touch but were paranoid about communications. They assumed everything was routinely intercepted.'

'And were they right?'

'They were once I'd been introduced as a trusted intermediary.'

'Strike Now! didn't find out it was you giving them up?'

Van Zyl shook his head and scratched his beard again. 'Not at the time they didn't. The Security Service played a low-key game and was happy for the most part keeping tabs on key people. Obviously, if somebody was about to throw a bomb or shoot somebody, they moved in and dealt with the situation. That meant moving the target out of the way if that was possible. Alternatively, engineering fatal accidents was a speciality. One way and another, they ensured no fingers were ever pointed at me.'

'What changed?'

'What do you mean?'

'You're giving me ancient history,' I explained. 'You said your cooperation lasted ten years. I assume after that they left you alone. So, what changed?'

'They discovered later I'd been turned. Don't ask me how and frankly it doesn't matter. The point is these people have long memories, so the passage of time is like the blink of an eye. The upshot was they came for me. But, following my experience with Moti, I was on high alert. I spotted them in time and took evasive action.'

'After which the logical thing was to go to your ex-paymasters and seek help.'

'You must get sick of being right all the time.'

I shook my head. 'I know the sun rises every morning, even if you can't see it.'

Once again, van Zyl guffawed. This time he combined it with slapping his hand on the armrest. 'Hell, I could get to like you, man!' he exclaimed.

Me, I kept my own counsel. 'What was the reaction from the Service?' I asked.

At that, van Zyl's mood abruptly changed, and the hand became a clenched fist. 'Hypocritical fuckers!' he spat. 'Initially, they said the past was the past and I could go screw myself. I told them I knew stuff that'd make things very uncomfortable for certain people.'

'How did they react?'

'Reluctantly, they started a dialogue.'

'What exactly were you hoping to achieve?'

'Relocation out of SA. That way I wouldn't spend the rest of my life looking over my shoulder. It had to be enough so I could buy settlement rights. Maybe in southern Europe. Or some place in the Caribbean. I'd have taken Amy with me. It would have been a fresh start for both of us.' Van Zyl looked up and saw the questioning expression on my face. 'I bet you want to know what happened.'

'And I believe you'd like to tell me,' I said evenly.

'Well, we got to the point of talking numbers and then somebody up the chain of command did a double take. Or I think that's what happened. Overnight, the conversation we'd been having stopped and they started another one about my coming in and saying they'd look after me.'

'My guess is you were a bit wary.'

Wary!-Are you fucking joking? I had no intention of getting anywhere near them. I was under cover anyway because of Moti's people. I wasn't planning on giving that up until I was out of Africa.'

'OK, so what happened?'

'They started looking for me. And their looking was in a whole different league from anything Moti could mount. When they put their minds to it, they can field a lot of people and money's no object. I've sensed in recent days they could be getting close and that plus no wheels meant I had to reach out. That was why I called you, man.'

'What will you do when you reach Botswana?'

'Leave Africa for good. I've enough money to travel and keep on the move for a couple of years. Maybe I'll get more sense from the government once I'm out of the country. If not, then I can sell my story naming names. I'm hoping it won't come to that, but you never can tell.'

'Suppose I say I've changed my mind and won't help you. What do you do then?'

Van Zyl shook his head. 'That's not the way I read you. You're an honest guy and you'll do what's right. The world needs more people like you. Perhaps if I had your advantages, I'd be equally principled. We've made a trade, and you've got what you want on those drives. Now it's your turn to deliver.'

He let his words sink in and, perhaps because my expression conveyed something he was unhappy about, I saw his gun appear in his hand. It wasn't exactly pointing at me, but the message was plain.

'Don't get me wrong,' said van Zyl, 'I plan for us to make the journey together. It's much better if I travel with someone rather than on my own. But, because time must pass before we can set off, I think it might be an idea if you give me your car keys.'

I said nothing and made no move to comply. Maybe it was out of weariness at the way people have such a capacity to disappoint.

'I'm waiting,' persisted van Zyl.

Reluctantly, I reached into my pocket, retrieved the keys and tossed them over to him.

About to open my mouth to say something, I was silenced by the sound of somebody rapping at the front door. In that empty place, the noise echoed menacingly throughout the house.

CHAPTER FIFTY-EIGHT

Van Zyl's reaction couldn't have been any less extreme had the Security Services themselves come knocking. He shot to his feet, dislodging the brandy bottle from the footstool as he did so, and, waving the gun like a madman, looked about him. 'Who the fuck's that?' he spat, shooting me an accusatory look.

By that time, I too was on my feet and had crossed to the window. Unfortunately, I couldn't see anything. I turned back to van Zyl. 'Wait,' I ordered and, without giving him an opportunity to respond, walked out of the room.

It was through the kitchen window I was able to establish an eye-line. There was a man standing on the front porch balancing a clipboard on the outcurve of his huge belly. With a pen held in a ham of a hand, he appeared busy ticking boxes. Dressed in dark pants, a white shirt and knotted tie, he'd arrived in a small, liveried van parked in such a way that I couldn't read the lettering on its side.

I hailed him from where I'd been accosted by van Zyl on my arrival.

'Must be my lucky day,' said the man turning his head. 'First time I've been here and found anyone home.' He looked me up and down. 'But I'm thinking maybe you're not Mr. Rob Turner.'

'You're right,' I said.

'Might you be acquainted with the said Mr. Turner?'

'I can't help with that either. What's this about?'

'Dues owing is what it's about. Payment of same to the Municipality keeps me employed and lets me keep knocking on doors.' The official bent to his clipboard and flipped over a page. 'There's a heap of money that's piled up,' he said sorrowfully. 'Our collection procedures grind slow, but they do grind. At the moment, this is going only one place and that's the court in George.' He paused to give emphasis to his words. 'Just for the record,' he asked, 'can I take your name?'

'Just for the record, no.' I forestalled his next couple of questions. 'Visiting a friend,' I added. 'Could be he'll have some answers for you.'

'I'm much obliged.'

I gave him a smile, turned on my heel, and retraced my steps.

The armchair occupied by van Zyl had its back directly to the door, so its bulk hid him from sight. Accordingly, it was only after crossing the room, I discovered he wasn't there.

Panicked, I raced out and, in the passage, felt a breath of air on my cheek. Locating its source, I found an external door that stood ajar. Pushing against it brought me out at the rear of the house.

It didn't take much working out where van Zyl was headed, and I set off in pursuit. Taking what I thought was the shortest route to the river, I hoped to head him off. But, despite plunging headlong down the side of the hill, it was to no avail. When I reached the riverbank, winded and furious, I found neither my quarry nor the canoe.

CHAPTER FIFTY-NINE

Though the sequence of events was unforeseen, I cursed myself bitterly for not having at least hidden the canoe's paddle.

There was no point hurrying the climb back up to the house. My phone still had no signal and besides I could do without explaining my absence to the man from the Municipality.

Fortunately, when I did make it back, I found him gone. The only evidence of his visit was the Final Demand he'd left under the door knocker.

I didn't linger but hiked from the house along the track for a half hour before I could use my cell. Some time later, a taxi turned up and took me back to the N2 and the lodges by the river. I had it in my mind that Reception had a rack of tourist leaflets and among those would be stuff about car rentals.

This aim was fixed in my mind until I noticed a small crowd by the riverbank. With eyes downcast, they were staring at something on the ground, though the something was obscured by the press of people.

Curious, despite myself, I began to cross over but my steps faltered when I spotted the Fiesta. It was parked where I'd left it hours before. Surely, that couldn't be because that was the reason van Zyl had run out on me. I mean if he didn't want my car what was he doing?

I didn't dwell on the matter. At that moment, my overwhelming emotion was one of relief. I'd got what I came for and avoided a long and tedious drive up to Botswana in the company of a man with whom I felt little affinity.

Retrieving the spare key to the Fiesta proved a pain. It was wrapped in plastic and secured beneath the rear bumper with duct tape. I'd put it there maybe two years before and it had accumulated a lot of dust and dirt. It took me several minutes to prise it from the bumper to which it seemed chemically bonded and then a few more to unwrap it from the plastic.

All this time, no one paid me any attention. The focus was the riverbank and that intensified when SAPS appeared. There were a couple of uniformed guys in a *bakkie* and a couple more in plain clothes who joined them driving an unmarked white Golf. Me, I wanted to be away, but rubbernecking won out, so I strolled towards the water.

'What's up?' I asked someone who crossed my path.

'Guy hit his head and drowned. Take my advice, bro, and stand clear. It's not a pretty sight.'

Because I'm seldom advised about anything, my direction of travel didn't alter but I did hang back until a gap between gawpers opened before me.

I saw a body lying face down on the sandy bank. Its head was turned to one side, and it was wet through. It must have been retrieved from the river and dragged the few feet clear of the water. Drowning could have been the cause of death, but I thought it unlikely. There was too much blood on the soaked hair at the nape and something red and rich was continuing to leak onto the sand from the torn-out throat. From that, it wasn't too much of a stretch to conclude the victim had been shot. What did seem a long stretch, at least initially, was the realisation I was looking at van Zyl.

CHAPTER SIXTY

After that epiphany, I moved away quickly. I didn't want to run the risk of having to answer questions, even if they were no more than about whether I'd seen anything.

Fact was I'd arrived after the killing and that was dandy as far as I was concerned. My life and van Zyl's had been too much intertwined and for too long. It was now time to make a decisive break and that couldn't come soon enough

I started up the car and pulled away onto the N2 heading east. But I didn't get very far before hunger overtook me and I stopped at the side of the highway.

The place was no more than a patch of bare ground where an enterprising couple served drinks and snacks from a mobile kiosk. They'd set out a few fold-up tables and chairs beneath an awning that had seen better days and close to it was a large perch where a talkative green parrot held court.

My mind though was elsewhere as I ate a *roosterkoek* and washed it down with a bottle of mineral water. The obvious question was: Who'd killed van Zyl? Unfortunately, there was no immediate answer. Besides, as soon as I made that deduction, I scared myself with the thought that perhaps the target had been me. After all, it was me who had hired the canoe and it was me who had set off in it hours before. It wasn't too difficult to imagine that someone had made a mistake and iced the wrong party.

Of course, this was a very negative viewpoint. And one I decided, after not a whole lot of thought, made little sense. My recent experiences of having been followed and then attacked had left me with some acute antennae regarding the wellbeing of Number One. In recent times, I'd become the guy who spent life constantly looking over his shoulder, or repeatedly conning the rear-view mirror to see whether he was being stalked, or taking any one of a dozen other initiatives to try and keep himself out of trouble.

With the parrot telling all and sundry Get a Life! I turned my thoughts in a more productive direction. From my observation of van Zyl's wounds, it seemed he'd been shot from the back, probably while paddling towards the riverbank. Recollection supported this deduction as I remembered seeing when driving away an empty canoe snagged in flotsam downstream from the pontoon. On that basis, I reckoned he'd fallen into the water from where he'd then been dragged onto the bank. If that was the case, he could only have been shot from the other side of the river, a distance of at least a couple of hundred metres.

Investigating this theory, for curiosity now outweighed caution, took me back to the lodges but this time on the other side of the river. All the same, I was only able to take the Fiesta along a stony track so far before it petered out and I had to walk.

I negotiated a gentle uphill gradient through stands of Cape beech and yellowwoods until I came unexpectedly upon a barbed wire fence. It stood tall and the horizontal strands were set close together to form a formidable barrier.

Frustrated, I tracked in the direction of the river and parallel to the wire. At a spot where bushes were intertwined with the barbs, I spotted something that wasn't right. It was one strand of wire that sagged because it had been severed. Closer examination revealed three others that had suffered the same fate but had been reattached using small pieces of masking tape. The message was clear: somebody had cut the wires, passed through and, upon returning, had been very careful to conceal their visit.

I pulled the strands apart with difficulty and then, with my back bent, stepped through the gap. Once more, I headed for the river and soon after saw a gleam beyond the trees. By that time, the sun was casting long throws of liquid yellow light across the surface of the water. I explored along the bank in both directions, heavy foliage above my head keeping me in deep shadow.

Did I find what I was looking for?

I mean spent cartridge cases, cigarette butts, discarded chewing gum, food wrappings, disturbed ground, beaten-down grass; any or all the signs of someone having spent time waiting; waiting for the target to appear.

The answer was no, but I confirmed the consummate skill of whoever had taken the shot. From any one of the three or four possible vantage points I identified, there was a clear view across the river to the lodges. The distance though was greater than I estimated and on any body of open water there can always be at least a breath of wind that has to be allowed for. Of course, the sniper would have used a high-powered rifle with a scope and probably a copper-jacketed bullet for extra penetrative power. The objective would have been a single shot into the base of the neck severing the spinal cord and precipitating a catastrophic failure of all motor functions. Death would have been instantaneous. More than that, nobody would be any the wiser as to what had happened as a rifle fitted with a suppressor would have made no more noise than that of gas escaping from an air hose.

The field craft and marksmanship told me that whoever pulled the trigger had been a pro; that the hit was the work of an accomplished assassin and executed with the assured skill of a surgeon cutting out an awkwardly located tumour. Those were attributes they nurtured in the military, and particularly Special Forces. Unless the sniper was rogue, the killing had all the characteristics of government sponsorship, or at least official acquiescence.

I reflected on that making my way back to the car. Sitting behind the wheel, with the late afternoon sun bright in one corner of the windscreen, I drew out the card Lydia Estleman had given me weeks before when I'd been stopped on the N7.

I had no plan as to what I was going to say to her and, in the end, it didn't matter as her number was disconnected. And it stayed that way, though I tried to reach her several times over subsequent days.

CHAPTER SIXTY-ONE

Four months passed before the news of the labour scam broke. When it did, everybody understood it would be the stand-out winner of the upcoming Vodacom Journalist of the Year Awards. Of course, there was the Moses by-line which provided instant credibility, but it was the subject matter that stole the show.

Me, I never anticipated the fire storm that would erupt after the appearance of the story in print and on-line. I guess, like many, I've become inured to the manifest injustices of everyday life in our Rainbow Nation and get kinda beaten down by the regularly displayed shortcomings of human nature.

But somehow this story struck a chord in the national psyche and immediately took on a life of its own. That then precipitated a wider debate around the usual spectrum of social issues. There were the things like the unacceptable frequency of child mortality, HIV and TB; why the murder rate was so high; the yawning chasm between rich and poor; institutional corruption and incompetence; and, of course, the staggering level of unemployment that meant the least advantaged could be so easily and ruthlessly exploited.

Fuel was added to the fire when a political activist and retired journalist, survivor of no less than 12 years' incarceration on Robben Island, made a foray into the public arena via a syndicated editorial in which he thundered:

Is this what we aspired to during the years of struggle?- That we would witness the tawdry spectacle of a democratically elected government suborned by a morally bankrupt and criminal elite? That we would have to confront, more than a generation after the ending of the evil of apartheid, the sort of abuses which have so recently been dragged into the light from the dark places in which they have festered, evidently with official connivance. Not only is there the vile exploitation of what can only be termed slave labour to be addressed, but there are also allegations of multiple murders to be investigated and prosecuted. It must be demanded in the name of the comrades who suffered and sometimes fell during the long walk to freedom that action is swiftly instituted using all the powers of the State to ensure speedy redress for the victims and punishment for the perpetrators of these egregious crimes.

From such an august source, this superheated blast got the attention of the President and, with another election looming, his usual reluctance to do anything that might be perceived as hasty got blown away in the gales of outrage that threatened to engulf him. Within a week, there was news of a presidential commission and a week after that a band of the unimpeachable, so we were told, had been appointed and told to get their terms of reference sorted out within a matter of days rather than weeks or months.

But with my cynical turn of mind, I was inclined to view these developments as little more than window-dressing. It would be years before such a commission turned in its report and what was it going to say but that villainy had run amok and that this should be addressed through rigorous regulation and control coupled with strengthened protocols regarding audit and accountability.

Notwithstanding, it was true that various people found themselves arrested and interrogated though for the most part they were small fry. The movers and shakers of this criminal enterprise both in the public and private sectors took evasive action either by fleeing the country or by getting themselves lawyered-up and gaming the system for all it was worth.

The only real short-term success was in the matter of nailing the individuals responsible for shoving injured workers out of helicopters. The State prosecuted seven murders regarding five defendants all of whom received long custodial sentences.

The final footnote in this affair was the one appended to the name of my client Mahumapelo Matsunyane. This saw the light of day, courtesy of the Herald, in the hardly reverential headline *Moti Meets His Maker*.

The facts regarding his demise weren't in any doubt. He'd been found floating face down in the pool in which I'd seen him on the occasion of our first and only meeting. There was a single bullet hole in the back of his skull, but he hadn't been swimming when he met his death because he was dressed in an expensive tux and patent black leather shoes. There was speculation that he'd got on the wrong side of one of his bodyguards in a dispute over the man's pay. One thing had led to another, and the outcome had proved fatal for the irrepressible Moti. While this account had about it a certain poetic justice, I was sceptical as to the veracity of the explanation.

CHAPTER SIXTY-TWO

Forever afterwards, I wondered about the timing of the call I subsequently received at home from Lydia Estleman. It came only two days after Moti's announced death. I'm not a fan of coincidence and concluded her contacting me wasn't accidental but probably designed to intimidate and/or manipulate.

'I tried to call you a while back,' I said, before she could grab the initiative.

'Oh yes. When was that?'

'After the death of van Zyl. Your number was disconnected. I tried it several times.'

'Must have been one of those administrative glitches. You know how it is in large organisations. The problem's solved now.'

'Is it?' I said accusingly. 'You're calling from a withheld number. What do you want?'

'Do you recall our conversation when we met a while back on the N7?'

'Vividly.'

'Tell me.'

I pursed my lips in exasperation. 'It was the one about your sequestering my assets and making me homeless. And, as I recall, if you had a real hissy-fit, I could end up stateless.'

'You've a good memory.'

'Elephantine for personal threats,' I snapped. 'Rather like most people I fancy. Was there some purpose to this call?'

Lydia paused before responding. 'I'm instructed to convey an official message of thanks,' she said simply. I detected reluctance in her voice, but I may have imagined it.

'For what?'

'Lancing a boil.'

That threw me. 'What are you talking about?'

'Your escapade in Constantine.'

'You mean Steganga.'

'Please, no names.'

'Your thanks aren't necessary. I was there for my own reasons, and they were unconnected to anything you might have wished for.'

'We know that now. SAPS told us someone had been held there. A length of chain was found attached to a wall.'

'Conveniently providing you with a credible cover story should anyone question you and the Service about what went down.'

'Better that than raising the ghosts of apartheid-era politics.'

'What about van Zyl?' I asked, changing the subject. 'Where did he figure in all this?'

For a moment, I thought Lydia hadn't heard me. 'Van Zyl was a greedy opportunist,' she said at last. 'A man who thought we'd pay up for his silence.'

'Silence about what?'

'Some of the people he encountered back in the old days. Before the transfer of power. Didn't you know he was involved with terrorism? I'd have thought he might have mentioned it. Possibly, that he might have shared with you some of the revelations he threatened to make public.'

This looked to me like a slippery slope with a steepening gradient. 'Absolutely not,' I said. 'What were these revelations?'

'There's not much I can tell you, but van Zyl was employed as a courier by a group called Strike Now! He wasn't part of the leadership, but his was a position of trust. We know from other sources it brought him into contact with a wide variety of people. Some of those individuals are prominent today. Indeed, some of the names, if revealed, might greatly surprise you.'

'Does it matter at this distance in time?'

'Anything that contributes to unpicking the social fabric is to be deprecated,' said Lydia. 'Do you not agree, given the Republic's fragility?'

'It depends on what we're talking about.'

'Some that might still result in criminal charges. But truthfully, it's more about past associations undermining key players in their current spheres of influence. And I'm not only talking about government circles. The role of Security Services is to provide intelligence on threats to national stability; the constitutional order; and the wellbeing of the South African people. That's what our mandate says. Maybe, you should take the time to read it.'

'I guess none of that mattered much to van Zyl.'

'It mattered to the extent that he thought we'd give him what he wanted.'

'But you weren't going to do that, so you took him out.'

For the first time, Lydia laughed. 'That's quite a leap, Mr. Nemo,' she said. 'You may not be aware but there was an inquest after his death. Evidently, you haven't seen its reported conclusions. The coroner made it crystal clear what happened.'

'Which was?'

'Van Zyl wasn't an experienced canoeist. It seems he got into difficulties when a pleasure craft passed by. Consequently, he capsized. It then appears the boat's propeller caused him injuries that proved fatal.'

Questioning this bullshit was pointless. Besides, I was more curious regarding one thing, and for me it was a matter of professional pride. 'Did I lead you to him?' I asked.

'No, you didn't lead us to him. Let's just say we were proximate anyway when your car arrived that morning and you paddled away upriver. We were intrigued and so awaited developments.'

'And suppose I'd paddled back down the river with him. What would you have done then?'

'Your question's hypothetical.'

'Nonetheless, indulge me.'

'I can't do that,' Lydia said.

'He wanted me to take him to Botswana,' I volunteered. 'It was in return for stuff he gave me about the labour scam. How far would we have got?'

'You're hypothesising again,' said Lydia, before adding slowly, 'It's a long road to Botswana, Mr.Nemo. I hear tell there are stretches where you can drive for hours without seeing another vehicle, particularly at night.'

Suddenly, despite the warmth of the day, I felt a shiver travel up and down my spine. Abruptly, I made some excuse, broke the connection and walked out onto the roof terrace.

The previous week I'd bought a pair of Zeiss binoculars with a list of attributes longer than the sales patter from a second-hand car dealer. They were mounted on a heavy-duty stand and trained on the ocean. Sometimes there were pods of dolphins to be spotted leaping in and out of the water parallel to the shore; as they've been doing since time immemorial.

But today I was out of luck even though I kept my eyes glued. Eventually, I gave it up and, turning away, saw Effie standing patiently by the sliding door. 'There was an email that came in a few minutes ago,' she said. 'It's from someone wanting to see you. Apparently, it's urgent.'

'I'm on it,' I said.

AFTERWORD AND ACKNOWLEDGEMENTS

Thank you very much for reading my book. I hope you enjoyed the experience as much as I gained pleasure from writing it. This is the second Sol Nemo story, and it follows chronologically from the first entitled The Chanteuse from Cape Town. Both titles are available in print and eBook format and can be read independently of each other as they are stand-alone stories.

I welcome feedback on my work, and I would be most grateful if you could leave a review in respect of my writing. It does not need to be much, but I know how helpful such insights, however brief, can be to other people. **Please leave your comments HERE at https://john-constable-author.com**. Rest assured I will read them and be very interested in what you have to say.

Writing is a solitary occupation. A novel stems from a single idea which over time develops into s setting, a cast of characters and a plot. Draft succeeds draft and slowly the whole work comes together into what hopefully turns out to be an engaging story. During my journey along this road, I have asked for feedback and would therefore like to take this opportunity of expressing my grateful thanks for the opinions and comments I have received from a range of people.

What's next? -Well, there is a third novel in the series which I am still working on and which I hope to publish early next year. If you would like to keep in touch regarding progress with the new work, why not join the Sol Nemo Readers 'Club? **It's easy to sign up HERE at https://john-constable-author.com and in return I will send you a free, stand-alone, Sol Nemo short story.** Lastly, if you do sign up, I promise to contact you only occasionally, I will never pass your details on to anyone else and if, at any point, you decide to unsubscribe you can do so easily.

I hope to hear from you soon.

John Constable

This book is printed on paper from sustainable sources managed under the Forest Stewardship Council (FSC) scheme.

It has been printed in the UK to reduce transportation miles and their impact upon the environment.

For every new title that Troubador publishes, we plant a tree to offset CO_2, partnering with the More Trees scheme.

MORE TREES
LET'S PLANT A BILLION TREES

For more about how Troubador offsets its environmental impact, see www.troubador.co.uk/sustainability-and-community